NIGHT VISION

A SOUTHSIDE HOOKER NOVEL—02

BAER CHARLTON

Pat Erickson, Cover Design, pat-erickson.artistwebsites.com
Rogena Mitchell-Jones, Editor, www.rogenamitchell.com
Mar Penner Griswold, Content Editor
Laura Reynolds, Illustrator

ISBN-13: 978-09849666-6-0 (paperback)
Published by Mordant Media, Portland, Oregon
10 9 8 7 6 5 4 3 — 2019 Edition

ALSO BY BAER CHARLTON

<u>NOVELS</u>

The Very Littlest Dragon: NEW 2019 Editions
(Newly edited editions available: an all-new full-color ebook, a paperback with
coloring pages, and a full-color Collector's Edition hardback)

Stoneheart
(Pulitzer Nominee 2015)

Angel Flights
What About Marsha?
Pirate's Patch
Dry Bridge of Vengeance

—

<u>SOUTHSIDE HOOKER SERIES</u>

Death on a Dime – Book One
Night Vision – Book Two
Unbidden Garden – Book Three
Boomtown – Book Four
One Day Under the Grass – Book Five

Southside Hooker Series: Books 1–5 Box Set
(Collector's Edition hardback & ebook available)

—

<u>THORNY WALLACE SERIES</u>

Ruth Estella Charlton

1920 – 1979

BOX

FIRST KILL

In the dark of night, red looks black, and the white of freshly exposed bone appears gray. Nothing is truly black and white. All is a variegated palette of grays. The evil actions of humans fall likewise into the palette between, and are rarely at the extremes—except, of course, when they are.

There is an old tale about a man wandering in the wilderness with a staff and a lantern. The lantern had no candle, and yet there was light. The light, it was said, could illuminate the darkest corners of a man's soul—an ancient story for an ancient and simpler time. Today it was as simple as the light from a passing truck spilling between the slats of a freight car shoved off on a rail siding waiting for its next train. Or perhaps it was a forsaken crucible for the unspeakable.

In the dark night, a truck rolls to a stop at the stop sign by the highway. The driver gazed across the highway to the field of broken earth beyond. Sparse clumps of tall grass were the only audience to the dilapidated, faded red-brown freight car. The man had noticed it Monday night as he headed for work at the Gilroy's spice plant. He didn't remember the door on the side as being open.

"Kids," he thought as his right hand reached across the metal dashboard. The cigarette lighter popped back out from the hole in the dashboard and into his yellow-stained fingers. The glow from the hot metal flared as he lit his cigarette. His eyes were on the door across the highway as his right hand found the hole in the dash from years of habit. The smoke seared sweetly as he took the first deep draw of the morning. His wife had never liked him smoking, but his truck was his kingdom. He confined the habit to his work commute each day, where there would be no dispute.

He absentmindedly fingered the turn signal and slowly eased the '52 Chevy pickup out onto the empty highway. Turning left, he headed for work on the graveyard shift. The rail car was no longer even a memory as he turned up the radio. The sounds of Tennessee Ernie Ford sang to his truck driver's soul as they crooned together about another sixteen tons of coal and being deeper in debt.

The light had swept along the walls, illuminating a Rorschach of bloody red flesh and white neon bone framing a silent scream and horror-frozen blue eyes. As the light disappeared back into the blackness of the railcar, the scene faded quickly to gray on gray. Life-giving air ebbed and flowed with a high-pitched whistle from the slit in the throat pushed and pulled by lungs nearing the end of their journey from life into death.

The slender claw of a hand weighed the long thin bone bound with human hair and flesh at the end. The movement was slow as if it were the balance of life itself being weighed.

The brush dipped again into the dark cavity of the body pinned like a bug to the wall of the railcar. Small crescent cuts opened into cups to pool the blood, marching down both sides of the torso. As one fountain congealed, a fresh one was cut—to renew the flow.

The killer hummed tunelessly, contentedly, in the thick silence of the night. Feeling the added weight of the loaded brush, the strong, boney hand moved carefully to the wall and continued the curious twists and turns, creating a terrible tableau. Drawings and glyphs stretched around the walls of the railcar. Quarts of blood turned into a maniacal scribe's ink or an artist's paint.

The gibbous moon played hide and seek with a handful of late summer clouds. Far in the distance, a lone coyote howled his tortured call of solitary desperation. Summer's last crickets were ominously silent.

The killer gave a little giggle at the final pass of the bloodied brush. Throwing the now useless tool over his shoulder, he sat down on the floor to watch this latest life drain away. To feel the essence of the spirit as it flowed from the old vessel to the newer, more deserving.

His left hand silently withdrew the short-bladed knife from the scabbard on his belt. His right hand dreamily plucked a hair from his head. The edge of the sharp blade slid along the hair in the moonlight, slivering it.

Without thinking, his right hand placed the hair in his mouth as his left hand returned the knife to the scabbard. His right fingertips danced delicately along the edge of his left Killing Boot in delicious anticipation. He could feel the stirring of his penis as the time drew near.

With satisfaction, the killer eyed the lacey fringe hanging from what once was a face. Every slice had been a symbolic stripping of the identity. Every strip had been a morsel for the killer to ingest the power and strength of the victim's essence. Each strip sucked of its delicate copper and salty nature before being swallowed. Every finger pad had been a delight of sensual touch on the tongue.

The hollow whistle of the shallow breaths now drew shorter and more rapid. Soon, the killer knew they would catch, stop, and catch again. This one was strong. This one might actually take a try at a third breath.

The moon slid behind another cloud as the blue eyes grew flat and dull. The catch in the breathing rattled one last time. The killer smiled at the strength and determination residing in the heart and spirit.

Dark eyes flared with a red heat, then lidded and rolled upward as the killer reached release. Breathing rapidly, his chest fluttered. He moaned.

Out in the field, a lone cricket rubbed its legs with the heat of the night. A fast hand pinched it to silence and then passed it to a faster death between yellow and black molars. The tiny juicy feast was much smaller than the

Master's but no less satisfying. The small figure shifted back into the small gully and became one with the tufted grass in the night.

The silence of the night was complete.

Most in the South Bay Area slept. However, tonight, one had died as another renewed his power.

If you're in your mid-twenties, at the peak of condition, with mornings beginning with a fast routine of weights and martial arts, the mind remembers. When mountains of soap bubbles applied with a Japanese wooden brush in a large shower follow, the memories are ingrained. The mind will even remember what breakfast for you might be dinner for them, before you start a long hard night of muscle-wrenching work.

However, getting up in the morning can be a bitch after three surgeries, two broken ribs, a cracked hip, a dislocated shoulder, a broken arm, and holes where the surgeons followed the eleven dimes shoved through your body from a twelve-gauge shotgun at the hands of a revenge-driven killer.

Your only salve for inching to the toilet is the knowledge the man who saved your life is also alive, and in the hospital, recovering from fourteen dime holes and more surgery holes getting most of them out. He will undergo his fifth surgery while you sit on the porcelain easy chair playing with your cat's only ear with your left hand because your right is still in a cast.

Box slid around the corner from his sandbox. Straight and bold across the tiles, he strutted his full twenty-some pounds of pure orange tabby male muscle. Hooker recognized their relationship as one of equals. He had seen what the cat could do to a grown man.

Box leaned his head into Hooker's better leg and smeared his scent from the side of his cheek along the calf. As the warmest part of the body reached the calf, he stopped and leaned in. Hooker's left hand fumbled down and found the ear. The instant purr resonated off the tiles and echoed in the battered chest above. For Box, life was good.

Hooker's blurred vision refocused on the crosshairs of the bathroom tiles. The cool of the ceramic reassured him he could feel his feet. Well, at least better than he could the week before. His left hand was getting better at playing with the fuzzy ear. He rolled slightly on the toilet as the one thigh twitched and jerked with a spasm.

Four dimes had sliced his jeans and then flipped and tumbled their way through his upper leg and hip. As each had twisted and turned, they had cut muscle, tendon, and nerves. The surgeons hadn't been sure he would have much feeling in his right leg and foot for the first week. Once the feeling had started back, they started reconstruction, another operation in the basement of Good Samaritan.

The long operation had gone well, putting torn holes back together. Everything except two dimes and a piece of a third had come to rest close to the spine, a major artery, and nerve cluster. The dimes were close enough to pure silver, allowing the surgeon to leave them in place. The change was close enough to twenty-five cents. The surgeon made some 'two-bit' jokes with Hooker during visiting rounds. It hurt Hooker too much to laugh now, but he knew, in the future, he would get some good mileage out of the same jokes.

As he swallowed the last of the glass of water washing down a dozen aspirin, Hooker looked at the wild pinto blotching of yellows, reds, pinks, blacks, and blues, which splattered his torso from the last round with the surgeons.

His hair was becoming almost long enough to cover the two long scars along his scalp where the hot silver had sliced open his head like a surgeon's scalpel. The left eye was still not totally focused but was doing better.

"You would make one ugly date right now," he said to the young man in the mirror. But inwardly, he was happy his facial hair was taking shape again, or at least, enough to shave it into his signature beard tracing his narrow square jaw. He did his best with his left hand, and Stella cleaned it up when it was too messy.

The green that had danced in his hazel eyes was now missing, leaving only a washed-out gray. The return of green would signal his return to health and happiness.

This color change in his eyes was something the two sisters and matching mother hens, Stella and Dolly, monitored to check his progress.

He snapped off the lights and slowly limped toward the closet where he knew two dozen, more or less, starched and ironed white T-shirts were ready for him, thanks to Stella. He struggled into one of the masses of white. He could hear terra-cotta plates being set down as quietly as possible on the granite countertop in the kitchen. He heard muffled conversation between the couple who were the closest thing to parents Hooker had ever had. This sense of *home* did more to ease him than the massive doses of aspirin.

Hooker tugged at the bottom of his T-shirt as he limped slowly toward the open door of his bedroom. "Come on, Box. Let's go see what Stella and Manny have whipped up for breakfast." The large, one-eyed, battered, and scarred cat purred as he followed his partner in life.

The two had been almost inseparable since the day Hooker had found the almost-dead orange tabby kitten in a box under a car in the alley behind the Almaden winery. He had apparently been savaged by more than one dog. The vet had strongly suggested euthanasia, but Hooker could only think of how the cat, with the last of its strength, had purred the entire way to the vet's office. He insisted she do everything she could to save this fierce little life and watched as she sewed him back together.

"Good morning, sunshine," Manny called from his wheelchair at the breakfast table. He put down his pen alongside the pad of yellow legal paper and reached for his large stoneware mug of coffee. He watched the shuffling mass. "And good morning to you, too, Mr. Zombie."

"Hello, sweetie." Stella reached her cooking arm, spatula in hand, around Hooker's shoulder as he leaned in for a side hug from his left where it would not hurt. "Go sit down," she muffled into his hair. "I'll bring you fresh coffee when it finishes."

He nodded as he turned taking in the fresh pot still brewing. "Box, out," as he lumbered over to the front door and opened it. The yellow cat sauntered out the door, as Hooker reminded him, "And leave Mike alone. He isn't old enough to know you can beat the snot out of him. Let him turn two in peace." The cat shot a sultry look back at his partner, but also the alpha of the team, and headed for his own yard of grass.

Hooker closed the door softly and rubbed his face with his left hand. Rolling his eyes wide, he commented to nobody in particular, "Why, oh, why, does Box love to beat up on dogs so much?" He padded his way to the table.

Manny watched his movements with an experienced eye. During his twenty years as a cop and detective, he had suffered many broken bones, more than a hand-full of gunshot wounds, and several knife scars at hands other than surgeons. All totaled, enough scars for his wife of even more years to nickname him 'Mr. Zipper' long before the final gunshot split his spine and ended his police career.

"We need to get you down to the whirlpool today. The scar tissue on your hip is stiffening."

Hooker looked at the short silver hair over the reading glasses perched on the bent nose. Manny's liquid brown eyes danced with an inner light which could only be described as gold. "Yeah," he nodded, "I was thinking the same thing. I felt it tear a bit when I rolled out of bed." He dropped his right eyelid and let it flutter to describe the pain he had suffered earlier. "Please, tell me it gets better," as he dropped and slumped down into the chair, "or just shoot me now and be done with it."

Stella came over and kissed him on top of his head as she set the large mug of coffee down in front of him. "Oh, no, honey," she chuckled, "it gets worse. Just wait until you turn sixty, and you start to really fall apart."

Hooker heard the flapping of the cat door in the sunroom. Box jumped up on the back of the long custom-made couch. Hooker leaned back and watched his partner saunter down the entire fourteen-foot length. The world was his empire and his to command. The kinked tail swayed like a slow metronome as he made his way to the end. Front paw out, he rotated off the end, just a longer step to an almost silent landing. It still amazed Hooker that a cat with no depth perception could still know exactly where the floor was.

The proud tabby sauntered into the kitchen and dining area. He sat down to watch Stella. Box always kept his eye on her but took nothing—no attention, no food—from her.

If Manny happened to be lying on the couch in the

sunroom, Box would occasionally honor him with a sniff or allow a brief pat on his head, but for the most part, Hooker was his only real friend in the house.

Stella reached in the refrigerator. The small white bowl had a rubber hood on it. She took off the hood and calmly walked over and set the small dish of chopped tuna on the table. Hooker frowned at the strange breakfast food.

Manny sipped his coffee and made a couple of more notes in the Manny style of shorthand. He looked at his watch and leaned back to quietly sip more coffee. "I think we might build the barn this year."

Hooker had heard about '*this*' barn—a family joke—for years. Manny had browbeaten his ex-partner on the phone about this barn just so a right-of-way would not go through their acreage. Once Manny had landed in the wheelchair, any need for a horse barn had become moot.

"Are you planning to get small horses to pull your chair?"

Manny gave Hooker the 'deadpan homicide detective' look, which quickly morphed into rolling his head back, open-mouthed in imitation of a zombie. It was the family joke for asking a stupid question—being as stupid as a zombie.

Hooker snickered as he watched Manny lean forward and pick up the small white bowl. Leaning sideways, he placed it on the floor. In the dining area—Stella's dining area—the cat stood, stretched, and approached the bowl. He started delicately licking at the tuna.

Hooker could not see Box, but he could hear him. The

cat was eating his tuna in the same reverential way he ate the small dollop of ice cream Hooker always shared with him in the cab of the truck. Even on the coldest winter nights, Hooker was known for arriving at the scene of a wreck with his windows rolled down and polishing off a sugar cone with French vanilla.

Hooker looked at Manny. "When did that start?"

Manny thought about it. It had become an unconscious routine. He looked to his wife. She leaned against the stone-topped counter, raising the hand still holding her spatula. She scratched her hair with the back end of the handle. "After you died."

Hooker chuckled. He joined in as all three went zombie. Box just kept on eating. The tuna must have been fresh.

Stella turned, still chortling over catching her favorite child with his mouth open and speechless. The scrambled eggs were just at the perfect stage. She lifted the pan and upended the contents onto a large serving plate. The pinion pine nuts were perfectly roasted to tan with tiny bits of darker brown. The tiny Canadian bacon strips were cooked just short of crisp and looked just like they were supposed to look. She stirred the grated mozzarella and parmesan cheese into the mix. She tasted a small bite —perfect.

With a stack of toast in one hand, rattlesnake hearts and flank steak with yellow guts omelet in the other, she returned to the table. Placing the food in front of her men, she stepped back for the fresh carafe of coffee.

"Oh, gosh, my soul, pioneer breakfast, and it is not even close to a special Sunday." Manny reached for the serving spoon.

Hooker held out his arm, and Stella leaned into his hug as she poured him more coffee. "Any day this side of a dirt nap and having breakfast with you two is special enough for me."

Stella topped off Manny's mug and sat. "Hear. Hear."

Manny raised his mug. "I'll drink to that."

They each took a bite of the omelet and leaned back to savor their favorite breakfast. "This is heaven," Stella said as she sighed, ignoring her usual rules about talking with food in your mouth. "Well cooked food, my two men both with smiling faces and a peaceful morning in which to enjoy them."

The two men raised their mugs, lightly tapped them together, and sipped on the great coffee.

In Manny's office, the phone rang. The ring echoed from the sunroom where the cordless extension sat next to Manny's place on the couch.

Stella almost spat her coffee. Her head whipped around and looked at the wall clock near the office door. Seventeen past nine. Not a good sign.

The phone would ring through another five rings before the tape machine would pick up.

Manny deliberately focused on his food and continued chewing. Hooker, ever the tow truck driver—who never got a slow meal, was torn between staying calm and shoveling in the only chance he may get before the machine answered.

Stella, too long at being a cop's wife, leaned forward and rested her elbows on the table and sipped her coffee with her face in the steam. The first ring had killed any appetite she had for any food. The world was holding its breath.

The tape machine in the office clicked. There was the five-second silence, as they all knew Manny's terse greeting was going out. *"Romero, you know the drill."*

The machine clicked again, and then there was a two-second tone. The voice was a not so disjointed spirit. "Manny Romero, if you still value anything between those legs, you will push back from my sister's table and pick up. You have five seconds."

Manny was already pushing toward the office at the first word out of Dolly's mouth. Stella looked at the clock again. She knew her sister should have been deep asleep until about five in the afternoon.

Hooker knew he was now in a time constraint. He started shoveling as his right hand reached for a second piece of toast.

Stella reached out and calmed his right hand. "Slow down. They can't get here that quick, and with your bum arm in a cast, you can't drive." She tilted her head and looked at him through the top of her left eye and raised an eyebrow. "Besides, you look ugly enough eating with the fork in your left hand, but when you hurry, even the kids in Africa lose their appetites."

They both strained to try to hear what was going on. Manny was too subdued for them to hear. It was not a good sign. Nor was Dolly calling in the middle of her night. Her days were running the city of San Jose from the night dispatch, an answering and dispatching company in the roughest neighborhood of the city from her custom-built oversized steel desk chair made to hold her quarter ton of boss. She knew where all the bodies were buried, and who had bones left to rattle. Nobody who was anybody disputed she was the heart and soul center of the city.

On her desk was a large tree limb with two words, *The Stick*, carved into it. It was a large stick the large woman stirred shit up with, and only Dolly ever touched it.

Manny rolled out of the office as he stuck the pen back in his shirt pocket.

He took a sip of coffee and loaded his fork. He looked up at his wife of twenty-three years. "They called her at home."

Hooker ate faster.

Stella put her coffee mug down and picked up her plate of food as she stood. She turned and then looked back at Manny. "Shit." She turned in disgust and went to scraping the good food into the garbage.

The temperature rose with Stella's anger. Manny looked over at Hooker. "If you're going to get a shower, now is the time. A deputy will be here with a van in about fifteen minutes. Dolly said the guy knew the way. He helps with the canning."

Stella stood leaning against the apron of the large farmhouse sink. Her arms were crossed over her large chest. "It's okay, Hooker. Just leave the dishes. I'll clean them up." She glared at Manny. *This crap was supposed to be over.*

He closed his eyes and stretched his eyebrows as his head tilted as if to say *these things happen.*

Her lips curled as she turned her head and looked out the window. The valley they loved stretched out for miles. What was once a green valley was now dotted with new homes. The developers had discovered heaven in the Almaden Valley.

She turned back. "How bad?"

He weighed what to tell her. Only one victim killed was not bad, but nobody in their right mind would call a retired detective in a wheelchair out for just a single dead body. He knew it, and he knew Stella knew it, too. It was the nature of the killing. It was the killer. And there lay the problem.

Manny looked in his mug as he took one last imaginary swig of coffee. He was stalling. He knew his time was up.

Quietly he placed the mug back on the table. He straightened his plate and the silverware.

Stella cleared her throat.

He looked at her. It was going to break her heart, and he knew it. Their eyes were locked.

Stella turned suddenly, raising her head. "Oh, shit, Manny." She stood holding onto the cold porcelain of the sink. "That asshole is back, isn't he?" Stella would have to pay heavily into the swearing jar before it was over.

Manny's voice was small. "Yes."

She stared out the window at the fountain in the entry. "Who?"

Manny chewed on the information. "A man." He chewed on his upper lip. "They haven't identified him yet. They may never. He has started peeling. He peeled the gloves and mask."

Over the years, Manny had learned Stella was a strong person. He had shared much about his job. It had helped her understand as the nightmares came and went. This killer, the one who had been nicknamed the Cowboy, still visited Manny and Stella on an almost nightly basis.

This was the killer who had put him in the chair seven years before. The killer had shot Manny in the spine to incapacitate him. Fortunately, Manny's partner had reached him in time to save him from becoming the killer's latest statistic.

Manny's mind raced where he didn't want it to go. They had stopped to check out an open door in an alley and had heard a noise. His partner was calling for backup, and Manny had stepped down the alleyway. Suddenly, there was a blinding flash, and his head hurt. As he wavered from the blow to the head, there was a pop, and his back was on fire. His last thought was how mad Stella would be. Him being getting home late to dinner, and the muddy water he was falling into would ruin his new shirt.

His partner had found him five minutes later, stripped naked. An 'X' of black electrical tape held a wad of cotton over the bullet hole to stop the bleeding. The eight-inch spikes used by the killer to nail up his victims were lying by Manny's side.

Manny and Stella jumped at the knock on the door.

Hooker, now showered and dressed, opened the door for the deputy.

CHAPTER TWO

The railcar stood shabby and sun-scorched in the late summer sun. It looked as if Butch and Sundance had robbed the train and cast this car aside.

The sheriff deputy pulled the van off the side road, easing it in next to the patrol cars and blackouts from the medical examiner's office. All the usual suspects were here.

Seeing the blacked-out Cadillac meat-wagon, Manny moaned quietly. "Oh, great, Doctor Doom is here." It was anybody's guess as to whether the county medical examiner got along with anyone, but the general feeling among the rank-and-file was a crime scene was more pleasant without him showing up in person. Not that any bloody crime scene could ever be pleasant, but it was the thought. The mere fact of him thinking to show up personally meant there would undoubtedly be some other high-profile brass standing around with their thumbs up where no tan lines existed.

Manny reached out and grabbed Hooker's arm as the young man groaned his way out of the back of the van. Hooker turned to look at his mentor and father figure. He very slightly jutted his chin out and up as if to say *What?*

"Never mind... You already know. I shouldn't have thought otherwise." The man's shoulders collapsed ever so slightly in resolve.

"Manny. I've got this. I have your back. Anything I say only goes to you. This is your domain, man. I'm just the Fun New Guy."

The older man scoffed. "Right, a newbie with two bits buried in him from taking down a serial killer. You may be young, but there's nothing newbie about you."

They held the look of mutual respect that was their bond. Slowly, a tiny curl began at the corner of Hooker's mouth.

Manny grumped to hide his smile. "Oh, shut up. Get me the hell out of here."

Hooker pulled the chair out, set it up, and then reached in and leaned into the other man's lap with his good shoulder. Manny reached out and grabbed, two-handed, at Hooker's belt. With his legs, Hooker dragged the man out of the back of the van. Manny knew the pain on Hooker must be intense, but he also knew Hooker was relentless—only Hooker touched the older detective.

The deputy who could have been there a few minutes earlier to offer some help started to say something. Manny snapped his head at the man and gave him his *'you are so dead meat'* burning eye. It was a look he had perfected over a couple of decades as one of the top detectives in the city.

The deputy withered and backed away.

Manny pointed to an unoccupied area. "Let's get back up on the asphalt and go over there. I want to look at this from along the road first."

Hooker and Manny moved along the road cautiously. The communication was perfect between them. Not a word was spoken. A nod of a head, a finger here, and a hand spread there. It was silent but rich in the depth of looking, instead of just seeing. It was one of Manny's favorite approaches to teaching.

Looking is what you do at a crime scene. Seeing is looking, but with an overlay of judgments, wants, needs, beliefs, and prejudices. The talent is just to look. Gather all the information you can before you start assuming.

They could feel most of the eyes watching them, wondering what they were doing eighty yards away from the crime scene. One voice called out, and it was calling Manny.

Manny didn't flinch, didn't even look up. He kept doing his job. His left hand rose with one finger up, and the middle finger going up and down. His old friend Paul Tanner knew the finger was Manny's code for *'be with you in a few minutes.'* For anyone else, it may have meant *'shut up and go away,'* but for the county commissioner, it was the former. He and Manny had been partners, walking a beat together back in the bad old days.

Had they known each other back then, he would have been Manny's best man when he married Stella on the dock beside the troopship, he then boarded ten minutes later. Ten minutes after Manny had boarded the ship bound for Pearl, he met the man on the top rack of the bunks, and they had become good friends. When they returned, Manny had convinced Paul the only place to live was in San Jose.

The soft-spoken eighth-generation Minnesotan hadn't even gone home to collect his belongings. He had his folks bring them out when he and Manny graduated from the police academy. The folks stayed for a month and then went home to sell the family farm. They had lived near the coast in Watsonville ever since.

The soft crunch of hard soles on gravel and sand let Manny and Hooker know from forty feet away they had company. The steps stopped, and Manny made one more critical scan of the field.

The fingers on his right hand kept slowly drumming. Drumming... And then they stopped. There was a slight intake of breath, and Hooker squatted down beside him.

Nodding out with his chin, Hooker knew the mentor was asking for his take. He gathered his thoughts and mapped the area. He nodded slightly toward their right. "There was no evidence of a car, but he came in carrying along that depression. He then moved left to about where Doctor Doom, in the stupid black suit, is standing. After t, he circled to see if the area was clear. But I don't see that he came out this way."

Manny nodded as he raised his left hand slightly and waved his old friend Paul in. Still, only to Hooker, Manny continued Hooker's evaluation. "The bent grass suggests you're right about him carrying the vic. But I think the deep weight-carry damage masked them leaving."

"Them?"

"Look along the sightline where the depression becomes a berm. There is some grass flattened there, too. I think we'll find a footprint, or at least a toe print along there before it becomes hard-packed and railroad ballast. The line you see off to the left is the lookout. Last night, the breeze was coming up from Gilroy, so the lookout took station downwind while our killer walked straight in with the vic on his shoulder."

"What do you have, Manny?"

Without looking up at his friend, he took in the entire scene. "Well, Paul, to gild the lily and put it in terms little schoolgirls like you and the stupid suits out there can understand, we have a cluster fuck." He folded his hands in his lap. "Ask Doctor Doom out there not to take a step. Then have your brightest boy go snoop around his feet for the barefoot prints I think he will find.

"As for the royal fucking, the prize would have to go to the two idiots standing at the end of the railcar drinking coffee. They've been milling around the past twenty minutes all over the tracks of your killer. The blond one even didn't like his coffee, so he threw it out, probably along the best place we could have pulled a pure boot print."

He turned around and looked up at the man. "But if you want to save anything from here, you can ask Hooker here to show your best caster where he can get an un-fucked-up print. Why the fuck would you guys come down here, dance all over the evidence for hours... and then call me? Do you really hate me so much for raping you at the last poker night?"

The man growled back with a deadpan face. "Fuck you, too, Manny. I would have called you three hours ago, but it was some tit-head in City Hall who thought it would be improper to have a civilian here."

He held Manny's stare until Manny nodded in under-standing. They had both worked against the machinations of those in City Hall, who had no clue about how things ran in the real world of the street.

Sighing, Manny returned his gaze back over the tableau.

Turning to Hooker, the commissioner acknowledged him. "Hooker, it's always good to see you son. How is the body coming along?"

"Stiff and hurts, but then again, there are the not-so-good days." They smiled at something all too true about the wounds only coming from being shot, stabbed, or beaten. The commissioner had his fair share of scars, also.

Pointing, "You see the guy in the gray jumper? His name is Harold. He is the best and brightest we have. Go see him about where you want him to cast. We still have to figure out how to get the deadweight up onto the railcar," he finished as he jerked his thumb at his former partner.

Manny grumped, "At least you didn't call me a sea anchor," referring to a bad comment made years before that had become a running joke.

They both watched as Hooker made his way across the field, scanning the entire time—something the police had failed to do.

The commissioner squatted down and rested his right arm on the wheelchair armrest, pushing off Manny's arm. It was the most extreme invasion of personal space for a person in a wheelchair, but Manny made no protest. They had too much history for privacy.

"He has turned into one fine young man."

Manny chuckled. "Between Willie, Stella, and Dolly, the kid didn't have a chance."

"Would you have pegged him for only sixteen the Christmas Eve he towed Stella and her girlfriend, Claire Osofsky, off the Guadeloupe Parkway?"

"I could tell he was young, but we all thought he was maybe a youngish nineteen or twenty. Only Sweets knew right off the bat, but then Sweets is Sweets."

Paul laughed. "I still wake up in the middle of the night. I'll get up and sit in the den and turn Sweets on and listen to the cowboy music of his and read. He even got me reading Louis L'Amour and the whole Sacket family stuff."

Manny looked sideways at him.

"Don't look at me that way. I know for a fact you have more than a handful of his books in your office."

"Reference books," Manny defended with a faux

grump. "All two-hundred books as well as some Zane Grey."

The two continued to banter and stab at each other like puppies who had gotten too tired or too old to play the physical rough-and-tumble.

The two smiled proudly as they watched Hooker walk straight up to the most loathed man on the county payroll to tell the medical examiner not to move an inch—until he was released. He pointed out the man had accidentally stepped into the middle of the most important section of ancillary evidence.

The two old friends watched Doctor Doom stiffen in his jet-black sharkskin suit. However, he didn't even turn his head as the tech took castings mere inches from his shoes. He knew he had screwed the pooch. As a very senior person, he had made a mistake usually marking newbies for their entire careers.

This will be the last crime scene he comes out to for a long time, Manny thought as a wry smile crossed his face and was matched a couple of feet away.

A large box delivery truck with county markings stopped on the highway. Shortly, as the two watched, it carefully started backing its way toward the railcar. On the back was a lift gate.

The commissioner rose stiffly. "I think your elevator has just arrived."

Manny reached out and gently backhanded his old partner's sleeve. The silent communication had the man follow as Manny wheeled along the road to the depression at the edge. He pointed at an unmistakable cowboy boot print, size ten or twelve, undisturbed in the sand about five feet away from them.

The toes pointed away from the railcar.

The two men turned and looked across the narrow-asphalted lane. The field beyond was a good hundred acres of burned off stubble from some crop that had failed a few years before. Manny guessed a poor try at winter wheat or sorghum. They moved for a closer look.

There was nothing there.

"A car would have been obvious sitting out here at night." Paul scanned about. "So, what are you thinking, they were dropped off?"

Manny's eyes searched the side of the field, looking at the dirt clods for thirty or forty feet in each direction. "I don't know yet." He looked up at the commissioner. "I'll let you know once I see the body."

"Body is gone. It left almost an hour ago." He knew what Manny was after. "Male, about five-nine, and hundred-twenty or thirty pounds. An easy carry."

Manny weighed the information. Turning the chair, he studied the road.

"Then get some cops out here and have them comb this line for at least a quarter-mile."

He held his hand up to shade his face. He looked across the field to a small stand of low trees in the distance. "What's out there, Kooser Road?"

"More like Santa Teresa." Paul saw what Manny had

spotted. "I'll have a team check around those trees and make sure they park a hundred yards off."

Manny spun and gave a hard push, still thinking. "Let's go look at the art gallery."

The sand and broken field weren't easy, and Manny had to let his old partner tilt him back on the large wheels and then drag him backward to the waiting truck. It was the worst insult for a person in a wheelchair. Surrendering control and doing it so completely they are moved like a broken stove on a hand truck. The commissioner never said a word, but both knew it was something that would always be between them. The same as the bullet in Manny's spine—he would forever have the upper hand.

Hooker pushed the button, and the motor whined as the three rode up the approximate level of the railcar. The driver had done an almost perfect job of lining up the lift-gate until there were only a few inches of separation. This distance was nothing for Hooker and Paul. They each took a side, and they were in.

The walls were solid graffiti in blood.

Hooker and the commissioner stood, with respect, in the doorway. They looked at the horror as Manny unhurriedly rolled the length of the railcar, his eyes cataloging every sweep of the brush strokes.

Manny gave a low whistle. "This is a hell of a lot more than he had to say eight years ago." He gradually pushed his wheelchair down the railcar.

"Did they find the brush hairs?" It was almost a

distracted comment. Paul knew it came from the second side of Manny that was just gathering the information.

"Over here by the door."

"Were they still bound?"

"Yeah." Paul shuddered.

"With what?"

"They will have to look at the lab, but they think he peeled the skin off the vic's penis."

Manny kept moving and cataloging. He sounded distracted, but both men in the railcar with him knew what they saw were the two heads of Manny. One, looking and recording, and the other, asking questions. When Manny and Paul had been working crime scenes together, Paul had always joked they were the Three Musketeers— Manny, Manny, and him.

Manny stopped. He sat a moment, and then spun the chair around, frowning. "What were they bound to?"

Paul scratched his head. "We're not sure. It was a small bone of some kind. It was very light and about six inches long."

Manny didn't even turn. "It's a wing bone from a raven. One showed up with the young girl. It just wasn't attached, so nobody thought anything about it. I always figured, because of the three days it took to find the body, a mouse or rat had separated it from the hair bound to it and moved it just enough away to appear as if it were outside the kill zone." He turned around, thinking about crows and blackbirds. "Hooker, do we have ravens here?"

He had caught Hooker unaware, and the young man

had to do some mental gymnastics to catch up. He knew it was a trick question of Manny's to bring him back into the investigation instead of just standing in repulsed awe of the writings on the walls. "Um, no... We have crows and blackbirds. Many people think the crows are ravens because they are large. A crow is much larger than our blackbirds, but the raven is even larger still."

Manny put his index finger in the air. "Paul, did you know that?"

The larger man looked at Hooker with a frown. "You sure they aren't ravens?"

Hooker nodded. "Ravens have a diamond-shaped tail when they fly, but our crows have a blunt square tail. People confuse them because they both have black beaks, as where the blackbird has a brown beak."

"Where are ravens found, Hooker?" Manny smiled to himself. He was now having fun with his former partner. He leaned in to look closer at a few of the writings in the darker areas. Only half of his mind was paying attention to the lecture path he had sent Hooker down.

"They should be here, but the crows and blackbirds seem to have pushed them out. Going south, there have been sightings down in Salinas, but more down near San Louis Obispo. In the temperate spring, you might find some venturing into the upper bay, but mostly they stay over in the Central Valley. There is a lot more grain over there, but the crows and blackbirds like the roadkill, and we have it in spades on Blood Alley."

Paul stood with his mouth open. He thought a moment and closed it. "How do you know all of this?"

Manny laughed. "How long have you been clearing bodies and stuff off Blood Alley, Hooker?"

"Ten years... thereabout."

Manny looked at his old detective partner. "It's like working the streets, Paul. Some things you learn in books, and then you learn the more important stuff by just doing it in the street."

"But how did you know he knew it?"

It was Hooker's turn to laugh. "One day, we caught Dolly out on something. And I'd never tell a soul what it was... just because. But I shot three or four birds. Maddie told me I had the wrong ones. They were only large blackbirds. She told me she would pay me a dollar if I could kill a crow. But then she added she would pay me a fifty if I could bag a raven. She knew there weren't any ravens."

"So how many crows did you get?"

Manny laughed. "None."

The commissioner frowned and looked back at Hooker.

Hooker rolled his eyes and shrugged. "Crows are smart. They can count up to three. So if you sneak up on them, they know it. They also know what a gun or rifle is."

"They can count?"

"Yup," Hooker nodded. "They count one... two... three... many. So if five men walk into a blind, they are many. If four walk out, they are many... and the blind is empty. But if four men walk in, and three walk out... the crow knows there is at least one still in the blind."

"So, you never got close enough to shoot one."

Manny was laughing even harder now. Hooker glared and then laughed, too.

"Oh, I did... once... I reloaded Betsy with hard bird buck, which is between the size of double ought with nine pellets in the shell and standard bird which is twenty-four or so. I had sixteen BBs. And I spent the day walking around the field with Betsy under my coat."

"So, what happened?" Paul frowned, getting a little antsy about telling war stories instead of solving a crime.

Manny *harrumphed* a snort. "He was right underneath the bird when he shot it."

Paul thought a moment. His imagination shifted from information to imagining. He chuckled. "Was there anything left?"

Hooker shrugged and rolled his eyes. "A few feathers."

Paul laughed, and then looked out at the other people looking in at the three laughing at a crime scene of a brutal murder.

He frowned as he thought it. "What did this have to do with Dolly?"

Manny smiled. "Stella was going to bake a pie for Dolly."

The penny finally dropped for Paul... "So she could eat crow."

The young tow driver and the man in the chair just smiled.

Paul smacked his face with his hand. "Oh, brother, she would have been on the warpath for sure."

Hooker nodded his head as if to say *do you think so*.

Manny wheeled back and down to the other end and returned, and then circled his finger in the air. "You think they got plenty of good photos of all this?"

Paul frowned. "Sure, why?"

"Because I need to go down now, over near the highway."

Hooker didn't have to ask. He pulled the chair up on its back wheels and jumped it down onto the liftgate and into the box of the truck. "Hold on to the bang boards," he directed Manny and then leaned out and around the edge of the truck. He whistled to the driver. "Take us out to the highway and stop on the side."

The driver fired up the truck, and it started to roll as the commissioner jumped over with a question on his face.

Hooker didn't have to look at Manny for clearance. "He's going to throw up."

The ex-partner looked around Hooker to see Manny grabbing the sideboards with both hands and had pulled his body out of the seat until his head was hard against the boards. His knuckles were as white as his blanched face.

Paul watched his old partner and still best friend.

It was a rare cop or detective who ever had a personal stake, much less personal experience in a murder. This one was too close for Manny. Manny and Paul had drawn this killer over a period of five years when he started.

The controlled violence of a true psychopathic killer is

like no other killer. Most kills are classified as a cold-blooded kill, such as a hit with a single gunshot wound, or GSW, to the head or heart. These are usually from someone who knew the victim, and the victim is usually found in bed with another person to whom they aren't married.

The next step up in violence and gore is the crime of opportunity. This spreads a whole class of gore. The cleanest is an armed robbery gone south. It is usually the nervous young gang punk who empties a gun into a liquor store owner and then runs, leaving the money lying on the counter.

The bloodiest is the wild bar fight that goes wrong if there is such a thing. A good bar fight is just fists and kicking until someone breaks it up. When things get out of control, bottles are broken and used as weapons. These usually result in ambulances and time in jail. The ones Paul and Manny saw were the ones starting with bottles and pool cues but soon turned to knives and a rare gun.

None of them is more than heated blood.

The psychopath plans and is metered. How the crime is performed is like a fingerprint. The fingerprint of this killer was a small four-inch scar on Manny's lower spine where the surgeons removed the bullet but couldn't repair the spine.

Several minutes later, the three stood on the side of Monterey Highway looking across a small field at the rail siding. Manny grumped quietly. "We need to contact

Southern Pacific and find out how long the car has been there."

"But this is a Northern Pacific and Burlington Northern line. Southern doesn't run up this far."

"That may be true, Paul, but look at the undercarriage. It's not made for snow country. It's a Southern." He looked up at his ex-partner. "I don't know if it makes any difference, but I want to know why it's here, how long it has been here, and when it was supposed to move next. I want all the information I can have on the car. I also want to know how often this siding is used. The ballast is all washed out, and I don't think the bed would hold much weight."

"I'll get them rolling on it. Anything else?"

"We need the officer and van for a few more hours. And I'd like copies of everything you find as well as all the photos out to the house this evening."

Paul smiled. "Is Stella home?"

"Call her and give her your request. If we need to pick anything up, like Sicilian sausage from Chiaramonte's, then she can get ahold of us through Dolly and the radio."

"I'll have it all at the house by dinner." He turned to leave and looked back. "I'll have the deputy bring the van over here to pick you up."

"Thanks, Paul. We'll see you for dinner. You can even bring a date. It'll give Stella someone to talk to who isn't talking about killing and blood."

The man waved his hand over his head as he walked across the field toward the rest of the circus. The troops had thinned out, but there would still be some kind of presence until they figured out how to move the railcar to an evidence barn.

"What do you think?" Hooker squatted and steadied himself by putting down his fingertips of his left hand.

"I think it's going to be a happy tummy dinner." Manny smiled at the young man.

They both knew Stella loved cooking extra special when there was a guest at the table, and the last guest had been Hooker's slave for two weeks. Squirt, was a young kid who saved Hooker's life a couple of months before, and who was having the fifth and hopefully, final operation this morning to remove some excessive scarring restricting the blood flow and use of his right arm.

"I was talking about this," Hooker pointed to the railcar and surrounds.

Manny pointed out across the fields. "I think they parked over there in the little clump of low trees. I think the killer did all the carrying. The other guy is just the watcher. I think he carried the vic all the way over here, and then I think the vic took a very long time to die, probably hours. This asshole has expanded, and he had a lot to say this time." He thought, and then looked over at Hooker as they saw the van arriving onto the highway. "And I think we need to go see your girlfriend."

"Uncle Willie or Dolly?"

"Both."

CHAPTER THREE

"I take it we're going up to William's first?" The deputy didn't even look in the mirror. His turn indicator started to click.

Hooker sunk back into the seat, and zombie rolled his head into the window. "Of course, you know Uncle Willie." Manny shot him a commiserating grin. Just when he thought Hooker had figured out how everyone in law enforcement knew everyone else, he made these little surprise discoveries.

The deputy looked in the mirror at the tow truck driver sidelined by a handful of dimes delivered by a twelve-gauge shotgun a few months before. "You know the 1952 Hudson Hornet over in the far corner under the green tarp? It's mine. I'm still looking for a Lincoln flathead sixteen to jam up to the fluid drive and pozzie rear end." He took the right turn to head up the hill to the house connected to the oversized barn of the garage he was talking about, and he glanced back at Manny. "But until then—William and Maddie are finished racing the convertible Dart GT that was yours—so I'm thinking of buying it."

"What the hell are you going to do with a nine-second car?"

"We thought we could get her down into the low eights... but instead, we're going to pull the 340 Hemi and stick a 318 in her, so I have a nice dependable daily runner." They didn't have to see his face to know he had a love-struck smile on his face.

Manny looked at Hooker. "I thought Willie didn't have any kids."

Hooker laughed. "It looks like Willie has been duping us all these years." As they pulled into the driveway, the subject of their derision strolled out into the sun in all of his glory. Hooker groaned.

His uncle's florid blue granny dress had a large burn hole at thigh height. It was high enough to see Willie was taking the day commando. The dress stopped short of the battered engineer boots with the bands of silver Concho hearts over the instep. The welding helmet was thrown up over his head, which pulled the skin on his face and accentuated the jagged scar started under the right side of his jaw and ripped a pinkish-white highway across the throat and up the side of his face in front of his left ear. The scar with its final star pattern was a souvenir of the meat hook from which he had been suspended for three days, before it finally ripped across his throat, tore through his shattered jawbone, and out of his face.

Ten minutes later, he had killed seven of his Viet Cong jailers, and then led and carried six other men through the jungle to freedom, a hundred and forty kilometers and seventeen days later.

Willie removed his large leather welding gloves and opened the side door. The deputy came around to help get Manny out of the van.

"Jeez, Willie, this one has got to be the ugliest dress you have ever dragged home." Hooker half covered his face in mock terror.

The deputy smiled and leaned in toward Willie and stage whispered, "He hasn't seen the pink and lavender one, has he?" Willie started laughing and slapped the man on the chest with the gloves.

"Ssstop!" he lisped.

Hooker knew Willie only let his Nancy come out and dance when he was among trusted friends and those he considered family. Hooker groaned more and held his head as he lay forward onto Manny's shoulder. "Oh, Gawd, Manny, the kid actually *is* his."

Manny sat stoically. He let Hooker play, but he had things more serious on his mind.

Willie sobered and looked at the detective. "You're coming from the railcar?"

Manny nodded.

"Chet stopped by about an hour ago. He's not officially back to work, but he was down there, too. They hadn't cleared the car yet. How bad was it?"

"He got worse." Manny thought about it. "They are

bringing duplicate photo sets of everything out to the house tonight. Paul is coming over for dinner. Why don't you join us unless you have a date?"

"Hank and I were just going to grill some roadkill here, but I can bring him and give Stella someone to talk to about cooking."

Manny hiccupped a laugh. "Oh, that's even better. She's getting the outside kitchen ready for the annual canning. I'm sure it's about time Hank receives the final indoctrination into the perverse side of this family."

They both smiled as Hooker buried his face in his left hand. The cast on his right kept his dominant hand away from his face.

"Perfect. Hanky can schlep canning stuff with the best of them." Willie turned toward his ward who was eyeing the large burn hole on the dress. "Do you need anything from your room, Hooker?"

"Willie, I spend my days barefoot in jeans and a T-shirt. But if there are any jeans here near wearing out, I could cut them down for shorts." He put his hand along his face and turned it to hide the dress.

The three laughed at the slapstick humor as the deputy joined in.

Willie hung his hand on his now out-thrust hip. "Don't knock the coolness of a chintz dress, young man." His Nancy was in full steam.

The other three men groaned and then laughed.

Hooker shot back. "But those boots and gloves offset any advantage you get from the dress."

Willie lifted the hem of his dress. "Not this advantage."

Manny just looked at the deputy with a pleading look. The deputy sprang into action and rounded the van. Climbing in, he acknowledged with a train conductor's voice. "All aboard! Next stop, Dolly's Dispatch."

The van nosed around and out of the giant driveway. Halfway down the hill, the deputy broke the silence. "If I may ask, why does he wear those dresses? He only destroys them with the welding and all."

Hooker chuffed with a short laugh. "It's economics. He buys them by the bagful at the Goodwill. They would cost him fifty cents each, but by the bag, they cost about a quarter. A pair of bib overalls, if you can find them, would run upward of two or three bucks. So, its dresses by the bagful or go pay retail for work pants. The pants wouldn't last as long as a shopping bag of dresses, and he doesn't buy them by the shopping bag—he uses the thirty-gallon trash bags."

"Hmm, I'll have to remember that."

Hooker and Manny both buried their faces in their hands. *He really must be Willie's love child.*

"Oh, I didn't mean for me. I meant for when I need to bribe him, I should make a run-through the Goodwill first." He rolled the steering wheel right and eased around the ramp onto the freeway. "Do you know what size he wears?"

Hooker growled back. "Anyone at Goodwill can tell you. They probably set those ugly dresses aside for him.

Nobody else would be caught dead in something so visually abusive."

The rest of the drive was thankfully in silence.

Dispatch was a gray cinderblock building hunkered down in the corner of a large parking lot. As per normal, there were only three cars in the lot. But Hooker had seen many New Year's mornings when the overflow of tow trucks, plumbing trucks, security vans, and cop cars turned the quiet side street into a parking lot.

As they got Manny settled in his chair and started toward the steel-plated door, it swung open. A quarter ton of Florida orange muumuu over bare feet walked out into the sunshine. Dolly lifted a large arm and shielded her eyes from the painful light.

"Who the hell are you two?"

Hooker took the lead and walked into the large hug and buried his nose down into the woman's fat neck. "Hello, sweetie. Miss me?"

Her right arm came up and trapped his head hard into her neck as she giggled. "Don't you dare tickle my neck like you do your fat girlfriends, you little pervert, just give Mama a hug. And don't talk. It will ruin the fantasy of you being a perfect child." They laughed together. Dolly was the surrogate mother for many young tow truck drivers who had no one else to care about them. Three weeks after Willie had caught Hooker trying to hotwire his car, she had taken over the duty of putting him to work. He was only fourteen but lied and had a bad fake driver's license saying he was twenty. She found him a better-looking license and a job jump-starting cars and running parts for a tow company. He had now been connected to them for over ten years. He let go of her so she could hug her brother-in-law.

She didn't have to say a word as she swooped down on the man in the wheelchair.

After a minute, Manny told her, "In nineteen states, this would be seen as a mugging. In two others, it would be seen as rape. In Arkansas, they would just call it incest, and it would all be good. But you would have to explain things to your sister."

Dolly backed her shaking jello into the shade of the door. "Get in here. I'm not going to stand out here in this heat." She looked out at the deputy. "Steven, are you coming in or are you standing out there like a stupid or crazed dog?"

"Coming, ma'am."

"Coffee is fresh, just made it last night."

The deputy doubled his walk. "Perfect, ma'am."

She shot him a stern eye for his obvious sucking up.

The three sat near Dolly's desk. Dolly held court from her custom oversized welded steel office executive chair that had four pneumatic rams instead of the usual single one that was only rated for two-hundred pounds. Her bare feet were crossed on the desk near The Stick.

"Chet stopped by earlier."

Manny sipped on his coffee. "He gets around for a guy who is supposed to be recovering from a gunshot wound."

She looked at Hooker, who was paying close attention

to the coffee in his mug. "Hmm, yes—seems to be going around lately."

She looked back at Manny. "How's my sister doing with all this extra work?" She referred to taking care of Hooker while he too recovered from gunshot wounds on top of tending to Manny.

Manny ignored the jab. "Oh, the canning is coming along just fine. We have a new tent that will be about sixty feet long by the same twenty. It should give plenty of shade when you come to peel potatoes. And with the Squirt out of the way, she's almost bored and looking for something to do."

She gave him a deadpan look before her head fell back into the zombie-head family response to dumb questions or statements.

The deputy giggled. Hooker looked over, and the word *Nancy* drifted through his head.

Manny braced his forearms on the arms of the chair and rocked forward to adjust the pressure on his rear end. To those who knew him, it was also his way of clearing his throat.

"Willie is coming over for dinner, along with Paul. I think it would be good to tap into Willie's Naval Intelligence thinking. With all that time he spent in the jungles of Vietnam, I think he might have a better take on some of this aboriginal mindset. Maybe we can finally get a grasp on all this message shit the asshole is writing."

Dolly, ignoring Manny's language and venting,

snapped her fingers and pointed to Hooker. "That reminds me, Father Damian has a message for you. Said that any night you could make it up for dinner at your usual time, let Candy know. Oh, and don't bring cigarettes, he's quitting."

"Maybe I can get up there tonight after we go over this stuff. If Stella won't loan me the Caddie, she can schlep me. She wants to meet Squirt's big sister, anyway. I think she's working on trying to get Candy a slot at the college for nursing school."

Dolly made her living listening to people and more of how they said things than what they said. She was listening to the tension in Hooker's voice.

"How long before you have your girlfriend back?" She was referring to the eleven tons of steel that were Hooker's tow truck.

Hooker sunk into his seat. She had scored a direct bull's-eye.

"Willie said that he couldn't even get three of the pistons out of the case because they were seized in there so bad. He'll have to drill and shatter them. The case will have to be sleeved to a larger bore, which means that we have to figure the stroke to balance her out. The pistons may have to be custom cast, and that would take until fall. So all told, I would say Mae West might be a Christmas present all over again. He was referring to the Christmas that they had found her in Oregon, and then the next Christmas when she became a tow truck. But to get me back on the road, Don is going to put me in a one-ton and have me just run service calls until the doc says I can pull regular duty."

Dolly looked at Manny with the same look that Manny knew all too well from his wife. The look that said *I lay this at your feet. You're the man. It is all your fault.*

Manny put up his hands. "I have nothing to do with this. Stella works his physical therapy, and what she says, goes in the house. You know that, I know that, and he knows that. Hell, even Box knows that... but he just ignores it. And he is the only male who can get away with it, too."

Dolly didn't have to say not to be trash-talking about her favorite fur chest warmer. She was the only person who could pick Hooker's cat up other than Hooker, and even Hooker avoided that kind of contact as much as possible. He had seen what the burly warrior cat could do to a human face or hand.

Hooker calmed the tension. "The truck he has is an automatic. I could drive it with one hand. So even with a cast, I can run service calls. Dolly, trust me. I won't lie to you or Stella if I am in pain. I am not a stupid kid... most of the time. I'll take it easy. I'm in for the long haul here, and I need my body to be right as much as I need Mae's engine to be right."

She watched him for a minute as she sipped her coffee. She looked at her coffee and then she looked over at the two women wrangling with the phone lines. Dispatch, being the answering service for most of the businesses in the San Jose area, was also the dispatch for all of the alarm companies, and most of the plumbers and electricians.

They were the only dispatch for all of the independent tow companies, and after midnight, the only dispatch for the auto clubs, sheriff, highway patrol, and ambulance. Most calls for the city police and fire department went through the city dispatcher but could switch over after the ten o'clock shift change if they needed it.

"Karen, is this coffee the new beans I ordered in from San Diego?"

"Yes, ma'am, they are."

"Don't let me do that again. There is absolutely no kick in this coffee at all. I'm falling asleep just sitting here listening to Hooker drone on about his girlfriend."

The two women at the switchboard looked at each other and smiled. "Lucky you, we think it would be yummy to fall asleep with Hooker." They giggled like schoolgirls.

Dolly ground her head around and glared at Hooker.

He raised his hands and cast. "Hey, you saw. I didn't get anywhere near them, much less nuzzle their necks."

"You three are incorrigible." She looked back at the two giggling girls. "Dina, you should be ashamed of yourself. You're newly married and pregnant to boot. Karen... Karen, you're just being nasty. Wait until I get home tomorrow and tell your father."

It had been a running joke for many years that she looked like Dolly's husband even though he could never have kids. However, the family that was made was every bit as strong as the family that was born. Only Dolly and Hooker knew that if Dolly passed away, Karen would own dispatch with Hooker as a partner. Hooker knew that he never wanted Dolly to leave him four walls and no window. He'd rather have the grief and love she handed out in fair amounts.

"Well, we ought to let the young deputy get back to real work, and I'm sure it's getting close to time to set the table or take a nap." Manny stretched as he spoke.

Remembering, Dolly snapped her fingers. "Hooker, there is a box of Chiaramonte's Sicilian in the fridge. I had it towed down when Stella called. Mike had to come bring me some new information for the company, so I had him run by."

Hooker got the ten-pound box of sausage as Dolly rose to get hugs all around. Each person always got a hug and a *stay safe* when they walked out the steel-plated door that had five bullets still stuck in it. It was a rough neighborhood, and Dolly knew, sometimes an even rougher city.

As she let Hooker go, she reminded him to call Candy and to go meet with Father Damian some night around midnight soon.

CHAPTER FOUR

Coffee was fresh and steaming in the office. The three older detectives and their protégé were pinning up photos on the large movable boards. Paul explained the larger crime scene board and the eight-by-ten photos. "We had these re-cropped to the most salient information. The four upper rows are the corresponding symbols starting with the first known kill site and working down to last night along the bottom. In these file boxes are the close-ups of each overview in case they can help. Today they shot the six large areas, which you see here, and then sectioned them off into twenty-four sections each. Those sections are in each of these six binders and are marked to coordinate to each of the overview shots. There is still no identity to any of the victims except for the second, which was the college girl hitchhiking down the coast."

"Melody Richards," Manny offered.

"Thank you." Paul moved to the other board. "This is what we have so far on this one.

"We think they got there sometime around midnight. By the dried blood on the hands and legs, we figure about twelve-thirty when he nailed the victim up to the wall.

"The gunshot wound was consistent to a twenty-two short, the same as you got in your back. The bullet was too deformed to pull barrel marks, which is consistent with all four, or five, counting Manny. The perp used a chunk of the vic's shirt to stop the blood flow and taped it on with electrical tape, consistent with the others. The lab is trying to see if there are any prints, but unless he got sloppy this time..." He looked at Manny, who was slowly shaking his head.

"After what you said today, we went back over the first three and did find a bird bone in the general cataloging of items in the kill zone. But because nobody gave it any credence, it was held into evidence as 'other.' But it was consistent with the one you picked up and had identified. I also noticed in the first case, they didn't even figure out the bloody bunch of the vic's hair was also the paintbrush."

Willie had been staring at the photos of the print castings. "What do we know about the barefoot prints?"

"This was the first time we had soil, so we got lucky on the lookout. The print indicates fine bones, and the weight to be under a hundred pounds. The shoe size would be about a men's size six. However, we really don't know if it is a small man or woman's print. We did determine, with the flattening of the arch there was no hesitation on walking on either the sand or stubble—they are always barefooted."

"Because of the desensitization of the footpad... as well as sandals being an unnecessary expense," responded Willie with a nod. "We saw a lot of it in Nam."

Hooker mused, almost to himself, "It would be consistent with any of the Mouse's tribe."

Manny nodded and looked back at Paul. "What did they find in the tree line over on Santa Teresa?"

"Good call there. We have tire tracks, the boots on what we assume was the driver side, and the barefoot was the passenger. The boots made for grinding of small stones to create trace grind marks, but there were none on the passenger side. There was a weight load shift, resulting in grind marks at what we believe was the trunk. After, we found they led off into the field. The field is being guarded tonight, and forensics will start working it with a group search tomorrow to see if there is anything else we can find."

"What about the tire tread?" Hooker leaned forward.

"Firestone 575-16 series, consistent with every small Ford, Dodge, Mercury, Chevy you can think of from 1962 forward, they all used this tire. It was the number two best-selling tire in America for over the last decade or more. Sorry, but we have a dry well there unless we find the car and match some unique tread wear."

"So the only thing new is we now know the raven bone is a part of the package." Manny leaned back and stretched.

Paul pointed at him, and then at the footprint castings as he sat down on the corner of Manny's desk. "And we know we have a lookout."

"And the cowboy boot prints are consistent?"

"They may be new boots or soles, but same make and model, and by the footprint, we don't think his weight has changed by more than maybe ten pounds heavier." Paul finished his coffee.

Willie frowned. "Why not a woman? Do you have evidence the killer is male?"

Paul's eyebrows rose as he set the mug on the desk. "Good point. It's the nature of the kill making us assume it's a male. In the Navy, you didn't have to deal with this kind of stuff, so this psychological profiling may sound a little out there, but it bears up.

"In the rare instances of a serial killer being female, they don't do it up-close and personal. They will use either a gun or something that doesn't make a mess, like poison. Also, female serial killers are about the kill. It's almost always a sexual thing, and they get a release. With guys, it is a very personal ritualistic thing."

The old Navy Seal snorted. "*Arsenic and Old Lace* syndrome."

"Exactly."

Willie nudged his chin toward Hooker. "So your explanation for the dime...?"

"The exception to the rule—it was an anomaly." Referring to the Dime Killer, Hooker continued with, "It was a shotgun but with overtones of personal and rituals."

Paul glanced at his watch. "This is all we have at this time, and if there are no other thoughts, I have an early meeting with probably the mayor and some other bite-in-the-ass in the early morning, if I don't have reporters camped out on my doorstep."

Manny hunched on his elbows translating into a slight hop in his chair. It was more of him shifting mental gears than any kind of adjustment in his seating. "No, we're good here, Paul. Thanks for all of the information and the briefing. If anything comes in, give me a call, and you know what time dinner is."

Hooker sat quietly. Something was just too familiar, but he couldn't put his finger on it... just yet.

"Hooker... have you got something, son?"

Hooker looked up at the commissioner as if he had just suddenly materialized. "Wha—? Uh, no... Just thinking."

Paul stuck his hand out. "Dolly can find me night or day. Since my Patricia passed, she has become my guardian angel." He sighed. Two years since he had lost his wife to cancer and the pain was still fresh. "If you get a thought, just give a holler... night or day. It doesn't really matter anymore. I don't really sleep much these days."

As the detective collective invaded the kitchen area, they were greeted by two grown children powdered with flour. The entire large square island was taken up with making food. More specifically—exotic cultural confections.

A very happy, but slightly embarrassed Hank, smiled sheepishly. "Hello, boys."

Willie eyed his partner, whom he had never seen wear anything more feminine than a white shirt but was now down to his jeans and barefoot with a frilly pink apron covering his wife-beater undershirt. The apron might have gone without comment except it was the joke apron Manny had gotten for Stella as a housewarming. The large bold letters relayed the sentiment: *If you don't like my food, you can kiss my grits.*

Willie cleared his throat. "And which part exactly *is* your grits?"

Hank turned red as a barn. Stella interceded. "Don't you boys have some toys to play with? Hanky and I are making kugel, and if any of you plan to have any on Saturday for dinner... you will shut up and go away." Stella had spoken.

Hooker turned to Willie as Paul squeezed Manny on the shoulder and slipped out the front door. "Willie, I need to go meet Father Damian at eleven, and if we go now, we can stop in and check on the Squirt."

Willie's right hand came up in a silent goodbye as he turned away from the force, he knew not even decades of being a tough Navy Seal could have prepared him for. He slapped Hooker lightly on the chest and pointed at his bare feet.

Hooker stopped by the door and tried on a pair of Stella's flip-flops. A wee small, but close enough, and he didn't want to spend another moment in the eye of Stella's storm. Manny was already beating a fast retreat to his office and the two doors, front and office, snicked shut at the same time.

Willie stopped halfway to the fountain dominating the center of the hacienda entry plaza. "Don't you want to bring Box?"

Hooker thought a moment about opening the front door, and then just stared at his uncle as he barked loudly. "Box. Go time." He smirked at Willie.

As they both turned to walk around the fountain and out the tall hand-hewn black walnut front gates, they could hear the SNAP-snap-snap of the plastic door on the other side of the house. Box had his own door but usually refused to use it for anything other than a necessity. Two things you never had to tell Box twice—*dinner* and *go time*. Of course, he was always ready to beat up another dog, too.

The large orange tabby was standing straight-legged on his small patch of grass between the driveway and the promenade walkway leading up to the front gates and entry into the traditional hacienda with its two-foot thick straw stucco walls. Hooker had never seen any other cat pee standing like a horse. Even dogs made arrangements, but it was as if Box was proud of what he could and was doing. Box was Box.

The cat scratch-kicked a couple of divots in the grass and looked to see what vehicle had replaced the giant tow truck.

Hooker opened the passenger door to the 1952 DeSoto convertible. It was the very same car Willie had caught him trying to steal over a decade before. Hooker wasn't sure if Willie held onto the car because he really loved it or it reminded him of where they had started. Either way was fine with Hooker; he had long gotten over the embarrassing story Willie loved to tell about finding Hooker hot-wiring the radio instead of the ignition. Hooker had come a long way.

He now stood at the door. "Box." The cat seemed to shrug as if to say, *I guess this one will have to do.*

The late evening was a joy in the top-down roadster. Even Box was enjoying the wind as he stood on Hooker's lap with his front paws on the windowsill and his face in the breeze. His one good eye was closed, but Hooker and Willie could tell the unique cat was in heaven with new smells coming at him at forty miles an hour.

The large old Detroit V8 engine rumbled and echoed in all three hearts. Hooker looked across the lights of the valley. He missed the much higher perch and deeper rumble of his true love, the eleven tons of his Mae West.

The 1959 Marmon truck was Hooker's first vehicle and first major love. He and Willie had rebuilt her up from scratch, so to speak. They had torn the old truck down to just the frame and built from there. The front nose of her was the largest ever made commercially. The engine was almost double the size and power of any other big rig in the San Francisco Bay Area. She was the fastest tow truck in five counties. Hooker floated her over the 120mph mark on a regular basis. With Hooker at the wheel, she ruled the night.

CHAPTER FIVE

The halls of Good Samaritan Hospital were clear of the usual flurry of family members coming and going, soothing or irritating the patients, and testing the patience of the nursing staff who were hoping to get their charges settled down to sleep through the night. The third floor was almost all post-op recovery and was usually a mausoleum by eight at night.

The two men walked quietly down the linoleum hall looking into dimly lit rooms with monitors blinking or the bluish-gray wash of color from televisions hung from the ceilings. The large shopping bag hung heavily from Hooker's left hand. The occasional movement in the paper bag was lost in the gait of his injured leg.

The doorway was lit, and the two entered single file. The nurse was holding the young man's wrist, taking his pulse. Her back was to the door. She stiffened at the sound of the hushed voices.

"I hope this means he still has a pulse."

"He looks like something even Box wouldn't chew on."

"Do you think he's still in a coma?"

"Was he before?"

"Well, he was stupid enough to dive in the way of a buck sixty in change."

"He must have been hanging out with you."

"Are you saying I'm brain dead?"

"Well, you are nothing more than a two-bit survivor of the same killer."

"You do know he has the same amount of change still stuck in him, don't you?"

"Are you calling him a two-bit zombie, also?"

A low moan came from the bed. The nurse was both amused and annoyed at the two characters for disturbing her patient. "Nurse, can I get a better room with intelligent conversation?"

Hooker laughed. "Squirt, you better stay here. Your nurse is the best looking one on the whole floor. But if you want us to leave you two alone, we can close the door and go talk to Helga, the night duty nurse, who has been known to twirl rectal thermometers in ice water before administering them."

The young nurse opened her mouth in shock. "She does not. I will have you know his night nurse is kind and caring."

"Must be you," Willie was warming up to the young lady. He wasn't attracted, but he did have a knack for drawing the best out of people.

"Well, um, yes. Yes, it is." She blushed slightly.

The smooth talker moved in close to her. Draping a gentle avuncular arm around her shoulder, he led her to the door.

"Well, we are glad you will be taking care of our young friend tonight after we are done with him. He will probably need a nice long sponge bath, as well as a very long special massage." He winked at her and smiled his winning smile. "But first, so you don't lose your job, and we accomplish what we need to do to the young man, you need to go find something else to do."

She turned and looked over Willie's shoulder as Hooker opened the top of the bag as a large orange missile ejected from it. "Is that a..."

Willie turned her out the door as he swung it shut. "Goodbye."

The cat stalked up the young man's chest as he sniffed around and between the hospital smells for a hint of his young friend. Only Hooker and Dolly had ever been allowed the privilege of touching him—until this scrawny kid walked into Hooker's life, and the picky cat had added him to his social circle.

"Hello, Box," the voice groaned from the large white ball of a bandage wrap. "Good to see your mangy butt—or is this your face?"

The cat stood on top of his chest and touched his nose to what should have been a human nose but was just an opening in the gauze. Box took in a long breath. Somewhere between the conflicting acrid and sweet odors of medical pollution, he found the familiar scent of his young man Johnny—who had become known as the Squirt, short-hand name cops usually hang on any new guy. The cat relaxed and lay down on his chest and began to purr his signature uneven rumble.

Hooker looked at Willie and smiled. All was right with the world.

The young man moved his one un-bandaged hand onto the cat and was soon asleep. The two older men sat quietly soaking in the tableau of their friend and the cat. They also needed the calming coming from such a strange yet familiar place.

A while later, the light from the hall split the gloom of the room as the young nurse silently slipped in, and upon seeing the cat, closed the door.

Willie leaned his head back and saw the concern on her face. "We're sorry, but he was uncooperative, and we had to knock him out."

At first, she looked shocked, and then she realized Willie was joking. "It looks like you did a good job of it. Why... he looks almost... um... catatonic."

Hooker groaned. "Oh, you went just a bit too fur."

Willie choked, and then offered, "I had to paws and think about that."

Hooker rose, putting an end to the *punishment*. "Seriously, we would leave the mange bucket here all night, but you will probably have to give the kid some more drugs later, and Box wouldn't let you near him. But for now," he looked at the drool coming from the kid, "I think he's good for a few hours."

He held the bag open for Box, who lay ignoring him. "Box, come on. We've been busted, so it's go time."

The cat jumped off the bed, grudgingly crawling into the bag, which Hooker picked up and carried. Turning back to the nurse, he shrugged. "It's a medicinal cat."

The two men walked down the hall. They had not gone far before the giggles settled in. The wiggle in the bag didn't help. The cat in the bag routine just barely made it to the elevator.

Box may have had only one eye and one ear, but his deadly claws were all intact. The bottom of the bag hung in loose shreds as the doors of the elevator closed on the three standing males.

Willie giggled. "Left him catatonic..."

CHAPTER SIX

The two priests sat uncharacteristically at the last table in the front window. Father Damian's usual table was in the back room. It was a quiet corner where he sought refuge from the daily noise. In addition, it was where the street urchins and crustaceans who washed along the great way of Winchester Boulevard knew they could find an open ear and a kind word. Some nights he heard more confessions in his middle-of-the-night booth than he did all week in the confessional.

The new location was Father Damian's choice for two reasons. The first was to create more seating, the restaurant had removed the four large booths and replaced them with five tables. This provided Damian easy wheelchair access by simply having a chair removed.

The second reason was he could see out the window and view most of the parking lot, an important aspect this night.

Father McBride, the old man at the watch, leaned back in his chair.

"Long day at the hospital, Father?" Damian knew the sun was barely up when Father McBride started his self-appointed rounds at the Valley Medical Center, the catch-all for the county derelicts and those who could pay very little or nothing at all.

"Aye, and not a good day, as it were." The balding man slumped into his chair. "We lost another of our flock this morning. I think it was one of the lads who occasioned his way in here. It doesn't feel cold, but sometimes when they lay on the concrete, it sucks the heat and life right out of them." He closed his eyes as he shook his head in denial. The heart-wrenching decades had taken a toll on the man, but even well past retirement age, he refused to stop. The younger priest prayed that one day, he too would find such strength in his faith.

The low rumble of a deep, powerful engine caught the older man's attention, and his eyes opened as he saw the large chrome front end of the DeSoto as it nosed into the driveway. He sat up for a better look. "Now, here is a real car."

The scars on the younger priest's face crinkled as he saw who was in the passenger seat. "It looks as if our young friend Hooker has secured the services of a chauffeur."

The man whose business it was to know or find out who people were, drew his smile up tight on one side. "I believe, my friend, this is the young man's adopted uncle. You two have a little history in common. You were Ranger, and he was Navy Seal. He also served in Korea, and then in the early years of Vietnam, he was captured and held captive for almost a year before escaping.

"I'm sure he talks just as freely about his service experience as you do. So I would say if you want him to talk at all, stick to what he really loves."

"And that would be...?"

"Why, Hooker or cars. Unless you are inclined toward his life's sexual nature or his predilection for..."

"Hooker, so good to see you."

"Father Damian, Father McBride, this is my uncle, William Knight."

Willie leaned forward with his right hand. "Please, call me Willie." He shook with McBride and turned to the younger priest.

Father Damian stretched out his left hand and right hook from his body and wheelchair. "Excuse me if I don't stand."

Willie said nothing. His right hand remained extended over the chair. His eyes and smile never wavered. "Hooker tells me you were also Special Forces."

The priest examined the large 'J' scar covering the man's throat and up the side of his face. Slowly, Damian moved his right hook into the hold, and they shook. "Father McBride was just giving me the sit-rep briefing on you, too." They both smiled. Everything was in the open now, and any pissing on the back of the barn was unnecessary.

Hooker passed around the back of the younger priest and pulled out the chair next to the window. Father

McBride cleared his throat and looked behind Hooker. Willie had sat down but leaped to his feet.

Hooker froze and then rolled his eyes. "I'm in trouble, aren't I?"

The soft voice behind him was pure warm biscuits and honey. "Only if you don't turn around and give me a hug, you big goofball."

He turned, and the scrawny, freckled waitress flowed into his arms. They stood silently. Neither knew what to say in front of the two priests or Uncle Willie. Finally, they separated enough for Hooker to give her a quick kiss before turning a tiny bit red. "I missed you."

"Well, mister, I've been right here. First, you get my brother shot up, and then you two just lay around like two big fuzz balls of gauze for months. What is a girl to think?" She gently dug her finger into what she hoped were ribs more ticklish than painful. Hooker winced and squirmed anyway. "If it wasn't for running into Willie and Hank occasionally, when I sat and watched you two drool into your bandages, I would have never been entertained."

She released Hooker and stepped back around the table. "Hello, Willie." She folded into his arms as well, and when she kissed him on the cheek, he didn't blush. "How is Hank?"

"Hank is a little sassy, but I try to keep him in line. I'll tell him you asked for him. He would have come, but Stella seduced the young boy away, and they're cooking as we speak. It was something disgusting with sugar, cinnamon, dough, and several other things to ruin a girl's figure."

"I'm sure you will survive."

Willie leaned back toward Hooker, and in a staged whisper shared, "Oh, and I forgot to tell you—don't ever play gin with her for real money. She's better than Hankie."

As Willie took his seat, Candy drew a finger gun bead at Father McBride. "Coffee and cherry pie...." Placing her hand on Damian's shoulder, "Coffee and Dutch apple. Moreover, Willie, what can I get for you? I already have Hooker's water and stale bread."

"I'm an apple man, Candy, and I guess I can indulge in one cup of black."

"Great, I will leave you gentlemen to your man talk stuff. Just remember—keep it clean. Hooker is still a virgin." She spun on one heel and with great drama, huffed off like a steam engine.

Willie laughed at her playful, dramatic movements. "Such a refreshing child!"

The other three chuckled. Sometimes it took a fresh set of eyes to remind you what it is you enjoy about something. Hooker smiled as he watched Candy's ponytail flip as she walked. The warmth in his chest moved north.

As the coffee flowed and drained away, and the dishes of food became just dishes ready for a wash, the conversation was light.

"What time do you have, Hooker?" Father Damian leaned forward.

Hooker looked at his watch. "11:48."

Damian's eyes were focused just slightly over Father

McBride's shoulder. "Hmm, interesting. A little early, but drawn in."

"What's early?"

Damian studied the young man's face. He hadn't really gotten to know him before, but could now see under the young face, the eyes and soul belonged to someone twice or three times his age. Softly, he confided, "Why, the reason you are here tonight, your important message." Looking out the window at Willie's parked convertible, he lowered his voice as it drifted off. "But let's give them a few minutes alone."

Hooker followed the priest's gaze. At first, he only saw the large blue car. As he looked closer, he noticed there was a large orange cat lying on the tan boot covering the folded down top. A second, careful look found the small whirlwind of dust and scraps of paper and street flotsam. This whirlwind wasn't moving with the wind. This one moved by its own volition. This bit of the night air and grit was named Peter, a man whose previous assistance had helped to save Hooker's life.

Peter was one of the lost people who floated in the world between reality and one they felt more comfortable in because they made it up. A former engineer of some sort, but now just a shattered soul. Most days, he found his way by touchstones, such as a midnight conversation with Hooker, and a bummed cigarette he had later passed to Father Damian.

Hooker watched the smudge in the air and his cat who could fillet a hand in one swipe. "What is Peter doing?"

Willie turned and watched the scene for a moment. "My dear boy, it would appear your feline juggernaut is becoming a true slut."

"Maybe we should go talk to him before there is trouble." Damian pushed back from the table and turned his chair. He pushed out toward the large glass doors.

Slowly opening the doors, Damian came out first. In a soft, reassuring voice, he attempted to calm the man from the streets. "Hello, Peter."

The standing swirl of dust and detritus turned his head. His hand continued to rub the ear and neck of the large purring cat. "He... hello... fa... fa... fa... Damian."

"Peter?"

"H... H... Ho... Hook... Hooker?"

"How are you, Peter?" The two carefully approached the midnight swirl of dust around the side of the car.

"G... Go... Good Ho... Hooker." The man continued to pet Box, who continued to purr loudly.

"You seem to like my cat. And more importantly, Peter, he seems to like you."

"Th... This... is a n... ni... nice cat." The man spoke as he continued stroking the cat. "Thi... this is... yo... your cat... H... Hooker?"

"Yes, Peter. He is my partner. His name is Box."

The man thought but didn't laugh. "B... Box... Box is a... v... very nice n... name. He is a v... very n... nice cat."

The three men watched the man's hand pet and scratch, rub, and smooth the cat's one ear and neck.

"H... Hoo... Hooker?"

"Peter?"

"Wha... wha... where... is y... your truck?"

"It's broken right now. It's getting fixed."

"L... li... like... like your arm?"

Hooker raised and looked at the cast. "Yes, Peter, like my arm."

"I... I... I'm so... I'm sorry you got shot."

Hooker looked at Damian. Damian just shrugged.

Hooker just had to accept things and information were passed on the network of the streets.

"Peter?"

"H... Ho... Hook... Hooker?" "Did you have a message for me?"

"H... Ho... Yes."

Hooker was used to the tiny steps as well as the missteps it took with Peter to get a discussion handled. The shattered mind flowed like the wind he seemed to exist in.

"Did you want to give it to me?"

The man stopped petting Box. He seemed to just freeze for a long moment. Hooker suspected it was for more than a few of the man's heart beats.

With exact movements, the man stepped back a step and then sidestepped once, and then once more. Hooker could feel the counting.

Peter turned slightly and then began to hum, but with an open mouth. The hum rose and fell, and then he spoke. "The killer is known. The dog gets a bone, Secure the death, but only when the debt is paid. They meet they will, on Fox's Eve, be by the old mill when the moon hits the trees."

Hooker wasn't sure he had actually heard the man rhyme and not stumble or stutter. It was the most amazing thing he had ever heard Peter say in the ten years they had known each other.

"Who gave you this message, Peter?"

"Th... the... Mo... The... Mow... The Mouse."

Hooker thought. He knew his sister. Or at least what was left of her inside the tortured body of what she had become—the leader of a gang or tribe of mentally unstable and barely human entities. They lived in the dark shadows of the land or city. They floated up and down in the lower half of the San Francisco Bay Area. But they were trapped from roaming farther by their own fears of crossing over open water, even on a bridge. In the south, the strong permanent smell of garlic kept most of them at bayside or at least from traveling south.

"Peter, I know the Mouse. She won't send me a message of a rhyme unless she also sent a side message that would guarantee the rhyme was true. Did she send a side message along with it, Peter?"

The man thought by looking at the stars. Hooker didn't think that was where his memory box was, but he knew Peter was obsessive-compulsive, and he would only do things if there was a touchstone for his compulsions or at least made sense once he finished.

He pointed to the sky. "Th... the d... the dog."

Hooker tried to help. "The Dog Star, Peter?"

The man nodded. "Trav.... traveler... traveler cross d... dog." His left hand pointing to Sirius, the Dog Star, as his right pointed east and moved across the other finger to the west.

Hooker saw the ancient art of storytelling in the man's hands. He knew there was more trapped inside of Peter than would ever get out again. "When the bright traveler crosses the dog, what will happen, Peter? What did she say?"

The man fell in on himself. "Yel... Hoo... Hooker? Yell... yellow ha... yellow hair." The man was very agitated, but Hooker needed to know.

The calming voice of Father Damian interceded. "Peter? Peter?"

The dirt swirl rallied. "Fa... Fath... Damian?"

"Peter, you are among friends here. Even the cat likes you. You are safe." He let those last two bits of information transfer. Box even stood and leaned toward the inhabitant of the night air.

Damian relaxed in his chair. "Peter, the cat's fur feels good, soft, and safe. Box likes you. You have a new friend." The slow, softer pacing had calmed the man, and he even reached out and ran his one hand along Box's head and back.

Damian and Hooker waited out the man and the cat. Finally, Peter took the critical steps back to the side of the car, so there was more contact with the cat.

Damian's voice was as soft as a summer breeze in the treetops. "Peter?"

"Da... Damian?"

"Peter... can you tell us what yellow hair is?"

The man continued to pet the cat, but his right hand rose near his ear and then fluttered as it moved downwards.

Hooker watched. He whispered, "Long hair... it's a woman." That was the complete confirmation Hooker needed the message was from his sister. The sign language was how they had spoken to each other as kids. Partly real deaf sign language they had learned from the other kids, mostly what they made up. The fluttering open hand was Hooker's sign for his sister's long hair that he loved.

At one foster home, the woman was jealous of her long hair, so she cut it and shaved her head. That night, as they sat on the opposite ends of the bunk beds, Hooker signed to his crying sister. He would always love her and in his eyes, she would always have her beautiful hair.

Hooker looked at the priest in the wheelchair. The man nodded. "Peter? What will happen to the woman?"

Peter petted the cat one more time, and then with his other hand, he reached out slightly to his side, and spreading his fingers, as if taking in the night air, he closed the hand violently into a white-knuckled fist.

Then there was nothing in the air. Not even a hint he had ever been there.

Damian and Hooker stared at the empty air. The two were still thinking as Box jumped down and headed across the parking lot toward the small bit of lawn surrounding the restaurant.

The glass door sucked open, and the two older men walked out. Father McBride stopped to put on his black fedora. Willie softly asked as he approached, "Well?"

Hooker thought as he turned. He looked up from the pavement into his uncle's face. "I think I need some help from your old work."

"What kind of help?"

Hooker pointed into the air. Willie looked up.

Looking back at Hooker, he chuckled. "The sky covers a lot."

"I need to know what satellite we have visible to the naked eye which Peter could see, and when it will be crossing Sirius from our viewpoint."

The older man washed his hand over his silver brush cut. He smiled. "The answer may be closer to home than you think. Hanky is more than just a starry-eyed young lad. He even has a large telescope in his garage. He eats this stuff up like you chew up large engines." The man leaned his head and gave Hooker a serious stink-eye.

"Ohhh shhhhift into third gear." Hooker saved himself from another quarter in the swear jar. He knew Willie was talking about the blown-up engine in the giant tow truck.

Turning around to shake hands with Father McBride, Willie stuck his hand out. "Father, it was grand to meet you and your associate finally. I will see what we were talking about and get back to you by the end of the week. Then we will have you two out for a Sunday dinner." Turning, he took in Damian. Once again taking the man's hook, he secured their bond. "We will have plenty of times to chat and get to know each other. But for right now, I need to get this boy home to his bed, and hopefully, rescue my boy from the grips of a woman who cooks."

The DeSoto nosed out of the driveway and headed south as the two priests waved goodbye. Box settled down in the middle of the front seat between the two laps and closed his eyes as he began to purr. Willie reached over and turned on the radio. The tubes warmed up as the second refrain began about tumbleweeds tumbling in the blue shadows—the kind of music only Sweets played. With a glance at his watch, Hooker confirmed the disc jockey friend was indeed working his shift.

A powerful old car, great music, his cat next to him, and one of his favorite people at the wheel—Hooker's left hand found the cat's only ear and absently rubbed it gently between his knuckles. He put his chin up and into the wind as his right arm in the cast rested on the windowsill. The temperature was T-shirt under leather jacket weather —if he still had a leather jacket. For now, the faded yellow-tan work jacket would do. All was right with the world.

Except for the rhyme was now rolling over again and again in his head.

CHAPTER SEVEN

The big car barely changed its tone while climbing the hill. Hooker finally broke the silence. "How bad?"

Uncle Willie thought for a moment. "Remember those pieces of bread you put in the toaster back when you were fifteen? The ones when you thought the toaster wasn't working right, so you batted the flipper down a third time?"

Hooker rolled his eyes and looked over his shoulder back at the lights of San Jose twinkling in the distance. "The ones that caught fire and burnt the house down?"

The older man stuck his index finger into the air. "Just the kitchen, young man, it was just the kitchen. I had to use a cutting torch to get the rest of the house to go up."

"But kind of like the toast, huh?"

Willie nosed the large car into the driveway and brought it up to the gates. He set the brake and turned off the ignition. "Not just like the toast, but exactly like the toast."

"Toast."

"You may say so."

"So the block is..."

"Cracked." The man opened the door and stepped out. "In five or six places I can see with my naked eye, two I can stick my thumbnail in. There is one crack I stuck a dime in, just for you." The man's humor could run to the macabre. Hooker had destroyed the engine in an effort to stop the killer who had nearly dimed him to death.

"What are the chances of finding another Marmon engine these days?"

"Working on it." They walked through the outside gate to see the house lights were still very much active. "Oh, Gawd, help me wrestle Hanky to the ground and drag him out of here."

The two were still laughing as they entered the quiet house. "Hello?"

"We four are in here."

Willie looked at Hooker and mouthed the word *four?*

The two empty wine bottles on the island were an indication. The empty quart Ball jar with the characteristic reusable glass and wire top was the final giveaway. Stella and Hank were lounging in the sunroom, plowed.

As the two men entered, the two drunks chorused, "Hello, dear."

Willie looked at his cross-eyed partner as he leaned

over to Hooker. "I'll bet they see more than two of each other."

Hooker giggled. He had never seen Stella so plowed. "Two bottles of wine, and then a quart of Maddie's moonshine.... It's amazing they are anything short of catatonic."

"What about Box?" Stella slurred.

"Nothing, dear." Hooker leaned into Willie. "I'll help you with Hank, and then I'm just going to throw a blanket over the other body."

Box entered through the cat door behind the large couch. Sensing all the activity was on the couch, he jumped up onto the back. He took one sniff and headed for the sanctuary of Hooker's bedroom.

The two men watched the orange commentator as he stalked from the room in stiff-legged disgust. Willie commented about him being a very smart cat, and then they laid-to on the aqueous body of Hank.

Hooker returned and locked the door. As he heard the big V-8 leave down the hill, he started turning off lights.

He stood in the archway of the sunroom. Stella was already snoring lightly. Hooker brought a light blanket and tucked her in on the couch.

"I don't think she has been tucked in since she was maybe twelve."

Hooker turned to find Manny sitting in the archway. "I'm sure she was looking after other people long before she was twelve."

The old detective pursed his lips as he thought. "I can't

remember which, and I would be stupid to ask, but Dolly is three years older or three years younger?"

"Dolly is the older, and it's five years." Hooker leaned over and turned off the three lights on the wall switch. He looked at the surprised look on Manny's face. "You didn't hear that, and certainly not from me."

"I was just curious as to how you knew."

"I saw a photo of when Dolly was six and holding Stella. If I hadn't loved them both already, I would have fallen in love with them then. Of course, neither one resembles those two little girls in any way, shape, or personality."

"And you would probably get slapped on the back of the head for even mentioning the picture."

"Got that right, buster," slurred from the couch.

They both froze and then listened to the resumption of snoring before they moved into Manny's office.

"How does she do that?"

"Scary, isn't it?" Manny forced his eyes open wall-eyed and crazy. "She's been scaring me since we first met. The scarier thing is she will never mention it again. I don't know if she doesn't remember, or if she just holds onto it until it's the right time to bring it back up."

Hooker shook all over and closed the office door behind them.

He walked to the chalkboard and wrote:

"THE KILLER IS KNOWN. The Dog gets a bone.

Secure the death, but only when the debt is paid.
They meet they will, on Fox's Eve,
Be by the old mill when the moon hits the trees."

AND THEN ON the other end, he wrote:

WHEN?
When the satellite crosses the Dog Star, Sirius?
What day?
A blonde woman will be killed.
Who? Where?

MANNY READ and then leaned back in his chair. "This is your sister."

Hooker nodded. "Even more interestingly, she fed me the message verbally through Peter."

"He's the night dweller you see at midnight and give a cigarette to?"

"The same."

"But I thought he was afraid of her? She beat him or terrorized him or something."

"I don't think she does any of it personally. I think it would be more of a psychological threat if it came directly from her. But it could have been one of her thugs. I think they are all afraid of her, anyone on the streets. I have no idea what the size of her tribe or army is, but I know it is more than a few dozen... um, bodies."

"So what do you think?"

Hooker sat in the large barrel chair. "Manny, I'm not really sure what to think." He leaned forward and laid out his right hand from the cast. "I've known Peter going on ten years now. I know when he tells me something, he has read... it's dull and flat. He is just reporting. But this was a rhyme. He recited it in a sing-song fashion. I could almost hear my sister's voice telling him the rhyme."

He pulled his hand and arm back in and chewed on his thumbnail. "And if she taught it to him, she would have had to go over it and over it many times."

Hooker's eyes were pointed at the desk, but his focus was a long way away and a long time ago.

Manny watched the young man think and then turned his chair to study the rhyme and questions.

"You capitalized the word 'Dog.'" He sat thinking about it.

"It was the way Peter sang it. It sounded like more of a name or title. I think it may mean something about the knee slave who is never more than a few feet from her knees. I seem to remember her calling him Dog. The whole tribe is about animals because they live like them."

Manny nodded. "Do you think she might be talking about the killing in the railcar?"

Hooker stopped chewing at his thumb. He rested it gently on the chair arm, thinking.

He looked up at Manny with a question on his face. "I

don't know. For someone who is always on foot with no means of communication, she has always impressed me with how connected to everything she is. It is like every street bum and night dweller is her personal radio station."

"Do you think she is asking you to meet her on this Fox's Eve at some mill?"

"The meet and the mill, I am sure of. I've met her there before. It is one place she can be sure we're not being observed by her people. But what I don't get is this Fox's Eve. Huckleberries, we don't even have any fox in this area."

Manny chuckled to himself. It always amazed him how the young man caught himself from swearing.

Manny considered the lack of foxes. "We don't have any ravens either."

Hooker stood up and wrote on the board *Raven bone*.

"Put a question on that—*how close*." Manny looked at the last line. "And I guess that would be moonrise?"

Hooker looked at the corner where the large bookshelves met the ceiling. "Moonset if it's in the next couple of weeks. The moon has been rising in the afternoon lately. And the trees are to the southwest of the mill so they would be moonset." He turned and made the notation followed by *when does the moon set*.

"So now we come to the satellite?"

Hooker chuckled as he collapsed back into the chair. "We'll get the information when Hank sobers up in the morning. Willie said he's an amateur astronomer who has a large telescope." He widened his eyes and made an 'O' of his mouth. The joke was lewd, crude, and exactly the kind Willie would make.

The two laughed.

"Have you ever seen your wife that plowed before?"

"Years ago." His lips sucked hard against his teeth. "When Paul and I worked the King and Story area. It was hard on her.

"When she kissed me goodbye in the mornings, she never knew if I would come home at night, or if she would have to go identify my body. When I made detective, it went in waves. She never had a drinking problem. It was more of a 'holding it all in' problem. Sometimes the dam or wall would crack, other times it would flat break." He leaned on his elbows and rocked his butt off the cushion. "After I got shot, and it looked like I would survive, and you decamped from Willie's, she got some relief. Her only fear was you might knock up some nice girl or something."

"But what about you?" Hooker asked.

Manny scrunched his face and farted. "I was out of the picture then. Get me up and dressed in a clean diaper. Feed me and keep me from drooling in my gruel. Stuff me in a corner for the day and put me back to bed with clean diapers. There was nothing to worry about anymore."

"So it was just me?"

"Kid, you were usually one glass of wine kind of worry. By the time you came to us, you were legal for driving. You hardly ever drank. You never smoked. Hell, I never asked— did you ever do drugs?"

"Is this the dad talk? Because if it is, then you're years

too late." Hooker thought a moment. "So this nice girl she was worried about, did she have anyone in mind?" His smarmy grin turned into a full Hooker smile, the one he used to get out of most trouble, even with Dolly and Stella.

"Boy, if you have the balls, ask her. But you better do it before Squirt and his sister move in." He slapped his forehead. "Shoot, I forgot. Put 'Trace Van De Camp' on the corner where I'll see it in the morning."

"You're tracing people now?'

"No. His name is Trace. Used to work bunko on the north end, but now he does small construction. I've forgotten to call him these last couple of months—what with you in and out of the hospital and all."

"So you two are serious about Candy and Squirt?"

"Why not? Stella and I could never have kids. We didn't even know we wanted any. Now, after inheriting you and Willie, we think we did all right. So why not rear up two more? All it would be is a reach back with a hand up. It's not as if we have to grow them through diapers or pay for their school or anything. And in the end, we are rewarded with a daughter who is a nurse, and we finally get a son who's in the family business."

"What, wearing diapers?"

Manny had felt the jab coming. He already had his hand on his tennis ball he used to squeeze all day for muscle tone in his hands and arms. The fuzzy ball hit Hooker square in the forehead and resulted in fits of laughter from both men.

Box scratched on the door.

A still laughing Hooker pushed himself out of the chair and opened the door just as the phone rang.

It was 3:37 in the morning, hardly ever a good sign.

Manny picked up the receiver. "Hello?" His tone was terse and short. He listened and hung up.

Manny turned and looked at Hooker who hung in the doorway. "Go to bed. Danny is picking you up for breakfast."

CHAPTER EIGHT

Danny was a force of nature. At six foot five, he was built like the most frightening lineman the Forty-Niners could ever dream of having. Incongruously, he was also the most settled person one could be around. His movements were spare, and he was the kind of guy who had about seventy words a day in him. Get to number seventy, and you'll have to see him tomorrow for the rest of the sentence. Unless, of course, if he is met at the door by Stella. She could make the dead talk like they were at a Toastmaster's meeting.

The door flung open, and before he could take evasive action, he had a large soft chest shoved into his lower half where other people would have a belly. Danny had a six-pack made more from steel than aluminum, but it was susceptible to being made happy with a very full-bodied hug from Stella or his mother, Tilly.

"Danny, Danny, Danny. You get better looking every

day. So much so, I just can hardly wait until next Sunday when you bring," Stella pushed back from him and gave him the eye, "your mama and Sweets out for dinner."

Danny stumbled through his memories. Not finding an appointment involving a Sunday dinner, he quickly made the notation. "Yes, ma'am. You can expect us about...?" he fished.

Stella flirted with a passing slap across his white shirt and chest. "Oh, shucks, Danny, any time after four is all good. I know Sweets sleeps until two or so. Now, come on in and have some coffee while you tell me how your mama is." She grabbed his hand before a *no, thank you* could escape his lips.

On seeing the giant black man in tow, Manny greeted him from his throne of the sunroom. "Danny!" he yelled with his arms raised.

Stella waved with her palm facing down. "Manny, I have told you a thousand times. The boys are black, and Danny's brother is blind. Neither one of them is deaf. But with your yelling at them, they will get there soon."

Danny leaned over and side hugged her as he kissed her on the top of the head. "I've got this, Mama." He strode into the sunroom.

Manny frowned with an ugly face. "Oh, lawd, you been losing weight?" Same old joke.

Danny pulled his custom-made shirt away from his sides near his belt line. "A little." Looking up with a worried face, he asked, "You don't think it looks good on me?"

The two laughed and shook hands. Old school respect —no thumb jig, none of the hand jive—just shook. It was the sign of the straight, simple respect the two had for each other—no fluff.

Danny sat at the other end of the couch where Manny was reclining. Hanging out on the couch was Manny's one vacation from the constant reminder he was not the man he used to be.

The couch was custom built for the sunroom when Manny still walked the halls of San Jose Police Department as a senior detective. On his days off, he enjoyed reading the paper in the sunroom with Stella. The length of the couch allowed both to stretch out reading or dozing.

They had designed the entire room around napping and enjoying the morning overlooking the Almaden Valley spread out below. The sunroom was the kingdom Manny and Stella took turns ruling, but on Sundays—it was a shared domain.

Manny sipped from his mug, the one with the gold detective badge molded onto it. Quietly, he asked about Danny's brother. "How is Sweets these days?"

Danny took the large mug from Stella as she sat on the ottoman to listen. He took a long sip and closed his eyes. The soft smile warmed and softened his face. It was the face of the man Stella liked best and held in her heart.

His life was of driver and bodyguard for his little brother. Blind since high school, his brother Sweets was now a night disc jockey for the local radio station. His popularity was legion. He could have had the more prestigious day shifts, but the night and the people who were awake and working then were what Sweets called *His People*. The simple fact was he knew he was allowed more leeway in the music he chose to play—even though it was against the company's programming.

Danny forced his eyes open and licked his thinned lips with just the tip of his tongue. Spare movements. "Sweets is doing okay. It's the end of a cycle, so he has to memorize the next eighty songs and their colors." He was referring to the new program routine where the owners of the company send out a new list every ninety days, and the DJ plays the songs by their color. Sweets had to have the list memorized because of his blindness. But he also played the music he wanted to play, a country-western sound, but more like a cowboy-who-likes-rock-and-roll kind of sound.

"Do you help him with that?"

"Not for the last few cycles. The East Coast finally got their heads around Sweets being blind, so they sent the list in braille. Mama helps him with the colors. The idiots still stick the color dot next to a line of braille." He did a fair imitation of Stella and Hooker's favorite physical commentary on all things dumb—he rolled his head with his tongue out in an almost perfect zombie roll. He ended up looking into the eyes of Box on the back of the couch. They held each other's stare.

Danny had never figured out whether Box was friend or foe. Box kept him guessing. Danny's calm disguised any fear, or maybe respect. The only thing he truly feared was his mother, Tilly Sweets, a force of nature to be reckoned with. Be on her good side, and life was glorious. Be on her bad side, and hell would be a nice vacation.

Box slowly closed his eye in measured disdain, walked along the couch back, and headed for the kitchen. He passed Hooker. Hooker only glanced at his partner and smirked. He knew there had been a face-off, and once again, the smaller fur man had won.

"Hey, big guy. I saw someone come in, but you've lost so much weight, I didn't realize it was you."

Danny stood and glared at the famous Hooker smile. In the last seven years, neither one had won this face-off. Once Hooker turned eighteen and was legal to tow, he stopped backing down from anything—tow or fight.

The two laughed and hugged. Danny growled like he hated it. It was a standing joke.

"We need to go. Mama put the quiche in as I was leaving."

Stella grabbed the man's tree of an arm. "What kind?"

"Don't worry. If it don't kill us, she'll bring you the recipe on Sunday."

Hooker called down the hall as they opened the front door. "Box, stay. Torment Stella and Manny." The cat stuck his head out of their bedroom door. The single eye was noncommittal, but the ear twitched. Hooker pointed his finger at him from the cast. "Behave. I'll be back soon and bring you some roadkill from Tilly."

Hooker had long admired the perfectly kept suicide-door Lincoln from the outside. The engine surged quietly as they headed down the hill of stupid to the Sweets home in Willow Glen. Hooker looked around the interior. His left hand stroked the soft leather.

Danny's eyes missed nothing—a small smile slid across his face. He settled back into his place in the world. This was his domain. Sweets may own the car—but Danny ruled it.

"Nice, huh?"

Hooker's eyebrows went up in appreciation. His hand did not hesitate its stroking of the smooth coolness. "It's softer than my jacket." He thought a moment and remembered what was left after the emergency medical units had finished cutting him out of it. He almost chuckled at the eight pieces of leather held together with surgical tape so he could wander around the hospital in his signature leather jacket—until Willie, in disgust, took it and burned it. "Was."

Danny frowned and then remembered, too. His right eye slowly closed as he made a mental note about birthdays. A few years before, his brother Sweets and he had taken Hooker out to dinner and his first truly legal drink. The date was in October, and it would be in his past datebook.

Hooker leaned against the door and looked out the window listlessly.

"What?"

Hooker looked back through the front glass. "I was thinking how nice the leather would feel in Mae when we get her rebuilt... then I was just thinking about Mae." He looked over at Danny. "Willie says I baked, raked, and snaked the engine. We have to find a new one."

The large man looked over at the depressed young white kid. He needed to be kicked in the ass and cheered up at the same time. Danny growled his throat clear. "Your scrawny bone for an ass would have torn up this sort of leather inside of a month. Probably wouldn't make it through the first week and a good fart. If you're going to have leather seats, you need some tougher stuff than what you get in your jackets. You'll need oil-tanned boot leather.

"Go over the hill to Santa Cruz to the tannery and pick up some yellow and blue leather so it looks right for that rig of yours. Any of the upholstery shops in town can reupholster the seats for you."

Hooker looked at the big man and laughed. "Danny?"

The man nosed the large car into the neat driveway with a perfect lawn on each side. He followed the short curve to the front door. "What?"

"Did someone adjust your word limit to a higher count?"

The big V8 burbled to silence. Danny stared at the front of the long hood. Slowly his head ground its way around to look at Hooker, who was on the verge of laughing. "Fuck you, fool." His imitation of an angry man made the response even more hilarious for Hooker.

Hooker rolled out his door, laughing. Danny steamed.

The front door opened as Danny made it there first. "What is going on out here?"

Danny squeezed past his mother. "Ain't talking," he grumped.

She turned to see her adopted white son. He was laughing so hard she knew it had to be something to do with her oldest and largest. Her fists found their usual resting place on her hips. "And what is so funny about you harassing your big brother?"

Hooker pulled himself together enough to stumble into her arms. He loved hugging her. There was no halfway or sort of with Tilly. When it came to hugs, she was in all the way. You knew when you were hugged by Tilly Sweets.

As they started to break apart, Hooker whispered in her ear. "Try to get him to say two more words today."

She knew her son. She rolled her eyes and then gave Hooker a 'Tilly' look as she slapped his chest with the hand towel. "Hooker, you leave your brother alone, or I will withhold dessert from everyone, including Sweets."

"Did I just hear my name being taken in vain?" The smooth-as-silk voice came from the front room.

Hooker closed the front door as Tilly headed back toward the kitchen.

"No, Sweets." Hooker strolled into the living room and was met in the middle by the slender man. There was a soft ticking sound coming from the man, and Hooker knew it was his sounding for objects around him, much like a bat. He put out his hand as he crossed into the room. "We were just commenting about being so late. We just knew you were probably starved and chewing on the furniture."

He took the outstretched hand and stepped in for a

hug. If you hug one of the Sweets family—then you hug all three.

Tilly sang out from the kitchen. "Quiche."

None of the four was bashful around food. Amazingly, for the size of him, Danny ate little more than Sweets did. But the pie dish was showing nothing but the glass at the bottom. The biscuits had been the most amazing, as they were sourdough without any mistakes.

Hooker pushed back from his plate. He was too full to get up and clear his dishes just yet. Tilly followed suit, and Sweets still had a few bites to go. Danny got up unbidden. Without a word, he cleared all the dishes. He returned with a fresh carafe of coffee and poured his mother's cup full. He likewise filled Sweets and his, and then set the carafe in the middle and sat down.

Tilly gave him a hard look. He just sat with a deadpan look. "Danny, be a dear and see if there is any milk in the fridge?"

Danny looked at Hooker. He shook his head.

"Is that a *No*, there isn't any or no, I won't do what my dear sweet mother who carried me for nine and a half months, breastfed me until I was..."

Danny bolted up. He returned with the half-gallon of milk and placed it beside the only person he knew who used it, Hooker. He went into the living room, leaving the three alone to talk.

Sweets looked to a place just above Hooker's head. "Did I miss something?"

Hooker folded his napkin and placed it on the table.

He confessed contritely, "I asked him if someone had upped his word allowance. He was unusually chatty. I guess he got mad." He started to get up.

Sweets reached out to the air near Hooker. "Leave him be. He's a big man. The conversation you entered started several days ago. It wasn't even your conversation, and you are right, Danny is a quiet man. He always was a man of few words. But this fight, you didn't start.

"About a week ago, I had Danny going through some old records back in the cold storage room. He overheard one of the engineers at the station explaining to someone else the reason he was so quiet was he didn't have much in the way of brains and had nothing to talk about or say."

"But that isn't even half true."

"You know it, I know it, and Mom knows it, but the engineer hasn't spent any time with Danny, and so he doesn't know it. But in his world, it is all about his perception, not ours."

"It's still a mean thing to say."

"True, but I doubt if I approach the man, he will ever see Danny as anything but a giant black man, and in his mind, that means Baby Huey." Sweets got a thoughtful look on his face. "As I said, the man has spent no time getting to know Danny, but you teased him because he had something to say."

Hooker had known it was wrong the moment he had said it, but he didn't know how to make it right. "And I feel like the stink on the bottom of a misstep on the lawn."

Sweets smiled his megawatt smile and made things all right. "I think you two are both man enough to get over it."

Hooker thought as they all three sipped. He noticed Tilly, the consummate mother hen, quietly watching over her brood.

"So what do you think his opinion of Sweets is?" Hooker smiled even though he knew Sweets was blind. He also felt Sweets could feel or hear he was smiling.

"I don't have a problem with, or from, the man. So I would be prejudiced if I tried to put words in his mouth. They might be right. They might be far wrong. I'm just not going to do it."

"This brings up something else I have wondered about for years—the name Sweets. It's your last name, but Danny and even your mother here call you by it."

Sweets' chuckle grew into a belly laugh. Tilly had tears squished from the corners of her eyes she was laughing so hard. Hooker joined in the infectious laughter with no inkling of what they had found so hilarious.

Danny walked in from the living room where he had been reading. His index finger marked his place in the middle of the book. He frowned at the other two and turned his glare on Hooker. "What?"

Hooker smiled, he had at least one more word out of the big man. "I only asked why you two call your brother by y'all's last name. You are all Sweets, but with you two, only Sweets is Sweets."

Danny thought a moment and looked at his family. The giant man softly shushed his chinos onto the chair and poured himself some more coffee. "It's his name." He glared at his brother and mother who were now laughing even harder. Sweets had even stopped making any noise. He was in silent convulsions. Tilly was threatening to bash her chin with her undulating chest. Danny sipped his coffee and growled.

Knowing he wasn't going to get any help or contradictions from his family, he put his coffee mug down and looked at Hooker.

He jabbed his right thumb toward his brother. "It started at the hospital. The wimp was in welding class in high school. Some ass..." He looked to see if his mother was listening. "Some ass-wipe dropped an oxygen bottle. The steel table sheared off the head. The bottle became a missile, and after bouncing off two walls and taking out four welding booths, it hit Sweets in the head." Hooker nodded. He had heard this part before.

Danny sipped calmly on his coffee. The memories made the vein in his forehead swell and pulse. "When I got back up here from USC, where I was on scholarship, I went right to the hospital from the bus station. His head was just a big ball of white wrapping, just like you were a few months ago. We still didn't know if he would live or die. Hell, I didn't even know for sure it was even him. All I could see was a big white ball with two scrawny little black arms hanging out down the sheets. They had tubes going in and more coming out. He looked like a Boy Scout knotting class gone wrong.

"Being the only smart guy in the room, I grabbed the

medical chart off the end of his bed. Some ignorant fuckhead…"

Tilly reached out and backhanded his shoulder. He turned on her.

"Then you tell it."

She laughed harder and rolled her hand in the air. She couldn't stand it. She leaned over and hugged her arms around his big arm and pushed her cheek into his shoulder. The left hand rolled again in the air.

Danny gave her a sympathetic look of disgust and turned back to Hooker. "They had him on the chart as Sweet Christopher. Not even Christopher Sweet… but Sweet Christopher—no comma."

Hooker frowned. His left index finger extended open from his hand. "His first name is Christopher?" His other hand took up the load of the mug, the cast working as ridged scaffolding.

"No. That's the point. They had him all screwed up. It was after visiting hours, and the head nurse came trotting down the hall to shoo me out. I spun on her like she was a right tackle. She might have outweighed me, but I had her by at least a head and shoulder. I put my finger on the name and quietly explained to her the grievous error of her ways and the ways of the hospital. I had her backtracked and hard up against the nurse's desk.

"I told her the name was Sweets—plural. Not rock candy, not gumdrops, not gooey cinnamon rolls, but all of them—Sweets. And when she started to point to the name Christopher, I snapped. I yelled his name was not Christopher… it was

Sweets. She asked what the last name was. I guess I growled or something. I told her in no uncertain terms... Sweets."

The whole table chorused. Then they all started laughing.

Finally, Hooker got enough control. "Then what is your first name?"

The three chorused the same. Hooker raised his hands in surrender. And laughed. He was sure he knew who the charge nurse was on the fateful night. He knew all the important fat necks to nuzzle. He rubbed his scars on his right side. They were still tender.

Sweets was first to break the contemplative silence. "When do you get the cast off?"

Hooker looked up. "One more week. They say the pain will be worse once I start moving those muscles."

Danny leaned forward. "I'll come rub the knots out. I can work out some stretches for you, too. I notice when you walk you're still bound up on the right side."

"I'd like that, Danny." He smiled. "So we're good now?"

"No." The twinkle danced in the whole family's eyes was there. "You're still underfed."

"Yeah, well, it's Stella's cooking. She has me on some crazy restrictive diet and all."

The two jabbed with the verbal sparring dance that happens with brothers. Tilly cleared the last of the serving dishes and unused silverware. Puttering around in the kitchen, she made a fresh pot of coffee.

Hooker noticed first. "You're awful quiet there, Sweets."

The man turned his face to where Hooker was. "When did you last talk to your sister?"

The laughs were over. The meal was eaten. The pleasantries were finished. It was now time for the work. It was time to get down to the real reason Hooker was in Sweets' domain.

"The Mouse? Just before I got shot. Why?"

"Any contact from her lately?"

Hooker's mind raced. *How does he do...?* It had long since stopped being creepy or even scary. It was now a great curiosity.

"Last night. She sent a rhyme puzzle. Actually, it was two of them."

"How did you get them?"

Hooker pointed into the air between them. "And there is the curiosity. She sent it verbally through an intermediary she used to torment. He's very afraid of her and her gang. But the way he recited it, I could tell she worked with him personally until he had it perfect. It was very strange."

"She needs your help."

"The Mouse. We're talking about my sister, The Mouse. The Mouse—the evil queen of all the night creatures and things crawling on two or four feet in the dark of the world. Help? Her?"

Sweets nodded. "She reached out through someone

who would rather die than deal with her. You know that, and she knows you know that. That's why she used him."

Hooker knew Sweets' injury was a give and take sort of thing. His sight had been taken from him. But in exchange, he had been blessed with an enhanced ability to remember every song, artist, producer, and other liner note information about music. But he had also been cursed or gifted with another kind of sight—he could 'see' images. Sometimes they were just wild extraneous stuff he couldn't attach to anything or anyone. Other times, they were very vivid and exact, meaningless to Sweets, but important to the person in the vision.

"What did you see, Sweets?"

Sweets sat stoically and then washed his hands over his face as if to clear his vision. "It was like Dorothy in the Wizard of Oz. She's running here and there with her little dog. In the air, I could sense the dark bird or birds. They were chasing her. She knows they will kill her, but not yet. So she is searching for you..." He sat back in silence, his face blank. If he could see, Hooker would have said he was just staring.

"What else, Sweets?"

He slowly shook his head.

"What?"

"It doesn't make sense."

"What doesn't?"

Sweets struggled. His voice was strained. "You had a big gun. A very big gun."

"Betsy. My sawed-off twelve-gauge."

Sweets thought a moment. "Maybe."

"I protected her."

"No." He shook his head. "You shot her... and she smiled. Then the whole area just turned to flames and exploded."

"You mean exploded and then turned to flames?"

"No. Everywhere was one big fireball... and then there was an explosion." He leaned toward Hooker. Danny was frowning as he watched his brother. He had seen this intensity overcome Sweets before.

"I told you it didn't make sense."

Hooker shook his head. "No. What does *not* make sense is me shooting Sissy."

Danny growled at Hooker. "I told you before not to call her by that name."

Hooker ignored Danny's anger.

"It's what I saw. You shot them both, her and the dog. And she smiled when you did it. It was like a relief. You were setting her free."

"Death is not freedom," Hooker growled.

Danny growled reflectively. "It is to someone who is truly committing suicide."

CHAPTER NINE

Hooker found Manny in his office. The large professional headphones covered the sides of his head. He was humming with the music and staring at the boards. The man was most alive when there was a problem in front of him to solve. Murder was the ultimate problem. Manny was at his best. He was at his most aware. It was as if every one of his senses was on hyper-overdrive.

Manny raised his right hand and then raised his index finger. Without turning around to see who was in the doorway, he called out loudly over the music only he could hear, "I figured out Fox's Eve."

Stella came up behind Hooker as he stood in the office doorway. Hooker turned to her. "How does he do that?"

She shrugged. "One of life's little Manny mysteries. You need anything to eat or drink?"

He smiled and shook his head. She knew where he had

been. He was more ready for a nap. Instead, he walked over to the oversized black walnut desk. He sat on the corner and waited.

Manny took off his headphones. "How was breakfast with the Sweets?"

"Good. Disturbing."

The man thought about the dichotomy. "Yeah, I guess it can happen with them. I can imagine the good. What was disturbing?"

"Danny talked straight for almost five minutes. It had to be over a few hundred words."

The man did not laugh. He grabbed his pursed lips, and his eyes roamed about the desk and walls. "He's worried about something. Did he say anything?"

"Sweets did. It was about some ass-jerk engineer at the radio station. Danny overheard the guy say the reason Danny didn't say much was because he wasn't smart enough to have anything to say. I just made it worse because I teased him by asking if someone had bumped up his daily word allowance."

"I thought you said he had run his mouth for five minutes."

"He ran his mouth after I had teased him."

"If he was pissed off, why was he talking? I would think he would just clam up for a few days."

"He did. He was in the other room reading Plato's *The Cave*. I recognized the book. It should be right there in the hole in your shelf."

Manny glanced over at the large bookshelf with the

four holes. "Hmm, I would have thought he would have read the Dostoyevsky first. Interesting... So what was the long speech about?"

"I asked why they called Sweets 'Sweets' when they are all Sweets." Hooker's eyes went up. "Yeah, it does sound silly when I put it that way."

"So why was Danny elected to be the mouthpiece?"

"He was the only one who could talk. I thought Sweets and Tilly were going to just blow gaskets right there from laughing so hard. I guess they thought maybe I knew."

"...about Danny marching Wanda Cutter backward down the hall?" Manny and Stella both chuckled.

"Now, there is an image." Hooker now had confirmation on his guess at it being Nurse Cutter. "A destroyer backing an aircraft carrier back across the ocean."

"I don't think even your Uncle Willie would have the balls to back-march Dolly or even Stella, much less Wanda Cutter."

Hooker laughed. "Oh, he has the balls. He's just not stupid." Hooker jabbed his finger at Manny. "You know, when I was on the third floor, and they would come to visit, I thought it was kind of strange Nurse Wanda 'I rule the world' Cutter would all but disappear."

Manny stroked his pursed lips and chuckled at the thought of her giving anyone a wide berth.

Stella rolled her head and leaned her hip against the door. Both men knew this was her giveaway tell she was going to stir up some fun stuff. "You know why they built Good Sam, don't you?"

"Because they needed another hospital?"

"No, silly. It was because they needed at least two miles of turf to separate Wanda and Connie." She was referring to the other strong nurse in the San Jose area who ruled the Valley Medical Center from her glass booth overlooking the emergency room—the place everyone joked was Hooker's second home.

They all laughed and then thought about what it would be like having the two domineering women running a hospital from the ground and third floors. The mental image made them laugh even harder.

Hooker shifted and stood.

"Well, it's been fun, but I need some aspirin and a nap. I'll talk to you in a few hours at dinner."

Manny hid his smile. "Sure thing, kid. I'll wake you when it's time." He silently counted three. "Oh, Hooker?"

The mop of curly black hair and droopy eyes looked back around the corner. "Yeah, Manny?"

"Have you ever heard the song... and I can't think of how the music goes... but the words are something like: *The fox went out on a chilly night. Prayed to the moon to give her light. Many a mile to go that night, before she reached the town-o, town-o, town-o. Many a mile to go that night before she reached the town-o.*"

Hooker frowned, thinking.

"Heard it before?"

Hooker thought blurrily. Shaking his head, "No, Manny, I haven't. Why do you ask?"

Manny waved his hand. "Nothing kid. Just thinking… Enjoy your nap."

He listened to the kid pad his way down the hall. Stella watched from the door. There was a muted conversation with Box, and then the silence. The man smiled and noted the time.

"That was evil, Manny Romero." Stella pushed off the door and headed for the kitchen. "I'm proud of you," she added with an evil smile. The constant take-no-prisoners and give-no-ground approach kept everyone in the family on their toes. It was refined to a very high and talented game. Most days, Manny was the Master, with Stella and her sister not far behind. If anyone were close to Manny, it would be Dolly—she practiced the game deftly with those who were in charge of her city.

The house settled into silence as Stella leaned over the island, sipping coffee, and reading the paper. This was her time of the year to scour the want ads for used canning jars for sale. One year she wrote directly to the Ball jar company, but the closest they could come to the prices she normally paid was a small discount off what the large chain supermarkets paid. Most of what she acquired was paid for in canned fruit or vegetables.

Manny opened one of the books he was currently reading. He had started back through the classics written in the nineteenth century. Sir Arthur Conan Doyle was one of four books he was dipping into, back and forth. Keeping the four-complex story-lines straight was his defense against boredom.

Manny looked at the clock when he heard the scream.

"Holy Chry... Sothamnus Nauseosa... on the desert floor!"

Manny smiled, *twenty-eight minutes*. Good recovery too... The Latin name for rabbit brush. The kid might have even hit REM sleep before the bomb hit his subconscious. He slipped the headphones back over his ears and chuckled. Some days he just loved being an evil man.

Hooker slid to a stop when his shoulder hit the doorjamb. "Damn it all, Manny, that was not nice."

He strode into the office in only his boxers and socks. "And knock it off. I know you can hear me. The tape isn't even running."

Manny swore under his breath. He knew he should have turned the reel-to-reel back on. It was obvious when the huge professional twelve-inch reels were moving. He looked up at the young man as he chuckled. Hooker was now very much awake.

"Yes. It was a nursery rhyme or something. She sang it to me when I was a kid."

"Full moon is Tuesday."

"I've got to call Willie."

Manny raised his open hand. "Telstar crosses Sirius every seventeen days in its orbit. The next from our point of view is Sunday morning at 1:17."

Hooker slumped back against the desk cursing. "Beans and wienies!"

The man in the wheelchair echoed him. "Correct, the pooch is fucked."

"She told us when. She even told us who... or what she will look like. But she held back the where." The two men thought about what all those points meant. "She did not intend for us to stop the kill, just to know she has the inside track on everything. Whatever she wants will be huge."

Hooker had grown up in seven foster homes with her. She had run away for good on her sixteenth birthday.

The foster parents had decided to have some fun with her for her birthday. The mother held her down while the father raped her front, top, and back. When they were finished with their fun, they turned her over to their mentally challenged adult son who was more violent and sexually sadistic than they were.

This was not the first time she had been abused in the homes. However, when it started, she knew this time, it was up to her to make it the last time.

During the exchange of the prisoner, she had made an escape, taking her to the sanctuary of the kitchen. She had started on the dim-witted son with a paring knife. As he sprawled screaming and bleeding from multiple minor cuts to the face and hands, she turned on the parents. The father had suffered the most with slashes to his crotch and face. The mother received only minor but painful cuts to her breasts.

Four months later, when they began to take their anger out on a thirteen-year-old Hooker, he finished what his sister had started. After no charges were filed, and during a transfer to a new home four states away, Hooker lifted the wallet out of the purse of the woman transporting the poor child and disappeared from the Greyhound station. Later, through some research about the homes they had been in, they realized he and his sister had always been *sold* to the next home. It had been a secret network of pedophiles and sadists. To Hooker's horror, he discovered the sexual abuse of his sister had been going on for many years and homes since she was nine.

Finding her had only been a matter of walking out of the bus station. She was waiting with a few new friends in the shadows. If he had gotten on the bus with the woman like planned—it would have been the end of their family.

Three months later, they had wound up in San Jose and were separated. She kept to the streets and the night, and Hooker had found Uncle Willie's car.

She had taught Hooker the power of the underground or street telephone, the passing of information from one denizen of the night to another—from the bum on the corner to the alcoholic in the alley. As their worlds separated with time, there was still a connection. They each knew they could somehow send a message to the other.

Just as she ruled a tribe of the creatures of the night, Hooker also knew and used the powerful tools of knowledge flowing openly in the street. For Hooker, it could be as simple as knowing where a derelict car was parked—no longer good for sleeping in. But on a more personal level, it was his lifeline to the only sister he had—even if she was not blood-related.

He looked at Manny leaning back in his chair, studying him. "What?"

"Care to share?"

"Share what?"

"You've been gone off into that head of yours for the last ten minutes."

"I was thinking about Sissy." He caught himself. He could hear Danny yelling at him to stop calling her childhood name. It was a name of derision, not just what a little boy calls his older sister. "... The Mouse."

"What about her?"

"She wants something. And if Sweets is correct, I'm not going to like it." He told Manny about Sweets' vision. Stella wandered back into the room with mugs of fresh coffee.

The two parents listened as their kid peeled the onion of his knowledge and of his pain. There can be no harder job than to be a parent who can't fix the tough boo-boos in life. Manny and Stella could only sit and listen and watch the slow train-wreck as it happened.

The afternoon sun lay slanted along the floors.

"Do you think there's any chance what Sweets saw could have been misinterpreted? I mean, he might have seen one thing and thought it was something else?"

Hooker pushed at the last bite of the afternoon snack. They had been talking for hours—over and over, all about the same things. They had looked from this angle or that. His eyes were blurry as he looked at his plate, but his focus was miles away. He was trying once again to read his sister's mind. Something they had laughed about as children—their ability to know what the other was thinking, without verbal communication.

"It's not how Sweets operates. He describes exactly what he is seeing. He can't interpret it, so he just describes the pictures. It's always as if his is in a museum or looking at *National Geographic* or *Life*. There are pictures in front of him, and he will tell you what he sees in detail. But he doesn't know it's a cow or car or building." Hooker looked up. "I guess he does know what things are and look like, but he saw a whole lot of flames as the world blew up. However, there is no perspective. If I were Box and sat next to the fireplace in there, it would be a big fire. Nevertheless, for us, and many feet away, it's just a fire in the fireplace. So he does not know if it's a campfire, a bonfire, or half of San Jose blowing up. He just doesn't know."

Manny moved his index finger along the grain of the table. His focus was closer and farther than Hooker's. "Let's hope it's just a campfire."

Stella cleared her throat but still croaked her words. "But he saw you shoot your sister."

Hooker slumped and nodded. "That's the part that scares me. He does know what that would look like."

"No doubt..."

"He was very clear about it—right down to my shotgun."

A heavy silence hung in the air. They were all talked out. It was now time to realize it and do something about it.

Stella watched as Hooker's jaw slid open and his head hung lower. The soft snoring sound effects were supplied by her husband. If she hadn't been so tired, it would have been funny.

Her chair purposely scraped, and the men jerked. Without spoken directions, plates were cleared, and the three headed for their respective beds.

The warm afternoon sun slanted across the dark slate floor. In the center of the warmest part, there was no cat to soak up the heat.

Life was twisting.

The quiet was a pressing gray noise, and the heat was building. Hooker knew he should look behind him but could not bring himself to turn. He was searching. What he was looking for, he couldn't find. You have to know what you are looking for in order to know when you have found it. The buzz of the heat reflected off the hot sand. Hooker could not feel his feet in the sand.

He knew he needed to turn around. He just did not have the strength to push his will.

The heat seared until everything was just white. Hooker looked for something. He knew he had to find it, whatever *it* was.

He knew he should turn around, but he didn't want to. He was afraid of what was there. He kept searching.

The white began to take parts of Hooker. He had to find it. He looked harder.

His legs ended at his ankles in the white of the sand. He wiggled his toes. He could feel the toes were now part of the sand. "I won't need boots next year."

The white sand washed against his legs and bound them together. The heat intensified. He pushed forward, searching for what he needed to find. He was trapped, but he had to find it.

The white around his legs drew snug. What was behind him drew near. The voice was urgent. He needed to find the thing and make the voice stop.

With a rush of adrenaline and determination, Hooker turned. He screamed as the shotgun exploded.

The expanding cloud of hot orange gas enveloped him and reached for his soul. He recoiled.

Hooker physically screamed, and as he recoiled in his mind, he jumped backward in the bed. He was suspended in midair for a moment. Then, in his mind, the shotgun blast hit him in the back and head.

His scream was cut short as his head and back hit the concrete floor.

Stella's shoulder slammed into the doorjamb and the half-open door. The door slapped against the wall, burying itself on the stopper. The noise was loud and explosive, like a shotgun blast at point-blank range.

Hooker's heart skipped a beat, and he passed out. His terrorized mind was certain he had been shot again.

Moments later, Hooker's eyes fluttered, and then he blinked. He was lying on the hard floor. His pillow was under his head. His blankets were neatly over him, and he was staring up through the spokes of Manny's wheelchair at the man himself.

"Just lay there. Stella is getting the ice pack."

Hooker closed his eyes. He tried to pull himself together, tried to remember. "Sorry for waking you two up."

"You didn't." Stella's face appeared over him, looking down. She knelt with a wince as her knees groaned and popped. "Why do you guys always have to end up on the floor? I'm truly getting too old for this nonsense." She placed a cold ice bag under Hooker's head.

A warm purr moved along his right arm. His arm and cast felt funny. Hooker wondered if a person could break an arm when it is in a cast.

Box placed a tentative front paw on Hooker's chest. Meeting no resistance, he placed the other on the chest and then sat down in the open armpit. It was warm and snuggly, but without the fuss of climbing on the chest.

Hooker frowned and rolled his eyes up to Stella. "What time is it?"

"A little past three."

"Day or night?"

Manny moaned, "Night."

Without looking, Stella reached over and rubbed Manny's hand. "It was one of those nights again."

Hooker looked through the spokes. "Getting shot again?"

Manny winced with a drawn back lip. The nod was almost imperceptible in the dim light from the hall. The man was embarrassed this kind of crap could go on for so many years. He looked out of the room's door at the black wall of glass and dim night lights in the courtyard fountain.

Hooker thought about how tough the man was, and how such a little thing could cause so much havoc in a life. He sighed deeply. "So, I guess this is never going to just go away."

Stella silently stroked his forehead and slowly shook her head.

Hooker smiled weakly. "So we are all up. I guess some hot cocoa would be out of the question?"

Manny harrumphed. "It tastes like crap with moonshine in it."

Stella rolled her eyes as she pursed her lips and nodded in agreement. "Guess I'll have to find where I hid bottle of dark rum."

Hooker sat up carefully.

"You dizzy?"

"Naw, I'm fine, just the bump hurts."

Stella stood. "Keep thet ice on it."

Manny chuckled. "Check the floor and see if there is a divot or dent?"

Stella tapped her husband's head as she walked out. "He's not your blood relative."

They all three laughed at the hard-headed family joke.

Hooker leaned back against the bed platform. He held the ice bag on his head. His eyes closed sluggishly, but without a sign of sleep. He was thinking.

Manny watched him attentively, deep in thought, immersed in his own brand of hell.

Hooker opened his eyes. He looked up at the detective.

Manny rocked forward on his elbows splayed on the chair arms. It was his way of preparing to talk. "The shotgun?"

Hooker nodded.

"It's strange, even if you are looking at the person who shoots you, in the night terrors, you never see the person... only the end of the gun, and a blast."

Hooker let the ice bag slide down his head, as he drew it out in front of him. He surveyed the cast. There were some cracks. It was at the end of its usefulness. The elbow had been feeling mushy for a few days.

"Have you ever figured out why people kill people they don't even know?"

Manny rocked back gently as he pursed his lips. "There is a belief in the Jewish religion that most people are good at heart. But there are a few who are evil incarnate. What makes them evil is anyone's guess. They are evil from birth. Maybe this guy is one of those. I don't know. All the years on the force, I saw a lot of bad things. But down deep, few of the people were bad themselves. Their circumstance may have been. They may have felt they had no other choice, but they weren't evil in the root."

Hooker slowly slid back up onto his bed. "I don't think mine was evil. He just didn't know any other way."

"Maybe you're lucky, and it won't follow you for long."

Hooker looked at his friend. "But you don't believe it."

Manny shrugged and closed his eyes. "There is always hope."

Hooker scratched his curly hair and finished the smartass remark. "Hope is a diamond."

Stella called from the kitchen.

Manny laughed. "Speaking of real diamonds..."

The three mugs were on the table. Stella sat at her place, shuffling a deck of cards—something Hooker had never seen her do.

He sat down as Manny slid into his area at the head of the table. Hooker watched her continue to break, separate, pile, and reshuffle the cards. She focused on the deck as if she were mesmerized by the moving pieces of card stock.

Hooker raised his mug and sipped at the heat and vapor of chocolate powder. As a kid, he had never tasted chocolate or hot cocoa. He had first tasted it at one of the other tow truck driver's houses. They had made it for the kids, and Hooker had taken a sip. He had almost given up coffee. The next morning, he was back to his old ways, but forever changed. He had stopped on his way home and bought some powder mix. When Willie had caught him, he threw the powder down the toilet. Hooker, red-faced with indignant anger, had stood the man up against the wall. As he was about to scream his venting spleen, Willie calmly shuttered his eyes and stated, "If you want hot chocolate, I will make you some. But it will be real hot chocolate. Never settle for an imitation. Always remember you are worth the real stuff."

A warm flood washed through Hooker. He realized

now Willie had been speaking about a lot more than just a mug of hot chocolate. He was talking about love and family and relationships, and basically, anything in life. It was about finding value within you. And, as Hooker realized the next day, Willie was reminding himself of that, too.

That was the day Hooker pulled the Congressional Medal of Honor out of the second drawer on the left under the sink. He had hunted around and finally found the photo to go with it and had taken it all up to the Phoenix Frame Shop. A few weeks later, he hung the framed medal, photo, and ribbon by the door. Every time they passed it, it reminded both Hooker and Willie—Willie had paid the price to be the man he wanted to be.

Willie had watched Hooker hang the frame. As he walked past, out into the shop, he commented in a grump, "At least you could have found a picture showing my better side."

Two days later, Hooker found a photo of Willie in the naval hospital with tubes and bandages covering most of his face and chest. Hooker had thumbtacked it to the wall beside the other, but recently, Hank had taken it down, stating how disgusting it looked. Then he had it framed to match.

Hooker sipped on the hot chocolate, thinking about how hot chocolate and chocolate chip cookies on a Christmas Eve was how Hooker had finally met Stella, and then Manny. Who could have known that two months later, he would be taking refuge in their home?

"Hey... Hooker?" Stella sat ready to deal.

"What?"

"I asked, are you in?"

Hooker looked with a frown at Manny and Stella. He was lost.

Manny leaned back. His right eyebrow rose. He summed up the situation. "We're playing gin until dawn."

"Gin until dawn?" Hooker was now really confused. He had never really played card games at all, and so this was a new game to him. "Is it like regular gin?"

Stella started to laugh, but Manny put his hand on hers and frowned.

"You were always working or over at Willie's. That's why this seems strange to you."

"Well..."

Stella rested her hands on the table, still holding the cards. "When Manny wakes up with the terrors, we get up and have hot chocolate. It always reminds us of the Christmas Eve you came into our lives. And we play gin... a penny a point. Manny owes me a million dollars he'll never pay. So we can start fresh with you and just play for points."

Hooker looked at Manny. "A million bucks?" He laughed. "You really are bad at this?"

Manny shrugged his eyes and shoulder as he raised his mug. "To Christmas and forgiven debts."

They laughed, and Stella dealt.

"So, what is the dawn part?"

Manny was looking at his cards. "The sun comes up."

Stella drew a card and discarded. "The terrors stop, and he can sleep again."

"Aha." Hooker nodded and thought about his cards. He was so savagely screwed. He drew and discarded.

The large clock in Manny's office could be heard ticking between the ticks of the cards. The night rumbled on with the soft thumps of the mugs of chocolate landing absently on the large table. Hooker could feel the soft soothing calm coming with the mindless play.

Softly, Stella laid out her cards. "Gin." She pulled the score sheet toward her and drew vertical lines.

Manny leaned toward Hooker. "I don't know why she draws those lines. Other than it gives us hope, maybe just one hand, we might put some points up."

Hooker laid out his hand. It was still a mess. At least Manny's was close.

The hands moved on. As Manny had predicted, numbers only filled one column—but it didn't really matter. Hooker realized he had spent very little time doing nothing with Manny and Stella. In fact, he and been a non-stop whirlwind since he first met Willie.

"What was it like growing up in the wild west of Nebraska?"

Manny stopped and put down his cards. He thought about the question. He rocked forward on his elbows, metering out a deep sigh.

"Main Street was a patchwork of concrete, board, and dirt sidewalks. Dad had a Model T truck we went to town in. He had paid a man twenty-two dollars for the truck and a battered trailer carrying a horse. The man saddled the horse and rode off down the street.

"I remember another day coming out of the dry goods store. The day was high heat, and there was a horse tied up to the rail on the bed of the truck." Manny looked at Hooker's frown of confusion.

"A horse?" Hooker nodded.

Manny snorted. "Don't worry about it... they were everywhere, and this horse was standing there tied to the truck with its tongue hanging out. My dad didn't say anything. He untied the horse and led him about a block down the street to the gas station. In those days, there was a large pan full of water to check tires and tubes for leaks. He led the horse to the pan.

"I remember my father standing there in his wool suit pants and a white long-sleeve shirt. His tie was one of those ribbons they just tied in a bow. His cowboy hat was pushed back on his head so he could scratch at his forehead. The back of his white shirt was stained into a gray cross from the sweat.

"He stood there, waiting for the horse to drink his fill. Then he led him back up the street. He tied the reins to the car behind us, and we drove off to home. I asked him why he had watered the horse. He didn't even think about it. He just told me it was because the horse was thirsty. He meant anyone else would do the same thing because it was what neighbors were for. Nebraska was that simple. You just looked after what needed to be done."

Hooker thought. "Like the canning."

Stella nodded and laid down her cards. "Gin."

Hooker thought about the horse and about the canning. He looked at Stella shuffling. "What about you?"

She laughed loosely. "The kibbutz?"

"What's a kibbutz?"

"It's a Jewish collective farm where many families live and work the same farm as a common family."

"I thought it was just your family?"

"Oh, it was. But with Dolly and me, it felt like a collective farm. For as unorthodox as we were Orthodox, we still got all of the lessons and stories as if my father were a rabbi."

"But he was a farmer."

"Farmer, lay veterinarian, furniture builder, substitute teacher, even a cop for a while." She looked over at Manny.

Manny laughed. "That's how we met. He arrested me for stealing a watermelon in the middle of the night."

"He caught you stealing?"

"Oh, heck no." Manny laughed. "He was the gym teacher. He knew it had to be one of the boys in the gym class. He just didn't know which one he had shot full of rock salt the night before. So he had both classes of gym running wind sprints up and down the football field. Pretty soon, the blood pressure is up, the scabs are weak, and were being rubbed off. I started bleeding. It was just small dots here and there... but he knew the pattern. He walked up behind me and slapped the cuffs on me. When I asked what for, he pulled the shirt up my back."

"What happened?"

"I served my sentence—the rest of the harvest was spent in his fields. I was very thankful someone took pity on me and brought me cooled tea."

"Stella."

She harrumphed.

Manny laughed and waved the back of his hand at her. "Oh, heavens no. She only had eyes for the Grader kid."

"Ralph."

"Yeah, Ralph. What a screw-up he turned out to be."

"Prison?"

"Nah, Congress." The two laughed.

They played cards for almost an hour in silence. 'Gin' was the only word spoken, other than when Stella stood at the stove and asked, "More?"

Stella sipped on her fresh mug as she reviewed her cards. She mused. "You know what would go good with this?"

Without looking up, Hooker replied distractedly, "Chocolate chip cookies."

Stella laid her cards face down and looked at Hooker over the rim of her mug. Manny decked his cards because he knew the look. They weren't going to be playing cards for at least a few minutes.

Hooker started to reach for a drawcard, and then realized he was the center of attention. Stella's face was completely unreadable, and Manny's was of light amusement. Hooker slowly withdrew his hand. He knew something was up, and it didn't feel good.

"What?" Hooker's breath was almost as loud as his

word. He was rapidly reaching panic under Stella's pressure.

Stella let him stew and worry a few seconds more. "What exactly *were* you doing out there that night with hot cocoa and fresh-out-of-the-oven cookies?"

Hooker had to replay what she had said a few times in his head. It didn't sound right. There was no trouble, no threat, and no condemnation, nothing... No trouble of any kind.

He swallowed and then cleared his throat. "It was Christmas Eve."

Her face was as animated as the stone fountain out front.

He laid his cards on the table and then slowly raised the mug to his mouth. Almost a decade playing this game with the two sisters had taught him the tricks. He sipped, never breaking eye contact. He sipped again, and then quietly placed the bright aqua blue mug on the thick walnut table. There was no sound from the placement.

Stella cocked her head slightly. Her eyes didn't betray her amusement at how well he had learned the waiting game. Rule one: whoever speaks first loses.

Hooker picked up his cards as if to resume the game. He moved two cards.

Stella smiled as she pushed back in her chair. "Really?" She laughed as Manny chuckled. "You won with the second sip with an empty mug. If I weren't rationing Manny's sugar, I would have sworn you had cocoa left to drink."

Hooker smiled softly at the acknowledgment of his prowess at the game they all played—he took the win. But his voice was soft as he spoke.

"Most people think the drivers volunteer to work the holidays for the extra pay. The truth is, there is no holiday pay, especially nights. The club calls pay a flat $7.41. $7.41 for a jumpstart, $7.41 for a flat tire, and $7.41 for a tow, even if it's a roll-over wreck down a cliff—$7.41 and the drivers get half if they're lucky. Most drivers came from situations not much different from mine. Most of those have a weekend or three to look forward to throughout the year." He laid down his unneeded pass cards.

"Even the summer I first started, I heard what the drivers looked forward to every year. It was your sister's ham hocks and black-eyed beans on New Year's Eve. Nobody ever asked what part of the South Dolly was from. She just said it was a family tradition and they didn't care. What they looked forward to is the confirmation that someone cares.

"Most of the older drivers can tell you how many days are left in the year. After turkey awful, Ace can tell you exactly how many hours until that midnight. It's a small thing for Dolly to do, but for them, it's the biggest thing all year."

He looked in his mug and started to get up. Stella waved him down and grabbed his mug. "Time to switch to coffee."

Hooker looked at her backside as she drew the coffee

mill toward her on the counter. He frowned at Manny, who was relaxed in his posture.

The man smiled and nodded his head behind him. He didn't have to look, and neither did she. Hooker looked into the sunroom. The previously dark windows were now a soft gray of fog. Soon they would be pink.

"I didn't stop listening." The antique mill growled as she turned the crank.

Hooker collected his thoughts. "Willie wasn't dating anyone then, so Maddie had come over and brought a bunch of fixings. We were baking up dozens of cookies, and there was at least a gallon of hot cocoa. I knew we would never eat and drink all of it, so I packed up the picnic basket and was out looking for the other drivers."

Stella plugged in the percolator and stood leaning with her hands on the counter. Her focus was hundreds of miles and years away. She was seeing a snapshot of her father taking the family and their Christmas dinner down to the Sheriff Station and county jail. There were two officers and the town drunk. The seven of them ate together in the larger holding cell because they couldn't let Junior Dirken out of the cell. The deputies had thanked her father for the best kosher Christmas dinner they had ever had.

Two weeks later Junior had come around to the farm. He told their father he was tired of being the town drunk and asked for his help. Their father had given him a job on the farm and made a place for him out in the barn.

Many years later, Junior still lived in the barn when he delivered their father's eulogy. He had recalled the dinner.

Sometimes, it is not the big things that make the difference, but the little ones.

She turned and sat against the counter. "So you were bringing them Christmas."

Hooker nodded. "For once, I had too much. It was my turn to share."

He turned toward Manny. "And I still have the Zippo money clip you gave me that morning."

Stella chuckled. "Was it the one I gave you the year before?"

He smiled wetly. "I was holding on to it for Hooker."

Stella croaked just as wet. "If there was ever any doubt about who is a member of this family... There is none now."

The percolator bubbled its finish as she collected and rinsed out Manny's mug and filled all three. Placing the two mugs on the table, she turned back toward the refrigerator. She took out Manny's insulin, and drawing out a larger dose, she said to herself. "I feel like pancakes are in order."

She walked over to where Manny was holding his undershirt up. She swabbed the alcohol pad over the area and pushed the needle in. "I'm feeling like chocolate chip pancakes."

CHAPTER ELEVEN

Stella walked into the gym room Hooker had set up years ago. She watched the giant black man from the back. Bored, Danny had stripped to the waist and was absent-mindedly curling the largest stack of dumbbell weight he could make as he watched Hooker struggle with the small kettlebell with his right arm.

Something was wrong with the picture. It took Stella a minute. "Where is your cast?"

Danny froze.

Hooker jerked at being caught and looked up sheepishly. "It got wet last night. It was falling apart in the sheets." He sat back up, resting the small weight on his knee. "I took it off before the sheets all turned to plaster concrete."

She cocked her head slightly sideways and gave him the eye. He smiled. "I put them in the washer. They should be dry by now. I'll put them back on the bed this afternoon before I take a nap."

"Hmm." She cocked her hip. Finished with him, she turned to Danny. She stepped over and rested her hand lightly on his massive shoulder. He twitched, unsure of what was coming. She bent over and kissed the top of his head. "Thank you for bringing your mama and Sweets out last night. I swear, I would have Tilly at my table any Saturday or Sunday you can spare her."

He looked up and around at her. "You can have her. But then her two foundering children would starve."

She leaned on him as she laughed. "I can see that."

"Danny is going to start dropping Sweets off, and then come out and work me over until I can work again. We might get Manny down here and work his upper torso, too."

Danny turned slightly toward Hooker. "You should have an upper torso like his. The man just needs to work on what he can't move." He turned back to Stella. "I've been reading some books about massage and stretching for better blood flow. I'll work on him and show you what you can do for him in bed."

Realizing what he had just said, he flushed. Stella felt the quick heat in his neck more than she could see any blush in his walnut skin. She hugged him. "I know what you meant. You don't have to do anything for us, Danny, and you and your family are always family and welcome for any dinner that doesn't have you two running off to work halfway through the evening."

"Speaking of work," she turned back to Hooker, "a deputy just dropped off four large boxes. I have to get Manny up and through the shower. Paul is coming over for breakfast. So, you two have about ten more minutes, and then get cleaned up for breakfast."

She looked around the large unfinished room. The wall of windows looked out across the valley and the lower driveway. The door entered from the garage, but there was all the plumbing for an apartment with two modest-sized bedrooms. The high ceiling matched the garage area, which was built to accommodate a commercial car lift in one of the three bays. Across the garage was a large storage room which over the next few months, would become stuffed with tons of canned food. It was Stella's personal food bank for law enforcement families in need. The access door from the outside had no lock. If there were a need, Stella damn sure wasn't going to be monitoring the flow.

"Thinking about Candy and Squirt?"

"Of course," she smiled softly. She would finally get the daughter she always wanted. "Thinking about them, starting work on the apartment in here, and I also need to get the tents delivered and set up. The vegetables are already rolling out of the fields so the gleaning will start soon. We need to have the canning kitchen set up and ready."

She headed for the door and then turned, frowning. "Where are you going to put all of this equipment when the apartment is done, and there are two or three cars in the garage?"

Hooker laughed. "Manny always wanted a barn." He pointed to the end of the driveway from where it wrapped down around the large sprawling hacienda with the huge concrete party deck. "We're going to bury it partially into the hill so it doesn't look so big."

Looking out at the hill, her mind worked in overdrive. "It might be better to make a permanent outdoor kitchen over on the side, and a larger storage area in the barn. Then you could have easier access to the gym across the way." She turned and walked across the two empty parking bays. She patted her pet Cadillac in the third bay. Her voice reverberated in the empty garage. "Ten minutes, then get cleaned up. Breakfast at nine o'clock...."

Hooker and Danny both softly echoed the rest of her spiel as she moved up the secret stairs. "If you are late, you starve." The two men chortled. Their mothers were so very much alike.

Cleaned and well-fed, Danny had taken off to get some sleep before Sweets needed to go to work for the night. The other three men gathered in Manny's office to go through the boxes of past cases of the killer secretly referred to as the Cowboy Picasso.

The boots had started it. At the third kill scene, someone had made the comment how the killer made his victims look like a Picasso painting, all torn apart. The name had stuck, but thankfully, had not made it into the papers, nor had much news of each killing. They were separated enough so the police had been able to present them as individual incidents, thus averting any public panic about a serial killer. The painted walls had never been seen by anyone from the news media. It had been one of the most closely guarded secrets of the case.

Hooker looked out the one window set mainly for light. The view through the narrow window was along the outside of the two-foot thick straw-bale and stucco wall. He could see out past the hacienda to the tan grassy hillside where the sun was pounding the South Bay Area. It was the twenty-seventh day with temperatures over the critical temperature for a crime: ninety-seven degrees, the true temperature of blood.

He knew from Manny that after six days of no relief from the heat, murders and other crimes of violence went up dramatically. He didn't watch the news or read the paper like Manny. For the most part, he had suffered enough of it in his early years and didn't need it vicariously now.

He rubbed his aching arm. Maybe it *had* been too early to take the cast off. And then there was the Danny factor. Hooker found it hard to be satisfied with working with a four-pound kettle weight when Danny was fanning himself with eighty-five pounds.

"I think Hooker would have a better take on... Hooker?"

Hooker swam back to the present. "Hmm?" he turned his head and raised his eyebrows.

Manny frowned with concern and then laughed. "Did Danny wear you out today?"

Hooker made a growling face and muttered something unintelligible.

"Paul was wondering if we might be looking at the kind of person who is technically untraceable, members of your sister's community or of that ilk."

Hooker scratched behind his right ear, and suddenly realized he was doing something he had not been able to do for the last few months. He continued scratching blissfully, then looked up, and answered. "It's possible. But then, they don't usually have any access to a car. In fact, they seem to disdain any contact with any kind of machinery. I'm not even sure they use knives, much less a small-caliber handgun."

"Hmm," Manny turned back to Paul. "I hadn't thought about that."

"Also, there is the boot issue. The lookout fits the type with bare feet, but not the cowboy with the boots. Even the Mouse doesn't wear shoes—and as a girl, she had tender feet. She at least wore sandals outside."

Paul filed the information away in his mind for later. "Okay, next in the boxes is our little friend, the raven. In going over the boxes, I found another. In kill number two, a raven bone was picked up but never cataloged. So now, we have three raven wing bones, and all of them are the leading long bone from the right shoulder to the first bend or the start of the finger bone. This makes it the..." He dug in his pocket. "Just a minute, I had it right here." Drawing out a small scrap of paper, he opened it and read, "It's the radius or the second bone. The ulna is the first."

Hooker smiled. "Just like us." He pointed to two points on his forearm. "Radius moves and the ulna is the structural bone. It could be there's something there about it being the moving bone," he pointed at the photos, "being a paintbrush and all."

Paul and Manny just stared at him. They weren't used to being taught things by a much younger man. They looked at each other and raised an eyebrow.

"Hey, I was paying attention when they were trying to put Humpty Dumpty together again."

They laughed as Paul took a set of photos from each box. "Now, what we have here is very interesting. Or, in the words of Charlie Chan, *most very interesting*."

He laid out seven photos of shoeprints and castings. "I had the lab reverse the casting photos so we would be looking at all of the same impression. I also had them adjust everything to real-life measurements."

Manny looked at all the photos. "Which kill are these from?"

Paul looked at him. "All of them."

"Can't be."

"Is."

"No boot or sole would remain the same over... what... twelve years?"

"Not if you wore them every day. No, they wouldn't.

But this is 1961, here is 1964, this one is 1966, this is yours, and here is the railcar."

Manny pointed to an artifact on the prints. "This notch is the same. On a regular shoe, it would get larger until it wasn't recognizable as a cut mark."

Paul pointed along the edge of the cast print. "Notice these three little V-notches. That is from what we call kill number two. Now, look here. There are four more. This is from yours. We only know of one killing between this one and yours."

Hooker gave a low whistle. "But there are four more. Somewhere, if this guy really is putting notches on his boot, somewhere, there are three more bodies."

Paul sat down and leaned back. "Exactly. Also, there are radical separations between his kills. Either this guy is hiding some we haven't found, or he's traveling."

Manny leaned back. "A serial killer usually starts with separations of long periods, but then, as he kills, the periods between become shorter and shorter as he searches for the same high, he got from the first successful kill. That is why they also become obsessive and compulsive about their kill routine. They are always trying to duplicate the feeling they got the first time. But with this guy, we had seen a huge gap between when he attacked me and the railcar."

"And if we understand The Mouse, he has accelerated even more." Hooker pulled at his pursed lips, a mirror image of Manny's habit. "So where has he been for the last six years?"

Paul looked at Manny. "So, how do you want to cut up California?"

Manny rolled his head toward his old partner. "I'll take straight over to Tulare and up into the gold rush country and work north. I know a few of these guys from Masons, so they'll talk to me without having to pull a badge. You take the south. I don't think you would have to call any further than Riverside or San Berdoo unless you hit pay-dirt down there."

Paul nodded. "I don't know if we need to figure out where he's getting the raven wing bones, but it is curious they are all from the right-wing."

Manny looked at Hooker. "Why don't you go visit your girlfriend tonight? She knows a lot of strange people. She might know someone in the Native American mystic community who could shed some light on the bone."

"I don't know about driving the Cadillac..."

"Whimper a bit. Stella will kvetch, but she will be happy to see her sister. And you better take the mange bucket, or Dolly will just clam up."

Hooker laughed as the phone rang. They all jumped.

Manny scooped it out of the cradle. "Manny."

The conversation was short. "Where?" He rolled his eyes up into his head as the person on the other end relayed the information. "Is a car on the way?"

He swung around and looked at Hooker. "Okay, we'll be ready. And Dolly? I'm sending Hooker and the mange bucket over to see you tonight. He's bringing a chaperone, so you two can coordinate about the canning. Paul said

Gwen and Peter down in Gilroy have already put up five hundred gallons of stuff. And I think the plant is kicking in a ton or something of commercially canned goods." He listened. "Okay. Love ya, sis." He placed the phone back in the cradle.

"Where?"

"Northside. The old rail docks."

Paul spat air.

Manny looked at Paul and then at the boxes of information. "They don't know this is all here, do they?"

"Hell, these new kids can barely find their asses with their hands and sniffing dogs." He shook his head. "No, they have no idea. Everything except the bones can stay here. They are all photocopies the lab-made for you. The old guy Johnson said it was the least they could do for you." He drew his lips tight against his teeth and scratched the last of the reddish hair in the gray. "They're making copies as anything comes through, but I have to take the bones back. The new guys are going to start learning soon."

Manny knew what kind of limb his old partner was out on. "Thanks, Paul. I appreciate everything you're doing here."

The man got up to leave before the deputy arrived. He put the bones in one of the boxes and put it under his arm. "Oh, and I noticed you had finally pulled the permit for the barn you busted my balls on a few years back. I look forward to finally seeing it raised."

Hooker chortled. "Heck, Paul, you can come out and swing a hammer with the rest of us."

He looked at the young man with elevated eyes. "I just might take you up on your offer. I hear there is some good food around here for an old bachelor."

Manny laughed and shook his hand. "We'll lay in some supplies."

Yellow police tape ran crazy patterns around and through the abandoned rail docks. A pathway, taped about a hundred feet wide, led out toward two large buildings about six blocks away through broken fields of concrete and old asphalt. The old sun-bleached concrete shone white-hot in the late summer sun. Hooker and Manny both squinted at the intensity of the reflection. Neither man had dark glasses to wear. Neither had had any use for them, until now.

Manny and Hooker were stationary as their eyes swept the scene. Their minds moved like the two players they now knew. They knew where the kill zone was, and so now, they were mapping out the placement of the lookout. After they found placement, they could start to map the entrance and egress routes.

"Where was the lookout?"

Hooker's head swiveled. "No real wind last night. I

already called the tower at Reid-Hillview Airport. So I would go with the onshore flow off the mudflats to the north."

He looked over the wide field to the south with the eye and mind looking for a place to hide, but where he could also see everything. He looked at three clumps of low bushes. The first one looked like it was only tall enough to hide a shoebox, and it was off to the west of the kill zone. The other two could hide Manny and him and were more to the south. He pointed to the low clump.

"Pretty small."

"I'll bet you a dollar to a donut there is a depression on the other side. It's at least a foot deep, and it's going to give up at least three good prints."

"Go get your boy."

Hooker walked off to find Harold, the casting expert he was positive would be there again.

Manny rolled along what was once a concrete road built to withstand the daily punishment of heavy trucks. The cracks, less than an inch wide, would not be open all the way to the dirt below. The heavy-duty roadway was eight to ten inches thick. The larger cracks yielded to brush, and the occasional tree start. However, long before the tree could do any damage to the concrete, the concrete had choked the life out of the tree's small trunk. The stunted three-foot-tall sticks stood here and there on the roadway.

Manny remembered this area had been part of the war effort. He looked off to the northwest as he caught a glimpse of a white P-3 Orion Sub Chaser taking off from Moffett Field. He felt old to know all of this. He remembered as a young boy, his father showing him a picture of the dirigible parked in what was fondly known around the bay as Hanger One. As a young officer, he was there for an event when a small stunt plane flew in one giant door and out the other. He was close enough to know it was a feat even a new pilot could have accomplished. The plane was small, and the doorways were five stories tall and an easy hundred or more foot wide. A real pilot could have flown one of the large Orions through it.

Manny eased the second set of yellow tapes up and over his head. He kept on pushing slowly down the road. His head was on a swivel, and his eyes were scanning for any little things out of place.

He stopped.

He looked along the broken curb. Forty feet back, a small waterway had formed. It had collected mud from somewhere. Not much, but just enough. It had flowed along the road, against the low curb. The small mudflat had only grown to about eight feet wide at the widest, then dried up, and left only a quarter inch of silt mud.

In front of Manny were seven perfectly preserved prints. Three were cowboy boots. One was a knuckle and thumbprint, and two prints of bare feet, a right, and a left.

Manny stared at the boot print in front of him. He bent forward. Captured in the perfect molding clay was a size eleven men's pointed toe cowboy boot. Along the arch were triangle notches protruding about three-eighths of an inch toward the center. They were uniform and evenly spaced. Manny counted, and his stomach rolled. There were an even eighteen. He looked at the next boot mark. It was too far away to be certain, but it looked like five notches cut into the opposite side of the opposite boot.

The white heat dimmed. All around him, clouds blocked out the sun. As the day grew dim and dark, his chest was in a vise. Each heartbeat tightened the vise. A hot brick was being pushed through his ribcage. Manny felt like he needed to throw up. He sat back and tried to call for Hooker. The breath wouldn't come. He tried to scream, but no noise came out. He tried to raise his arm and wave, but his arms wouldn't move. The world circled and became darker. He knew he should be able to see the coastal range of hills. In the dark, there was only the gray as it got darker. The brick stopped moving, and Manny could feel its hard edges. The edges scraped on his lungs with each shallow breath. He wondered why he couldn't yawn. Stella was taking a long time to bring him his soup.

The siren in his head sounded wrong. He was headed to an emergency, but he should have been driving. Paul never drove. Manny should be driving. And the stupid siren needed to be fixed. It sounded like an idiotic ambulance instead of a squad car.

Someone was talking. The radio—it wasn't Paul. The radio sounded funny. He knew the voice, but it was wrong. Hooker wasn't a dispatcher or even a cop. Why was Hooker talking to him? He was on his way to an emergency. Couldn't Hooker hear the siren?

"Pulse is 140 and thready. His blood pressure is 154 over 110. His heart sounds good, and the monitor says he has a great beat. Lungs are clear. Pupils are responsive."

"10-4, 2-7-5. Continue to monitor and fluids. We'll see you in five. Valley Medical out."

The medic tapped the microphone key twice in a fast double-tap as he turned to hang it back up.

"So it's not a heart attack, not a stroke, so what?" Hooker watched Manny with the oxygen mask and a needle in his arm. He hadn't seen him when the Cowboy Picasso had snapped a .22 slug through his spine, but Hooker's imagination drifted toward the time and thinking this was what it had looked like.

The medic kept reading the numbers as he rechecked the blood pressure. He took the stethoscope from his ears and hung them around his neck. Looking up at Hooker, he shrugged. "Hard to say. If I were a doctor, I might suggest a panic attack had caused some hysterical paralysis."

"If you were a doctor..." Hooker grimaced.

The man nodded. He leaned over. "Sir? Can you hear me?"

"His name is Manny."

The medic didn't even acknowledge Hooker's contribution. It just fed smoothly into the drill. "Sir? Manny, can you hear me? Manny?" He patted Manny on the cheek. "Manny, can you hear me? Do you know where you are?"

Manny grunted. "Where's Hooker?"

"Right here, Manny."

"Prints in the mud."

"I saw them, Manny. I got Harold on all of them before the medical pukes got there." He didn't even have to look up to know the medic didn't care. He knew the drill between departments. Only your department was the best. Everybody else was lazy and over-stuffed on donuts.

"There were more."

"I saw them.

"There were eighteen on the one, five more on the other. The guy has been busy."

"Shush," Hooker hissed.

"But..."

"Manny. Shut up before I make this poor medic knock you out."

The ambulance wallowed into the driveway, slowed, and then backed up to the doors.

Hooker got out and could only watch helplessly.

"Jeezus, Hooker. First, you go stabbing kids in the hand with forks. What now, a spoon through the heart?"

Hooker didn't need to turn around to know it was the receptionist who always looked like she just rode up on a horse, her blond hair long enough to sit on. The tight jeans flared on the sides of the thighs, with the special horse rider's muscle.

The rest of the package was sexy in a horsey sort of way. Hooker had tried to get a date for several years, but they were just acquaintances with some history of flirting. Hooker was in no mood for her scalpel between the ribs crap today. "Well, if it isn't old Cynthia Eye Candy. How are you doing, Cyn?"

The slow burn with her never took long. She spun on the toe of her ubiquitous shit-kickers, before speaking. "This best not be any of your doing, Hooker."

Hooker followed her into the maw of the large door. Thankfully, the Sunday and time of day provided an almost empty emergency room—it was one of the few times Hooker had ever seen it this way. Even with the empty waiting room, there was a certain hum in the air of moaning and a low tide ebb and flow of the sounds of people in pain.

Connie came down out of her glass booth. "How is he?"

Hooker shrugged. "He was talking. But we don't know why he keeled over like that. One of the cops just happened to look down the way. He was almost a hundred yards outside of the search area. He was lucky."

"I saw it was Jeff Kowalsky who brought him in. What did he think?"

"Maybe hysterical paralysis combined with a spike of blood pressure from a panic attack."

The older nurse pursed her lips and looked down as she thought. "Sounds about right." She looked around as if someone had more authority than she did. She pushed Hooker toward the doors leading back to the emergency area. "Go ahead. You're as close to a son as the man has. I'll go call Stella and talk her down from the tree Dolly probably talked her up."

"Thanks, Connie."

"Just take care of the man."

"Trying, Connie, trying."

By the time Dolly tracked Stella down at the grocery store, they had moved Manny up to a room.

Fortunately, or unfortunately for Manny, it was the third floor—old home week. Thankfully, it was Valley Medical instead of Good Sam and Nurse Cutter.

The older nurse spun around and glared at the man. "Gosh damn it, Manny Romero, if you don't shut up, I'm going to intubate you and then start pumping Thorazine down your IV."

He closed his mouth.

Hooker snickered. Nurse Petite spun on him, only to find a deadpan look on his face.

Stella walked through the door. "I've got this, Lydia." The nurse frowned and left.

Stella sat down next to Hooker. She softly took his hand. Hooker knew it wasn't a good sign.

She leaned over as if she were going to take comfort by resting her head on his shoulder. He did not turn his head. He knew the look in her eyes.

Her mouth was only inches from his face. The whisper probably didn't carry past a few feet. But there were large pieces of metal in the hall Hooker knew bent from the intensity.

"What... in sweet biscuits were you thinking when you left *my* man out there alone?"

Hooker tried the deadpan delivery. "There were sixty other cops..."

"How dare you talk back to me!" The tip of her finger

flashed an inch from his eye.

"He sent me to do something else."

"What?"

"Get castings of the other footprints."

"Did you?" Her voice was pure glacial ice.

"I found Harold and got him started, then went looking for Manny. That's when the cop saw him."

"How long was he lying there—alone—on the ground?"

"Seconds."

She waited. He turned and looked at her. "Stella. I swear. It was only seconds. The officer saw him go down. We thought he had been shot. We ran. We all ran." He searched her hard eyes.

"Leave him alone." The croak was a whisper from the bed.

She rose. Her index finger and hard stare pointed at Hooker. She wasn't finished with him. She turned to her man.

The knock at the doorway saved Hooker. He rose and walked out to Uncle Willie. "How...?" Hooker took him by the arm and walked down the hall. "He seems okay. But nobody will let him talk. I think when he saw the fresh boot tracks, something just snapped. I think all the crap from his dance with the asshole just came rushing back."

The man with plenty of experience with bad memories and events nodded his head as he also ignored the swearing. "Sometimes it can be those stupid things like the way the string beans are arranged at the market or the smell of hot gasoline on a muggy day. You just never know."

"How did...?" Hooker frowned. His face cleared and he rolled his eyes and head on his neck in the zombie act of attrition. "Dolly."

Willie laughed at Hooker. "Wow, the boy takes a few days off and blam-o, he forgets the reach and power of his girlfriend."

"Which reminds me—she wants me back at the table on Wednesday." He looked at his adoptive uncle. "I need wheels. I can't have you and Stella schlepping me all over the place."

"I think Don's new truck just got out of paint. I'll call him in the morning."

Hooker looked hard at the man.

"Okay, okay... I'll call him tonight." The man pushed on Hooker's chest. "Just for you." A hint of the man's Nancy slipped out. Hooker knew he was relaxing.

"Thanks, Willie."

Willie nudged his chin back toward the door to the room. "So what did you guys find?"

Hooker looked down the hall. "We'll know in about sixty seconds. Did you ever meet Manny's old partner Paul?"

Willie turned. "Of course, I know Paul. How are you doing, young man?"

"Mr. Knight, great to see you again! You look younger than when I last saw you." Paul spoke as he approached.

"Well, it was with all the fretting and worrying over young Hooker and his boy Squirt. Paul, it just wears a person down. It just gets right in and grinds the soul to grist. I don't know why I worry so about this little ingrate, but I do."

Hooker rolled his eyes as Paul, and he both tugged up their pant legs. "Holy Cap'n Crunch on scrambled eggs, Willie, can you get it any deeper?"

The mock horror of suffering washed over Willie.

Paul stopped him. "Can it, William. I caught the act the first time." They all laughed.

Hooker pointed to the envelope in the commissioner's hand. "Is that what I think it is?"

The man nodded.

Hooker put his finger up for the signal for one minute. He turned and stuck his head in the door to the room. "Stella, Willie is here. We're just going downstairs for some coffee. We'll be back."

She nodded, never taking her eyes off Manny.

Hooker faced the two men. "Let's go see Walt."

"Walt?" The commissioner frowned, his freckles turned into wrinkles.

Willie slapped his arm around the man's shoulders. "The janitor—he's in the basement. He happens to be a coffee snob—so much so he roasts his own beans."

The aroma was still intoxicating twenty minutes later as they looked over the photos.

"Holy crap! I would have had a seizure too if I had seen this boot mark. This guy has been busy is an understatement. We go from five to eighteen in six years?"

"No—we go from five to twenty-three in six years. You forgot the other boot. But even that is wrong. He still gets to carve another in the boot after today." Hooker leaned his head into his hand.

"He has to have been somewhere else." The commissioner sipped on his coffee as he thought.

"Have you called around yet?"

"Started. I got five of the counties. They should have gotten back to me by this time." He turned around to look down the long room. "Hey, Walt, do you have a phone I can use?"

"Hooker can show you, sir," the man called back from the workbench with a small TV over it. Perry Mason was addressing the jury.

Hooker held one eye almost closed as he raised his eyebrows. "You don't mess with Walt's Perry Mason, even if you are a county commissioner." He laughed and pulled out a drawer of the workbench next to where they were sitting. "It keeps the phone from getting stuff on it or broken from falling tools."

Hooker could see him make a note to himself. "Willie can tell you nothing will protect a phone when you throw a three-pound piston at it." The two laughed about an incident when the phone kept ringing because Moffett Field Naval base kept looking for their construction crew. They were only supposed to assemble the former hanger—Willie's new garage—and leave. The facts of there were no end walls and Willie had a great swimming pool combined with plenty of beer and a barbecue after four in the afternoon had nothing to do with the work dragging on until the end of summer. Of course, having twenty buff young men around the place didn't exactly upset Willie either. Three phones in the shop never survived the summer.

They watched the commissioner who was rapidly running out of paper to write on. Hooker reached over and opened another drawer and pulled out a pad of yellow legal paper.

The commissioner eagerly waved it over. "Uh-huh... yeah... the date again was... okay. I'll be back in about twenty minutes. We had one of the investigators end up in the hospital this afternoon." He listened. "Yeah, Romero, Mansfield Romero—pull his file. He's retired, but we are using him as a consultant, so the department should be picking up the hospital tab on him. Also, while you're running things to ground, open a folder for the other consultant." He looked at Hooker for his real name. He just got a glare. "Just put it under 'A' period Hooker. Right. Just like the working girl." He rolled his eyes. "Right—I'll finish this when I get in."

He hung up the phone. He suspected he wasn't going to win the staring contest, but he had to try.

Willie saw what was happening and started to laugh. "Paul, you are never going to get it that way."

Hooker smiled but didn't blink. Paul finally slid his eyes over to the older man.

"Hieronymus as in Bosch the painter who painted Dante's Hell, and it couldn't have been more apropos. Octavius, as in Caesar Augustus, the first Roman Emperor, and then the name runs off the rails with O'Keller. Now, what would you call the kid—Harry or Tavi?" He looked at

Hooker, who was busy trying to ignore the conversation. "What did you tell me your name was that day?"

Hooker looked at the man he loved deeply, and whom he knew every day he owed his life to this man. He thought back to the day Willie had returned to his prized convertible to find a scrawny butt in worn jeans peeking up from where Hooker was experimenting at trying to steal a car. Willie had smacked him on the butt and told him to scoot over—they were going to lunch. When Hooker had just stared at him, he had told him he was certain Hooker was starving, because he had just spent five minutes trying to hotwire the car's radio.

"Ralph."

Willie held his look for a moment then slid his eyes back to Paul with the *see what I must put up with* look. "Ralph."

Paul chuckled and eyed Hooker calmly. "Well, Ralph, you're now on the payroll for a while. Keep all the receipts if you talk to anyone over a meal or coffee."

Willie laughed. "Hooker knows where all the free coffee and meals are."

Paul stood. "Well, it looks like our boy was busy up and down the Central Valley. We even got a call from Reno. So I have some long phone calls to make." He turned and finished with, "Thanks for the coffee, Walt."

The man raised a distracted hand. There were six minutes left of Perry Mason. "Just leave a dime on the counter."

Paul looked at Hooker, who was shrugging.

"He never charged me."

The man heard more than they thought. "You weren't on an expense account like Mr. Commissioner there."

Paul laughed. "Man's got a point." He laid a ten-spot on the counter. It was always good to know where good coffee was available and better to make sure it stayed available.

They walked out to the elevator. "I wouldn't tell Manny tonight. Let him sleep."

"We'll just check-in, but since I need to talk to Dolly, I'll stay out at Willie's tonight—just to keep him honest. If you know anything before noon, that's where I'll be. If I'm on the move, Dolly or dispatch will know how to get ahold of me."

They parted at the first floor, and Hooker and Willie rode to the third. Manny was sleeping, and Stella was passed out in the chair next to him. They were still holding hands. Hooker grabbed a blanket out of the closet and covered her.

The young black-haired nurse who came on shift a little earlier, walked past as they were leaving the room. She whispered in a hushed nurse's voice. "Is she still asleep?"

Hooker nodded, knowing his voice would wake Stella.

"We'll wheel a spare bed in there in about an hour. She isn't going anywhere tonight."

Hooker took her hand and mouthed *thanks*.

CHAPTER THIRTEEN

The dim pools of light in the darkroom gave the two women at the switchboard an eerie cast as if they were witches enchanting a wall of snakes. Their disembodied conversations were an almost constant murmur. The late evening was a busy time at the dispatch, as tow companies were still busy and other responders became more active. The fever pitch would be between 10:30 and 11:40 and then die. The slow time was midnight until the drunks left the bar to start their cars or drive them into telephone poles if other drivers were lucky.

Dolly was reclining in her custom-built steel desk chair and across her expansive chest was her favorite orange fur blanket, Box.

"Stella knew you might be tied up at the hospital, and she knew she wouldn't be home to feed him, so she dropped him off for me to babysit."

Hooker took the plate from Willie and walked into the

oversized kitchen with a large dining table that sat twelve every Wednesday night for dinner. Dinners were by invite only, and the players changed every week, except for Hooker, the anointed one. Everyone knew there was a reason you were invited or not. The joke was Dolly ruled San Jose by night, and only loaned it back to the minions to take care of it during the day while she slept. Hooker knew the joke was more truth than humor. Elections and power had been won and lost around the table. Arthur in Camelot had only dreamed of such a table.

"Just put them in the sink, Hooker. I'll wash them with our dinner plates."

He rinsed them off and stacked them with the coffee mugs.

Turning off the kitchen light, he walked back into the dark room. He continued the evening's discussion. "So we thought you might know someone in the Native American community who could shed some light on the use of bird wings. If there is something more specific to a raven—that would be even better."

Dolly looked at the large school clock on the wall. "Dina, get me Doc White down in Paso Robles, would you, dear."

She looked back at Hooker. "Doc taught American Indian Anthropology at Stanford for over thirty years. He's retired now and doesn't go to bed until after Johnny."

"Line three."

"Thank you, dear." Dolly swung around and picked up the handset as she pushed the blinking light. "Yut ta hey,

Doc," their standard greeting since she had taken a class from him as a young girl. She explained what Hooker was looking for.

Hooker could tell the conversation was going to run on for a while, and figured Box could use a grass break. "Box, grass?"

The cat looked at Dolly, and she heaved her chest. He jumped as much as fell out of her chest lap. The two partners strolled to the steel-clad door. Hooker checked the peephole as Dolly checked the TV monitor of the outside security camera. "You're good, Hooker."

"No, I was just telling Hooker he was clear to open the door. He had to take my cat outside."

Willie walked over to the switchboard and sat down on the third rolling chair next to Dina. He watched the routine of pulling a cord out and plugging it into a hole in the wall, throwing a switch and answering the call, then plugging another cord in another hole if she was transferring a call, or using the radio if she was dispatching a call. The night rolled on. Willie still marveled at how they could keep everything straight, no matter how many cords were plugged into how many holes, and phone calls and trucks dispatched, and where they even were.

During a brief lull, he leaned in close to Dina. "How is the baby?"

She smiled and took his hand and held it on her large tummy. "He's sleeping, but I think he's his father's son. He tosses and turns."

Willie could feel the small convulsions of the child.

She was only six months along but looked more like ten. He smiled at feeling something only a father would normally feel. He knew that with Hooker, his life had blossomed into a very large family. He knew that his longest and best friend, the librarian, Maddie, felt the same. Their solitary lives had been blessed with the arrival of a young fourteen-year-old boy who only looked like a man. With Maddie's help, Hooker had become the man Willie had seen in him the first day.

Hooker knocked on the door. The thick steel on the solid oak door resounded only slightly louder than a sigh. Dolly had been watching the small security camera monitor and buzzed him and Box in.

"Just a minute, Doc, Hooker just walked back in." She lowered the handset and laid it alongside Box's body as the cat settled back in. "Hooker, he wants to know if you know which wing it was."

"Raven."

"Which side?"

"Right. It has always been the right radial bone."

"Doc, he says the right radial bone." She gave him a sharp questioning eye as to how he knew what the bone was called. He just shrugged.

She listened for a moment. "Doc, just a minute, let me put you on speaker so you can teach the whole class." She spun in the chair and punched the button, and then cradled the handset. "Doc White, this is Hooker. Hooker, Doc White."

Hooker sat on the corner of the large desk. "Glad to meet you, Doc."

"Same, son. I've heard nothing about you, so it must all be true." He laughed. Dolly rolled her eyes, and Hooker assumed it was one of the man's standards."

"So the right radial bone of the raven? How exactly is it being used?"

Hooker looked at Dolly. She held her palm out at the phone. It was as much permission Hooker needed. "He's cutting a clump of the victim's hair, and then binding it with some of their skin to the bone. He then is using it as a paint-brush to paint symbols on the wall with the victim's blood."

Over at the dispatching board, Dina turned toward Willie. Her eyes rolled into her head as she closed her eyes and wished she could close her ears. Her mouth had a full look.

Willie quickly reached down and grabbed the metal trash can full of crumpled call and run tickets. He held it up toward her.

She slowly gained control and opened her eyes. Looking into Willie's eyes, she grew a question mark on her face. He slowly nodded, confirming what Hooker was saying was true.

Karen reached over and rubbed her back.

"Can you describe the symbols?"

"They are kind of hard to describe."

"Okay, son—let's try it a different way. Do they look like numbers or something written?"

"Both, but it looks like mostly writing."

"Any other stuff, or is it just him writing in his diary?"

Hooker's eyebrows rose, and he looked at Dolly. She gripped her lips together in a smug smile. She knew her people. She petted Box.

"Man, you are good. There is a large circle with other smaller circles on the line and some other larger symbols in and out of the large circle."

"Just a minute, son." They could hear the professor had just put them on speakerphone as well. The sound of him pulling books and flipping pages was a soft background.

Dolly swung her chair around and lifted her coffee mug. She looked in it at the cold last swallow. Curling her nose, she held it out at Hooker. She slowly closed her eyes and nodded to let him know he had time. She knew the professor, and Hooker had just sent him on a hunt.

Hooker took the mug and rinsed out the old coffee. He stood leaning against the sink, thinking about the walls in the railcar. The fact of the 'ink' being the victim's blood was gruesome enough, but the writings were creepy and disturbing in a 'thing under the bed in the night' kind of way. He shook and then picked up the carafe for coffee. He put the mouth of the cup under the spigot of the large coffee urn and started to fill. The dispatch went through over a pound of coffee in a twenty-four-hour cycle. The second urn was already cleaned and ready to go when these twenty cups were low or old.

Hooker thought about his sister and what she

demanded. Her minions were subservient and basically under control. But if one or two were breaking out of her control, there could be trouble that could spread through the whole community. He didn't want to think about what kind of fallout could overflow into the regular community.

He carried the carafe in his left hand. He placed Dolly's half full mug on the desk with the handle turned away from her. She drank with her whole hand, holding the body of the mug and her three fingers in the handle. Her bent pinkie finger rode stiffly on the outside of the handle.

Quietly, he filled his mug, and then the other three. He expected Willie to cut him off with only a half cup, but he took it all. Hooker suspected there was something up because Willie was not a true night owl.

Returning from the kitchen, he could hear a chair squeak and books plopped on a desk. "So, we have a few things here." The professor was still lost in his world. "If you look here, you see the..." He seemed to remember he was all alone with a phone on speaker. Hooker could imagine the man with wild hair looking over his spectacles at the empty room.

The man chuckled. "Sorry, I was talking to my cat, I guess."

Dolly and Hooker smiled as they looked at the rumbling cat on her chest. "It's okay, Doc, we have one here, too."

"Oh, Dorthia, when did you acquire a cat?"

Dolly shot Hooker a hard look before he could even

think to mouth the name *Dorthia*. "It's Hooker's mange bucket, Doc. He just foists the derelict on me for safe-keeping."

"Oh, I see." He fidgeted with the books. "All right now, so—are there any patterns that have an arc like a sun with rays and it's resting on a flat line?"

Hooker thought with his eyes closed. His head was turning slowly as he tried to picture the walls. A part of him swore because this was the one time he could have used the Squirt and his photographic memory. "I don't think so, Doc. Would it be big or small?"

"Um... small, I think." The sound of three large books slamming shut bounced over the speaker. "All right, we'll hold Zuni and Navaho in limbo for now. So I'm looking for objects with an arrow coming out of them. Usually, it will be pointed in an upward direction."

"Yes." Hooker sat up excitedly. "I remember there were three in the railcar. Two were smaller, but not as small as the writing. One was a little larger, near the floor, so I just thought it was easier to paint it bigger."

Two more books landed on an auditory stack.

"All right, we are not in the Pacific Northwest then. Is there any hand print or something similar to a handprint?"

"No. We would have checked it for fingerprints, and there were none."

"Good, so the Plains Indians are out now, too. I didn't want to have to go get the ladder, anyway."

Dolly licked her lips and raised her eyebrows in a

memory about how the professor was so refreshing about his likes and dislikes.

"This might be taxing, but I'm looking for a specific symbol. It would be in the writing, but I think it would have stood out. As you look at it, it would be a snake-like an 'S' connected to a 'C'... or wiggle with two humps on the left and one on the right. Standing very close but not touching would be a straight line up and down, except the bottom would reach down farther like the tail on a 'g' or 'y'."

Hooker stared at the wall. The concrete melted away and became the wood of the rail car. "Could it have an arrow starting in the middle right curve that projects right through the line?"

There was silence from the speakerphone. Dolly frowned and looked over at the dispatching board and Karen.

Karen looked on the board and shook her head and shrugged.

Dolly rose to a more sitting position. Box turned his head and scowled at her. The purring stopped. She held her large hand along him as she leaned forward. "Doc? Doc, did we lose you?"

There was a pause, and then a very soft pensive voice responded. "I'm here, Dorthia... just thinking. Look, hang tight for a few minutes. I have to make a phone call, and I'll call you back in about ten or fifteen minutes."

"Okay, Doc..." She knew she was talking to a dead phone.

The clock ticked slowly as they waited. None of them wanted to talk. The last-minute had seemed to step off the sidewalk of reality into the superhighway of strange. Hooker knew they had just landed in the universe of his sister. Dolly suspected but wasn't sure if she really wanted to know.

Willie got up and stretched his legs. Looking at his coffee mug, he wandered into the kitchen. Hooker watched as he got another cup of coffee. Hooker turned and looked at the large clock. He was now positive Willie was truly up to something in the middle of the night.

"Dispatch, this is Dina... just a moment, Doc. I'll put you through."

Dolly's finger was hovering over the speakerphone button.

"What do you have, Doc?"

"I called a professor friend of mine. He has been doing some work over in Nevada and the long valley in California running along the border. They share some tribal grounds running the length of the Owens Valley, out through the many valleys north of Death Valley and into the Nevada desert. These are basically Piute Indian lands, but there are also factions. Some of these factions even reach west into the Central Valley.

"You may recall a few years ago there were some unsavory types who were rounded up out there in the desert. They called themselves a family, but they were more like a mangled collective who acted like a tribe. The leader was a guy named Manson."

He let the meaning of it soak in.

"The symbol you described would fit not only one of the more deviate factions of the Piute nation, but the Manson tribe, as well. The symbol is a hybrid of a shaman and a warrior. It represents the god of vengeance taking a mortal visage to put the world back in balance."

"By killing?"

"By not only killing, my boy, but killing in a much-ritualized manor. The entire process about creating the magic that will grant the power back to the mortal to become a god again. You said the victims were nailed up to the walls. I would hazard a statement of the number of nails always being the same, and it wasn't just the hands, but nails through the arms and legs as well."

"Correct." Hooker was drained and subdued.

"You mentioned the hair was bound to the raven's bone with a part of the victim's own skin. Would the skin have come from some sexual area such as the penis, vaginal lips, or breasts?"

"Yes."

"Then you have a very sick individual on your hands. There have been similar killings in the Central Valley. My friend was consulting on a few. They were hushed because they didn't want to frighten people about a serial killer. But you could check with the Fresno, Bakersfield, and out in Tehachapi and Mojave area."

"I thought a shaman was supposed to heal people? Like a witch doctor or something."

"Normally, they are. But with this faction, they are about the blood and killing."

"Where does the raven bone fit in to all of this?"

"The fact he uses it consistently is an indication it is a talisman for him. It is something that is very personal. If he is of the tribe, it may have been his vision quest marker. You will have to catch him and ask him to get any real definitive clarification on it."

"So, where would someone go to get a specific bone of a bird?"

"If I was one of my smartass students, I would say an ornithology supply. But I'm not, so I'm as stumped as she would have been."

Hooker looked at Dolly. She didn't acknowledge the comment, but Hooker was certain there was a glow creeping up alongside her ears.

"Do you think there would be some kind of company who could supply something like it?"

"There might be. Check with a museum. They may have a source for bones and things for restoring old skeletons or something. But I can't see them being cheap enough just to throw away every so often."

"Okay, Doc. Thanks a lot for your knowledge and research. If we need to contact the other professor..."

"You'll find him at the federal penitentiary just outside of Carson City. His last four numbers are all zeros." He laughed.

"He's an inmate?"

"Well, yes. It's a case of it takes a thief to catch a thief.

He's in solitary confinement, but he has a direct phone line into his cell. He does a lot of consulting work for police and the FBI."

"Okay, Doc, you are officially a member of my family of weird people who know even weirder people. Thanks for your help."

"No problem, Hooker. Any friend of Dorthia's is like family to me. Goodnight."

Dolly poked at the phone, and it was silent.

She shuddered. Box meowed a silent protest. "Personally, I think it's creepy."

"But what Sweets had to say was creepier."

She raised her hand and pointed at Hooker. "True."

She turned slightly and peered into the darkness. "Karen, who is on the table this week?"

Karen looked up at her cheat sheet. "Drivers—Mike P, Ace, Stan, Joe, and Terry; Cops are Chet and Micha. We have a call into Whelan's office, but they said he might be back in DC still. Peter and Dutch are in, and we need them to look at the switching problem in the alarm room. Hooker is the head, and we have two opens."

Dolly swung back to the two men now standing. "Bring Sweets and Danny. On second thought, Karen, Whelan has jerked me around one too many times. He's out—and I do mean out. We aren't supporting his next election. Find someone new who will work with us."

Hooker listened and thought about how the table worked, and the power it and Dolly wielded. Every Wednesday night, there was a special mix of players at the table. Twelve, now eleven that Hooker was back, that Dolly could make or break depending on how she arranged the board. He also knew next election term, there would be a new person sitting in the seat in Congress. His rock and foundation were cast on the solid nature of the person sitting in front of him.

Dolly looked back at Hooker. "Tell Danny I want, or you want, I don't care, which ever works, all three of them to be here. We'll have Sweets fed and out the door in plenty of time for his shift."

Hooker took a mental stumble. As far as he knew, she had never invited a woman to the table. Even Dolly never sat at the table. "Tilly? A woman?"

"Sure." She gave Hooker the special look Hooker felt he should know, but it just added acid to his stomach. "It's about time I shake things up in this town. As the song goes, the times they are a-changing."

Hooker saluted his obedience. "Box..."

She placed a hand on the beast who had tensed. "You're busy. He's fine here. I have plenty of roadkill to feed the mange monster."

"Okay, it's your kitchen."

They were halfway up the hill to the giant garage with the small house attached when Willie broke the silence. "A woman... Has she...?"

"Not to my knowledge." Hooker looked out over the quiet, twinkling valley as the big car nosed onto the gas station sized driveway. Hooker tensed. The large door was slightly open.

Willie put his hand on Hooker's arm. "It's all right. Maddie rode her old Matchless motorbike up here. She's working on the Granny car. In fact, there is some stuff out in Minden-Gardnerville area I need to go pick up. If we start early, we could stop off at a certain prison."

Hooker softened and opened his door and stepped out of the car. Closing the car door, Hooker sighed with his relief. "I'll get the door."

As he pulled the large steel door all the way back, he thought about Dolly and about the coffee now sitting uncharacteristically in Willie's gut. *Something is up.*

CHAPTER FOURTEEN

T he moon had finally set about the time the 1940 REO Speed Wagon truck barreled its way past Kit Carson Lake. The scenery changed to a slightly drier forest on the eastern side of the Sierra Nevada Mountains, as Willie and Hooker dropped down through the Faith, Hope, and Charity valleys. Even with all the tall pine trees, there was still high-country fall color to entertain the eyes. This beauty was not lost on either male.

Willie mused as he looked across the expanse of Hope valley. "Maybe next summer we should all come up and go camping or something."

Hooker harrumphed. "Willie, I've known you long enough to know that is code for rent a room, and maybe go take a walk around a lake like we did a few summers ago on Echo Lake. As for Maddie, I know she doesn't want to suffer through our cooking attempts over a fire pit again.

We only survived because of the little diner down the road."

Laughing, Willie shot Hooker a hangdog face as he glanced over. "Well, who knew they had some good steak to offer?"

"Maybe it had something to do with the big-assed sign saying *Best Steak West of Kansas City*?"

"It was a cute place."

"I was just afraid you were going to steal some of those red and white checked tablecloths and ask Maddie to sew you up a dress or two."

Willie flashed a wide-eyed look of mock shock. Both men knew Maddie didn't even know much more than sewing on a button, and even then she would drive it over to Willie and have him do it for her.

The miles and tall trees disappeared with the teasing and remembering of times gone by. The terrain leveled out, and large ranches became the landscape as the brush was replaced by long stretches of perfectly lined barbwire fences. In the distance, the occasional large hay barn hulked near a smaller three-story farmhouse with deep-set wraparound porches. Most of them were painted red with white trim.

About every mile, a road came out to the highway. Arcing over the end of each driveway, and connecting the fences was an arch made from large old telephone poles. Hanging in the middle the arch, high enough for a stacked hay truck to pass under, was a sculpted brand or the occasional sign.

Willie slowed as he approached each ranch entrance. "It's along here somewhere. Look for a large *R* lying on its back followed by a *C*. The ranch brand is Lazy RC Ranch."

Hooker frowned. "Isn't Lazy RC the ranch you get meat shipped from?"

Willie looked over and smiled hugely.

Looking back at the road and the next arch, he recalled, "I served with Steven in Korea. He was a great cook who had a bad habit of burning field rations."

The Speed Wagon slowed, but the arch revealed only a ranch humorously named Lito Ponderosa, or Little Ponderosa. The two men laughed as Willie asked the crude question, "Who would advertise they only have a little wood?" They drove on. Not much worth seeing.

They finally found the Lazy RC and pulled into the barnyard. A large man with long gray braids strolled out of the barn door. Hooker could tell he had an educated eye as he looked over the Speed Wagon slowly curving in front of him. Willie shifted into reverse and backed toward the barn door and parked.

"The extra two inches you stuffed in the nose really looks nice, William." The giant ran his hand along the hood. "Where did you clip it in?"

Willie winked at Hooker before he slid out of the driver's side. "Stupid asshole, you know I'm not going to tell a Ford man how to build cars right. It might upset the entire Detroit balance."

The giant laughed as he took one step toward

Hooker. "Ignore him. He was always an asshole, even before Korea. The name is Chief Steven Seven Toes, but you can call me Steve or Chief." He glared at Willie. "Only my wife or another asshole can call me an asshole."

Willie laughed. "Idiot, you've met Hooker before."

The man's face exploded in shock. Snapping back to Hooker, he smiled and looked at the man Hooker. "Oh, my gee-whiz, it is. Son, you done growed up."

The memory suddenly snapped clear in Hooker's mind. "It's the beard. It was much larger then." They laughed about the mutual teasing of a brief evening when Hooker was only fifteen but already towing.

He turned to Willie. "He lies like you do."

"Nah, there is a librarian who won't let him. But he *has* learned the word elaboration."

Steven waved a large paw at the Speed Wagon. "Leave this for now. Lunch is about ready, and we can load this after."

Willie took on a serious tone. "There is a little bit of a time consideration here."

"What?"

"Hooker needs to go up to the prison near Carson and talk to an inmate."

The giant turned to evaluate Hooker. "Friend?"

"Nah, the guy is an expert on a certain serial killer we are hunting. I have some pictures requiring his knowledge-able opinion. We would normally mail them, but time is a factor."

Steven looked back and forth between the two men. "Do you have an appointment set up with the prison?"

Hooker shook his head. "Evidently, this guy is a regular consultant with the FBI and others, so we figured we'd just come on over."

The man laughed the kind of deep belly laugh only large men can do with effect. "Not fucking likely. That kind of access usually requires a couple of weeks of red tape, unless you are married to him or are a blood relative."

Turning, he shrugged. "Well, come on in, and I'll call over and see what I can work out with John Red Feather. He's the warden over there. Meanwhile, I can smell the tamales Maria is making, and it's making me some kind of powerful hungry."

Hooker looked at Willie, who was chuckling and shaking his head as he followed the man toward the house. As they drew closer to the house, Hooker picked up the delicious aroma and had to agree about the powerful hunger.

A short while later, Steven cradled the phone back on the hook. "I'll be going to Texas. John said come on down." Steven pulled his chair out and sat back at the table filled with the remains of lunch. The four ranch hands had returned to their work, leaving the three men to discuss the prison and the engine they came to get. "Evidently, you're right. This fella has people stopping by all the time. He even has a phone line in his cell so they can call him at any hour."

Hooker just nodded with a smile.

The chief grinned. "Yeah, but you already knew that."

Hooker rolled his eyes and shrugged.

Willie wiped the last piece of invisible food from his smiling mouth. He nodded toward the barn. "Shall we load the engine so we can be on our way?"

The giant rolled over to one hip and fished out a small clump of keys. Tossing them to Willie, he countered, "How about you two take my truck, and we'll load all the Mopar scrap we can find into your Speed Wagon. That way you don't have to waste time when you pass back through unless it's close to dinnertime."

Willie thought about the idea. "The keys are in the wagon. The engine is fresh, so keep it under eighty or a hundred." The two smiled, knowing their history.

"How fresh?"

"Keep it under the speed you flipped the MP's Hudson Cruiser."

The former staff sergeant saluted with two fingers as they all got up. The chief cleared his throat. "And you remember even Nevada has the new stupid fifty-five law."

As they walked toward the barn, Willie showed Hooker the very distinctive Cobra key.

The reputation of the 427 engine was not exaggerated. Nor were the stories about the Ford Cobra. Hooker wasn't sure if his face would ever unfreeze the smile, but it was fun putting it there.

John Red Feather, who looked more like an accountant lost in some back office than the Piute Indian Hooker had envisioned, escorted them into a large interview room. The conference table had places for up to fourteen people.

"This is where the parole council meets. Usually, when Charles meets with people, they have a lot of stuff to spread out and look at. The large table helps."

Willie looked the man over. "Do you usually sit in on his consults?"

"Occasionally, I have a certain knowledge set in Piute lore and shamanism. I'm a sixth-generation shaman in our tribe." His stare was only slightly challenging, and he saw it had no effect on Willie. "When Steve told me you were coming, I had a chat with Charles. He thought I might be a bit of help."

He looked over at Hooker. "I guess he spoke to you or someone the other night?"

"Indirectly, actually, I was talking with a Doc White in..."

"San Louis Obispo... yes, Doc is an old friend of ours."

Somewhere outside the room, a bell rang, followed by a clanging, and garbled voices over speakers. The bell rang again, and a large metal door clanged shut. There was a knock on the door, and John stood up to open it.

A slender man with a mop of curly hair over thick glasses stood in the doorway. Dressed in an orange shirt and pants over a pair of fuzzy slippers, he looked more like a young child than a convicted killer.

John waved him in. "Come on in, Charles, we were just about to start."

The man entered shyly with a soft-spoken, "Hello." Hooker and Willie stood.

John performed the introductions. "Charles, this is Hooker and Willie. They're here to talk about the killer in San Jose."

Hooker sensed John was talking to a mentally challenged person, instead of a college professor. As he watched, Charles transformed physically into a more assured man. The shift was uniquely disturbing but explained something Hooker was familiar with—multiple personalities. The many facets of the man were at once explained.

"Hello, I'm Charles." His self-assured hand shot out to shake Hooker and Willie's hands. "So, my naughty boy has become busy again, I understand." Waving at the chairs, "Please, be seated."

Hooker pulled the photos out of the folder. "These are pictures of the walls of his latest kill."

The man pushed his thick glasses high on his nose and looked closely at the photos. "Good, good... I'm glad they took color this time. Those last ones you brought were useless. I need to see the blood. Anybody can paint black paint..." He shuffled the photos. His dialogue seemed to be with someone other than those in the room.

Hooker looked over at John with a frown.

John held up his palms. "He isn't here right now. We can say almost anything, but he can't or won't hear us. I'm not sure where he goes, but he is reviewing and comparing the case from the start and all the information he has gathered or has been brought since. This process takes longer and longer each time as more information is layered on top of all the previous evidence, and then is integrated. So, while we wait, can I get anyone something to drink?"

Hooker's face screwed up in curious resolve. Hooker looked to Willie. "Coffee?" The former Naval Intelligence Officer nodded as he watched the former professor.

The disjointed voice chimed in, "Yes, please. Coffee, please."

The warden patted Charles's shoulder, as the man remained bent over the photos. "Yes, Charles, of course, you want a glass of hemlock. Would you like some arsenic and old lace in the hemlock, Charles?"

The drone nodded silently.

John shrugged and quirked his face and mouth. He shook his head. "I'll be right back," as he slid out the door and a guard silently stepped inside to take his place.

The coffee was long gone by the time the 'professor' part had returned to Charles. Hooker was glad he had bought a second and third legal yellow pad as the first had filled fast.

"Wait... so you're saying even though he is presenting mostly Piute shaman characteristics, he probably didn't originally come from this area?" Hooker frowned. "How does that work?"

Charles smiled as he found the photo he was looking for. "Look at this symbol here. This circle with the arrow (which is actually called a carrot) is pure Piute. But you see this little wavy line it's resting on—it isn't Piute. It's more

Chippewa. It's not even a symbol or part of a symbol, as much as it is a dialect mark."

The professor rotated his glasses up onto the top of his head. "I've heard you say the word y'all seven times while we have been talking. Willie has never said it. You also just asked the question, 'How does that work?' Based on the wording of that question, and the use of the Southern term y'all, I would say you lived in Southern California around the San Bernardino area originally, but up on the hillside like Mentone or upper Redlands, and your family work involved the orchards." He sat waiting for Hooker to confirm his theory.

Willie just watched Hooker, curious about the possibility of learning something new about his ward. The clock on the wall ticked as Hooker weighed how much he was willing to share about his personal life and past.

"I was left at an orphanage in Ramona. Most of the foster homes were in the area until I moved into the Central Valley. I never thought about it before, but we were always near some kind of agriculture."

Charles smiled softly. "Thank you for sharing something I can tell is very private with you." Leaning back in the chair to not appear threatening, he continued. "You slipped and said, 'we were near,' so you were protecting a sibling. I would assume it is female and younger."

"Older. But yes, I'm very protective of her."

"Good, but not blood-related."

Hooker nodded.

The professor watched and processed some information which was only known or important to him. "So, just like your language, these little extra pieces keep showing up in our killer's writings, and they tell a very different story than we see initially." He turned to the Warden.

"John, this block here... what is he working on?"

The warden leaned over and scanned the photo. "In Piute, this is the story of the coyote bringing fire, but he has the bear taking the fire away to the moon."

"So it would just be scrambled eggs of thought?"

Turning it around for Hooker and Willie to see, he drew his finger along the symbols. "This is the coyote and the fire. Think of the coyote as a medium-sized dog instead, much like a fox. So when we add in this mark here and here, we have a fox crossing, not the desert, but a large lake instead. He is still bringing fire to the Chippewa, but it is in the form of enlightenment instead of flames.

"The bear here works with the fox to bring enlightenment which will rival the white light of the full moon. So it's about working together in combination to produce greater power. The sacrificial body contributes the blood so the shaman can paint the symbols to create the power."

Hooker ran his fingers through his hair. All of this information was more than he had bargained for or could take in at one time. "So, what about all the rest of this—is he just saying the same thing over and over again? Is this writing 'I will not spit in class' a hundred times on the chalkboard?"

The professor had seen the overloaded student look

many times. "Essentially yes, but..." He jumped up and started excitedly moving the photos around.

The other three men sensed a shift and stood.

"There. That's how he painted the inside of the boxcar."

Hooker stood stunned. He purposely had not told the man where the killing had taken place. "How did you know it was in a boxcar?"

The man turned and gave him a parental stare. "Please. I've been in my share of boxcars."

Turning back to the photos, Charles once more became the animated professor. Extending his right hand and arm with the fingers splayed as a starburst, he started. "The sacrifice, victim to you, was at this end of the car. He starts his writings close and works left, unlike a native English speaker, who would start to the right of the sacrifice, and work right."

Willie lowered one eyebrow. "So you are saying he is a foreigner?"

"No, I'm saying English is his second language. Arabic is his first language."

Hooker screwed up his face. "What? Then where does the Chippewa come in?"

Charles stood straight and buried his glasses back in the mop of curls on his head. He rolled his lips tight to his teeth and then puttered them out. "I said, Arabic was his first language. I didn't say he grew up in Arabia. Most likely he grew up in Wisconsin. His mother is Arabian, but early in his life, his Arabian father disappears. He's later replaced by a very strong figure in the Chippewa nation, probably a shaman. My guess would be this happened when he's probably nine or ten years old, a very impressionable time in a boy's life.

"Learning a new language written in a new set of symbols, such as Chipewyan, was not a hard stretch for him. After all, he has made the jump from Arabic script to Judeo-Spanish writing. The most seductive part of Chipewyan and Piute language is the power and building of strength when combined with certain other rituals."

"Such as human sacrifices." Willie looked up from the photos.

The professor pulled his glasses down and looked at Willie as if for the first time. "Well, yes... but it's not about the sacrificial body. It's about the blood." They stood looking and taking the measure of each other. The large scar across Willie's neck and up the side of his face held a fascination for the murderer, but the professor was in the forefront at the moment. "Yes, that's right, it's the blood."

He leaned over and started at the far right. "Here he is talking about the blood of a lamb. He is specific. So if we could find his original kill or kills, they would be either animals or children."

Moving to the next photo, he pointed to a small cluster of symbols in a larger circle. "Here he branched out and took two children at once. He hoped for a Gemini effect, which is more synergetic than just a doubling. You might call it quantum mechanics in killing. It's a very advanced thought process."

Hooker wasn't sure he was listening to the detached evaluations of an academic or the salivations of an admiring devote of ritualistic serial killing. Either way, Hooker found it a bit too creepy to be comfortable.

"So he started with children, and then graduated to adults?"

The man looked up and then stood. His eyes blinked, focusing behind the glass. Hooker guessed the serial killer stepped out of the way of the professor. "Yes but think of it as driving. You start by riding a tricycle. Stop, start, and turn—it's all safe. Then you move up through bicycles with training wheels, and eventually, you drive motorcycles and automobiles. But he's even beyond that. He's up to jet airplanes now.

"Basically, killing small animals or neighborhood pets is how most start because it's safe. You don't have to explain when a cat goes missing when a raccoon could have gotten it.

"Once the dynamics of how to kill are worked out, the killer progresses onto much larger game, like a child from another part of town." Absently, the professor's hand and index finger drifted to a very specific symbol set on the third photo. The action did not escape the ever-watchful eye of the quiet warden.

Willie was becoming agitated, as well. "So what are we looking for now?"

The academic resumed in force as he scanned over the writings. "Based on his progression, I would be looking for a male with Sephardic features, in his middle thirties, probably affected clothing with a fetish for their killing knife."

He drew his face closer to the last photo in the line-up. "Based on this, he's counting his coup on his boots or shoes. He's making ritualistic cuts. He also has moved into the last phase of some kind of stars and moon alignment. He's getting close to his belief in his becoming a king, or god if it's empire-building that he is doing."

The professor rose and once again raised his glasses into his hair. "My supposition is he's very egotistical, narcissistic, and psychopathic. He may even be sociopathic, as well."

Hooker furrowed his forehead slightly. "You said 'their killing knife'—did you also mean he has multiple personalities?"

The man slowly rose, blinking rapidly. "I did? Well, I meant to say his killing knife." Hooker saw a shadow of anger hiding in the eyes of the man before him as the professor slipped the thick glasses back down to his nose.

"What about the bone from the raven's wing?"

The man snapped. "I don't know anything about birds."

Hooker decided it was best to let it go. He turned toward the warden. "John, is there anything else to add to this?"

The man hesitated, and then looked at the back of the prisoner who was markedly ignoring him. He softly shook his head. "No, I think the professor has covered everything in his usual exquisite detail. Good job once again, Charles."

Hooker noted the man barely nodded his head in acknowledgment of his prowess. He felt sure the killer part of the man's personalities now stood fully developed in their presence.

The warden opened the door and addressed the guard. "You and Paul can take Charles back home now. I'm sure he needs his rest. It's been a long day." He swung the door wide open and stepped back to give the professor a wide berth. Hooker noted the guards did not touch the man either. A ticking time bomb came to Hooker's mind.

As the door swung shut, the warden leaned his back against it. Resting, as well as waiting, listening, and counting. Outside, the voice over the speaker followed the ringing of the bell. The large steel door slammed open, and then shut. The warden's eyes remained shut. Hooker and Willie waited. The room stank of unburned fear or tension.

With a deep sigh, John finally stepped forward and pointed to the last photo. "He wasn't completely forthcoming about everything in this set of photos. Here your killer is talking about a mouse or a mouse tribe or a tribe owned by a mouse." He looked up at Hooker with a question.

Hooker nodded. "I noticed he ignored talking about the photo, and yes, thank you, the mouse is real. And she has a tribe. And I fear she's in grave danger."

CHAPTER FIFTEEN

Thanks to its oversized engine, the heavily loaded Speed Wagon easily climbed the grade on Echo Summit out of Meyers. The last of the afternoon light stretched east of them toward Lake Tahoe. Both men smiled at the decision to change the route on the way home as they snuck quick glimpses of the majestic view.

Finally, Willie gave up and pulled into the overlook.

As they walked to the thick rock retaining wall, their mouths were at half gape. The gold sparkled across the lake some five miles away. A mist or haze played through the forest to create an ethereal, dreamlike beauty.

Hooker sat on the wall. "This is the kind of view you want to show your girlfriend."

The older steely eyes never wavered from the view. "Or just someone you care about."

The air was thick between the two men. Neither

needed to say more as they watched the long shadow of the mountain reach out to embrace the valley.

"So, why did you?"

Willie knew exactly what Hooker wanted to know. It was years coming. "Why did I what?"

"Why did you take me in that day?"

Willie spun on Hooker in mock horror. "You vandalized my DeSoto."

Hooker duck-lipped a raspberry. "Bull pucky!"

"With your little butt in the air, fixing to rip the wires out of the radio."

"I was trying to hotwire the car."

The older man offered out his palm. "Well, there you go. There's your answer."

"What, stealing cars?"

It was Willie's turn to duck-lip the raspberry. "You had no idea what you had in your hands. You didn't even know what to do with a stolen car—even if you could have hotwired it. But you were willing to try. You were willing to reach out and learn."

"With my tiny butt in the air..."

Willie rolled his eyes. "Oh, let's not go to any extremes. It may have been smaller than mine, but it was by no means tiny."

"But a small target of opportunity for your newspaper to smack..."

"Those papers weren't a newspaper. Those papers were my death sentence."

Hooker frowned in confusion.

Willie looked down at his hands picking at each other, and then back out at Lake Tahoe where the shadow reached out like a wraith from Hades. In his mind, it was a metaphor for the day over a decade before.

"It was the lowest day of my life. Those papers informed me I was no longer needed. I was flotsam on the sea. The Navy kicked me out. The only option I saw at the moment was to go home and crack open three or four quarts of Maddie's moonshine or drive the DeSoto off a cliff."

"Until you saw my butt..."

Willie nodded and looked back to Hooker. "Until your butt..." His lips curled in tight, white against his teeth. "I was mad already, but I got white-hot about someone trying to steal my car. You sat only a second away from me, pulling your ass out of the car and beating you to death right there in front of the post office.

"One minute, I was ready to commit suicide and the next murder. And then I saw what a screw-up you really were. I almost laughed."

"But you hit me, instead."

"I smacked your jeans... where your brains seemed to sit. I needed your attention and for you to not pull on those wires. It would have taken me hours under the dashboard to put the wires back so I could have my radio. You do realize the DeSoto is my only vehicle with a radio, don't you?"

Hooker had never thought about it. He pictured the plain expanse of smooth steel of the Speed Wagon's dashboard. As he mentally ticked through the many cars that had passed through Willie's large garage and hands, he realized all had been *radio delete*. "Yeah, why delete?"

"Because you can't have a radio on a racetrack, it would be distracting."

"Okay, but it still doesn't explain why you took me to lunch, and then gave me a home."

Willie looked at the hands continuing to pick at each other. He sighed. "As I said, you were trying. You didn't know what to do next. I didn't know what to do next. All my life, I wanted to be in the Navy, and then they didn't want me. I may have been pushing sixty, but I felt like twenty. I'd recently stopped seeing a man who wanted to try being married to his wife instead..."

"Ralph or Randy..."

Willie nodded looking back at the last light on the hills on the Nevada side of Lake Tahoe. "Randal. I didn't know what to do. Those papers were the final nail in my coffin. I knew in the moment, I would never put on my dress whites again. My daily khakis would never come out of the closet again. I was adrift, just like you, but you were down under a dashboard digging around for a new career. You were reaching out. You. All alone. You were going to take control of your destiny by your own hand.

"I guess the moment I realized what you were doing—I wanted to be a part of your life. I never thought about showing you the way. It was always about my being a part of your life. I had no idea you would turn out to be such a gearhead." He looked up and smiled warmly.

"So you adopted the screw-up."

"Ho, by no means were you a screw-up. I had years of experience of dealing with screw-ups, both below me as well as up the chain of command. Out of the gate, I just needed to show you a path and stand back. Although, I did have my doubts about securing you a bogus driver's license until you went out and got a job with it. It was a bit of a shocker. Even Maddie raised an eyebrow, and you know how nonplussed she is about doing things."

Hooker laughed. "I think down deep, even Don knew I wasn't nineteen. But after I hooked and towed the Opel around the yard and backed it through some holes, he had to admit I drove better than at least two of his other drivers."

"Yeah, Don called me. If you had just put it in the parking spot, it would have been fine. But you had to show off by backing all the way through three rows of cars, and the holes weren't lined up."

"Oh, hell's bells, Willie, what fun would simple stuff job have been?"

"But where did you learn to tow? I sure as hell didn't teach you."

Hooker laughed. "I sat on top of the warehouse next door to the yard for a few days. I watched them hook and unhook, and the backing part... I don't know... it just seemed as natural as driving forward to me. Scary the first hole but by the third hole I was having fun."

They laughed softly and watched as the last rosy mountaintop slipped into the shadow of night. The lights of State Line were beginning to glow. As they stood to resume their travels, Willie asked the important question. "Dinner in Placerville or Strawberry?"

Hooker opened the passenger door. "I'll let you know when we get to Strawberry."

The roll down the mountain to Placerville had been quiet. Both men seemed to have a lot to think about or remember. Willie had noticed the frost already forming on the large box stuffed at the back end of the truck bed. He guessed it was probably summer hog. Steven didn't slaughter beef until after the first snow in November, then hang until the New Year. He hoped for some blood sausages, so Hank could try out his new recipe.

Placerville never seemed to change much. It was the same sleepy town it had been in the late forties when Willie first found his way around the lower Sierras. The diner along the highway was the fresh take on the old railroad car with the wheels knocked out. The quilted stainless-steel skin made it look somewhat like an Airstream trailer, a look not lost on many travelers. There had seemed to be no need to get creative with the name of the joint, as they all seemed to be called a diner. It was the food luring them in. The sandwiches were good, but the berry desserts had drawn them past Strawberry and down to the larger city.

The heavy-duty white plates sat stained with hints of black and raspberry cobbler. The ice cream tidemark was homemade French vanilla.

Willie pushed the handle of his coffee mug from finger

to thumb as he stared food-struck into the dark brown liquid. He didn't have to look to know his movements were mirrored the next seat over. Stella had laughed at their unconscious mimicry.

"What prompted this sudden question about my actions?"

Hooker's finger stopped mid-track. His mind ground through the question and selected the reference. He chuckled softly. "The Squirt."

Willie looked up at the back bar of milkshake machines, coffeepots, and other food prep all neatly placed along the stainless-steel counter and back wall. He thought about how the Squirt had come into all of their lives during the spring, and ended up saving Hooker's life. He still lay in the hospital, but soon he would need a home to go home to.

Willie sipped his coffee. Slowly putting the mug down, he looked over at Hooker. "So, where are you going to stick your new child, daddy?" He smiled softly, a tease, but with an honest heart.

Hooker raised his eyebrows as he stared ahead and sipped his coffee. "It seems I have no say in the matter. Stella has all but staked her claim on the kid."

They both nodded and said in unison, "Heaven help him!" They laughed and sipped their coffee in mirror image.

As the Speed Wagon nosed out of the town limits and across the agricultural prairie of the Central Valley, Willie leaned into the open window mirroring Hooker with his arm out the other side. "So, how do you feel about being a benefactor?"

"I'm happy I have Stella and Manny to back me up, but it feels a bit daunting. I can look after myself, but to look after someone else..." He looked out the window at the rice fields whipping by in the black night. "It's why I had hoped there was some wisdom coming from you. But I think I'm far past smacking his tiny butt with some paper like a puppy."

Willie laughed at the image and analogy. "You went way past that mark the second you drove a fork into his hand in front of his sister who you hoped to take to bed. Yessirree Bob, that ship done sailed a long time ago."

Hooker groaned. "Oh, great, play the nasty memory over and over."

Willie laughed but took pity on the apple of his eye. "Look, I don't know if there is anything particularly wise I could ever tell you. When it came to you, I was making it up new every day. It scared the hell out of me. Maddie was of no help. She just kept asking why the hell I was asking her about raising up a kid. She had been the baby, and her dad just threw her in overalls and tossed her under the hood of a car like she was just another one of the boys. But what I can tell you about the Squirt is: you have your hands full. He's not like you. When he gets his head of steam up, you better give him a wide berth or hold on tight. I think he's got a whole lot of potential, and he isn't going to slow down until he fulfills it."

Hooker rolled his lips into his teeth and scratched at

the new scars on his head as the nerves knit. "That's what I was afraid of. I'm glad he's going to be out at the hacienda, so Manny can fill his head with cop stuff." Hooker laughed at the memory of Squirt lying in the hospital reading his letter of acceptance into the police academy while he was petting Box and sipping the moonshine Hooker had snuck into the hospital. "You should have seen his face when he realized one way or another, he was going to get his dream of being a cop."

Willie glanced over at the man the kid had become. He smiled softly and cherished the filling ache in his chest. Yes, Willie knew a little something about dreams coming true.

CHAPTER SIXTEEN

Willie stood in the kitchen in a frilly apron and his favorite boxers saying "Kiss My Grits" across the back. Hooker had groaned so many times, he almost didn't see them anymore. Finally, he just stopped trying to retrain the seventy-year-old.

Hooker smelled bacon. Either Willie was feeling energetic, or Hank was coming over tonight. Either way, Hooker was just happy for him. He walked up beside him and put his arm around the naked shoulder and squeezed. He leaned over and kissed the man on the ear. The reaction was quick and predictable. Willie had the most sensitive ears. It sent shivers all the way to his toes, and he squirmed cross-legged.

"Gosh damn it, Hooker. I've told you a hundred times my neck is *not* fat. It makes me feel perverted or something." He slowly squirmed, shaking his legs back into working order and went back to his cooking.

Hooker walked away with his mug of coffee. "I've told you a hundred times not to wear them boxers... but I know you won't change, either."

Hooker could hear Willie doing something, but he wasn't going to turn around and give the man any satisfaction. He pulled the chair out and sat.

The thrown boxers landed on the table in front of Hooker. Chuckling, he took the fork from Willie's place and fished up the boxers and tossed them to the large trash can. "Besides, Willie, you already are a pervert. Just ask Hanky Panky... it's your most endearing quality."

"You, sir, are just prejudiced."

"Well, it isn't from your choice in wardrobe." Hooker looked up at the ceiling. "Although, there was a lavender dress you were sporting—that was a nice one. It brought out the highlights in your hair."

The man grumped as he turned the bacon. "It burned up Friday."

Hooker stopped and at the risk of going blind, turned around. "You sure burn up a lot of clothes."

Willie didn't turn around. "It doesn't matter. The dresses are only fifty cents or less at Goodwill."

"Why don't you buy some bib overalls like Maddie has?"

Willie served the eggs and bacon and came to the table. Thankfully, the apron was long enough. "They want two bucks for pants and three for bibs. I can buy new jeans for ten."

Hooker just nodded. He knew the rest of the story. "And they would burn up just as fast."

Willie reached out and rumpled Hooker's hair. "Oh, how cute. The boy has been paying attention."

Hooker dodged out of the head petting. "Speaking of Maddie, what time did she leave last night?"

"Who said I left?"

Hooker looked over at the usually prim and proper librarian. Her hair was a wild mess with only an attempt at control. The T-shirt only barely covered whether she was commando or not. It did nothing to hide the ropey mass of scars where the surgeons had put her legs back into some kind of working order.

The summer she had turned twenty-one, she had attempted to set a land speed record. If she had gotten to the end, she would have been the first woman to drive a motorcycle faster than one hundred and forty.

Halfway across the salt flats, the front end developed a high-speed shimmy, and she stepped off the machine as it passed down through the hundred and sixty mark. She lay crumpled in the desert heat for over six minutes until an ambulance could drive its top speed of eighty to retrieve her shattered body from the sand.

Willie had spent all of his leave time for the next three years at her side. She relearned to walk using his arm as much as a cane.

Many years later, the two had taken the Granny car to Monterey for some seafood and too much alcohol. The corner was the same corner Willie had taken many times before, but it had never been full of a deer and two fawns before. The result was Willie's retirement from the Navy and a year of Maddie learning to walk again.

Maddie petted and then kissed Hooker's head and then Willie's as she rounded the table to get herself some coffee. Sitting, she folded her hands and bowed her head. Hooker was used to her version of saying grace. "Smells good. Let us prey successfully. Amen." She raised her head and stuck out her hand in time to take the bowl of scrambled eggs from Willie. "Thank you, William."

As they ate in silence, and Hooker could feel the eyes on him. He started running his assignments over in his head. One popped up. His report on the Fall of Cromwell and the following reformation of England was a week or so past due. He looked up at Maddie in horror.

His look was enough for her. She nodded. "You have had extenuating circumstances. Please have ten pages typed and in my hands by the end of next week."

Hooker didn't know if he was lucky to have an ongoing education about seemingly random things, or whether Maddie was just a frustrated schoolteacher with a sadistic streak. But one thing he did know—he was a better person for her guiding hand, along with Willie as Sergeant of Arms, and Manny as Mentor.

Hooker took a bite of the scrambled eggs. "Oh, my, what did you put in these?" His eyes were wide open, as he reached for the glass of water.

"Some of Hanky's cardamom and chili powder—gives it a nice little kick, doesn't it?"

"Little? That's like calling Mae a midget racer." He drained the glass and got up for more. "Oh, wow. Where has Hank been all our lives? Who needs coffee when you can wake up to this?"

The man sat in his frilly apron as delicately as a debutant. He fluttered his eyes. "Exactly what I thought, too." He chewed another bite, and then drained his glass and stuck it in Hooker's stomach before he could sit. "Maybe not so heavy next time."

The two had tears in their eyes, but in a household where one wears a dress because it's a quarter the price of a used pair of jeans... food was never thrown out.

Maddie barely even blinked. Her tolerance for hot food ran in the same circle as her taste for the high-octane moonshine for which her family was known. She ignored the two men as she reached over and grabbed the tops of the salt and pepper shaker in one hand. She placed the bottoms in her other hand and upturned them over her eggs.

The day was bright and sunny, and the convertible rolled down the freeway as if it owned the world. The two men relaxed, knowing all eyes were on them and the car. Hooker guessed the reason Willie loved the old DeSoto Firedome so much was for moments like these. Every time they rode around on a day like this, Hooker allowed himself to slip back to those feelings as an almost fourteen-year-old kid, and the day he discovered someone genuinely cared about him as a human being. It took several years for Hooker to understand why Willie would take on a young boy he knew he couldn't touch, take him into his house, and raise him as his own. Hooker was the heir and validation for all the man had stood for and had given so freely to his country and to Hooker. All he asked in return was Hooker be the best man he could be.

The Congressional Medal of Honor Hooker had framed for his uncle hung by the door leading to the large garage. It reminded both men who they were.

The large chrome grill nosed into the parking lot of the hospital. The big V8 engine shuddered into silence. Willie sat a moment. He looked through the front glass at the large concrete and glass structure. There was nothing graceful about the building. It was as pretty as a cast on a leg. They both had got the job done. "I swear. Between you, Squirt, and Manny, this place is starting to feel like a second home."

Hooker gazed west along the building to the Emergency Entrance. "I know a certain blonde who would tell you it's my first home."

Willie studied Hooker's head where the hair didn't quite hide the scars on his scalp. "She might be right."

The two men were laughing as they turned in the door to Manny's room. The curtain between Manny and the other bed was pulled. They could see a foot under the blanket. They sobered up and moved beside Manny's bed.

"I see they moved Stella out and gave you a new roommate." Hooker nudged with his chin at the dividing curtain. "Was she trying to run the hospital from here?"

Manny smiled and shrugged.

Willie plowed in as he sat on the edge of the bed. "Well, this brings back memories—you in a hospital bed, unable to kick Hooker's butt, and unable to talk. They did find a heart this time... didn't they?"

The dividing curtain slid open from the wall end. Stella sat in the chair, and Squirt was sleeping in the bed. The traction on his right arm and left leg kept the young man looking like he was half tossed into the air. The look on Stella's face was anything but peaceful.

Hooker laughed. "Hello, sweetheart."

Willie smiled his canary smile.

"Not funny."

Hooker confided. "We saw Winnie on the way up. She gave us the heads up you were consolidating your chicks into one place." Hooker nodded his chin toward the kid.

"Fine." She relaxed. The mother hen was where she was the most comfortable. "They brought him up about an hour ago. He will probably be out until after dinner. They had to go back in and scrape the femur. There was a scar ball starting to stop the blood flow. He's better now, but he'll be on morphine for about a week. And just so you know—you are not allowed to make him laugh or do anything to make him cough. It is very painful and can cause him to pass out."

"But he is finished with all the surgeries?"

"They had hoped. But they will be watching to see if he is prone to growing large scar balls."

"Well, we already know he has the other kind in cast iron and huge." Hooker owed his life to the kid knocking him out of the way, taking the two loads of dimes from the shotgun and still killing the killer—all while diving out of the cab of Mae West eight feet in the air. Stella didn't reprimand Hooker for his crude reference. She simply patted the boy's hand.

"So what did Dolly say?"

Hooker looked down at the detective. "Oh, so now you can talk?"

The man chuckled. "You didn't expect me to spoil Stella's fun, did you?"

"Naw, fair is fair."

"And... did she know anyone?"

"She called an old professor of hers who used to teach at Stanford."

Stella's forehead worked into a cluster of wrinkles. "Was the guy something like White or Whites?"

"Doctor White."

"Right. Doc White. He taught Indian stuff up there. I had never seen a man wear so much silver and turquoise jewelry before in my life."

Hooker cleared his face and returned to Manny. "Where to start..." His eyes rolled up into his head as they closed. He washed his face with his hands, trying to remember it all.

"We were right about it maybe being a native Indian

thing. He pretty much called it right off. It was a shaman thing going on. As we talked, we narrowed down the tribe, so we could get a handle on the kind of ritual or something.

"He asked about a snake line next to a straight line, and I remember seeing those but with an arrow in them... when I told him, he about had a heart attack. He pushed us off and called another guy who is serving time over in Carson City area but has a direct phone line."

Manny smiled. "Charles Pells. He killed his wife and her mother before hunting down five of her lovers and dismembering them. The guy is brilliant and poses no threat to anyone else, so he's given free rein to do research for police departments all over the world."

"Right. So anyway, this guy has been working on a series of kills stretching up and down the Central Valley and over many years. All of it has the raven bone and hair of the victim bound with their skin from their sex organs.

"So Willie and I went over and had a chat with him."

"You saw him?"

Hooker nodded. "The guy had some serious insight into our killer. It was as if the Cowboy was his son or something. There was some serious psycho stuff going on there, but we got our information and got out before the guy blew a mental gasket or something."

Manny thought for a minute. Finally, he looked at Hooker.

"So, now what?"

"So, tonight I go meet up with The Mouse and see what she has on her mind."

"Where?"

"The old mill."

"Think she'll be alone?"

"Pretty much. It's why we've used the mill before. It's when she wants to talk to me without the regalia of her contingent group."

"No backup. Wouldn't it be dangerous for her?"

"She knows I'm not a threat to her. But it gives her standing that she would one, meet me alone, and two, do so at the old mill."

Willie's forehead crumpled. "What makes this mill so bad news?"

Manny turned. "It was actually part of an old meat-packing plant. They also packed some fish there back in the olden days, but it is the killing floor that has them freaked."

Willie frowned even harder. Hooker picked it up. "They don't see themselves as humans. They are in touch with the animal world, so the slaughterhouse was used to kill what they think of as their kind."

"So if they take on the names of animals, and they think of themselves as animals, could this raven thing be connected?"

"It's possible."

Manny looked at Hooker. "You didn't tell Paul about The Mouse, did you?"

Hooker stood silent. Finally, he shook his head. "I didn't see any reason to get her involved before I heard her out about what she really knew, or if she was involved."

"So we know The Mouse told us when and who, just not where, and you think he doesn't think she's involved?"

"I don't know. But she's my sister."

"Okay, okay. So we wait until moonset." Willie sighed.

"No. I go alone."

CHAPTER SEVENTEEN

Hooker sat at the counter of the diner. He ignored the harsh light knifing off the Formica and turned the page. The 1961 Marmon shop manual was turning out to be a better purchase than just the ten cents he had fished out of his jean pocket last summer. The man had wanted a quarter, but after seeing the yellow and blue 1959 Marmon rumbling at the curb, he must have decided Hooker was the one person who might put the book to good use.

With the giant engine for his truck, now nothing more than so much scrap metal, he needed to know more about any new engine he might find. Willie had run an ad in Hemming's Motor News, but still no phone calls. But then, the most recent edition Hooker had glanced through was dated in the latter part of 1968. Even with all the downtime he was getting, he was far behind in his reading.

He also knew many of the other motorheads were just as up to date in their reading as he was.

The thin hand placed an open magazine on top of the manual. Hooker looked up at the soft but worn face of the closest thing he had going as a girlfriend. "I've told you before—I don't read Cosmo." He smiled warmly as he leaned back to look at her better.

The twenty-six years had worn hard on her, but she carried it more with pride than as yoke. Most men would walk past her on the street, but to Hooker, the quirky smile, the ropey body, and thin arms spoke more about inner strength than just another skinny girl. Her hand waved back a piece of flyaway hair at her ear.

"It's Vogue, not Cosmo."

"Same girly magazine."

"It's not about the magazine. I was thinking about cutting my hair like that."

The page had turned over, and the image was of some guy with a girl hiding behind his shoulder. Hooker laughed. "It would make you look more manly than your brother."

She looked down at the tight hair cut on the guy. She flipped the page, and it got worse with an Afro standing out past the model's shoulders.

Hooker looked at her with pursed lips, studying her face. "Yeah, that might work..."

She turned a few pages and found a model walking on what Hooker guessed to be a sidewalk in New York City. The dress and coat were hound's tooth wool, and the hair was cut scooped just below her neck, but not quite onto her shoulders. She planted her finger on the picture and glared at Hooker.

He thought about how short it was cut and how thin her neck was. He didn't have the heart to tell her the two didn't match. "I hate short hair. I like the way you have always had it. It doesn't get in the way. It makes a nice-looking ponytail, and I think it makes your... um... rear end look great."

"Men." She swiped the magazine back up and steamed off.

But Hooker watched, and he noted the playful sway of her hips was still there. She had liked that he liked her just the way she was.

Hoping to salvage some honor and tranquility, he offered. "I can bring Willie back in, and you can ask for his opinion."

Her head appeared over the waitress back station. She glared at him. "I might as well go out and ask your mother."

Hooker leaned back and thought. Maybe it was about time she "*meets the parents.*"

"That's a great idea. How about Sunday dinner out at the house? I'll pick you up about four." He knew it was her one day off.

She sidestepped out from the large cabinet. "Are you serious?"

"Sure. You might as well meet the folks. If you want to stay over, you can sleep in your brother's room."

She grabbed the pot of coffee and slowly walked down

the aisle toward Hooker as she thought. Her forehead worked into a frown. "Johnny has a bedroom out there?" Her one eyebrow arched up as she cocked her head and watched Hooker with the other eye.

"Where did you think he slept for the week... out under the truck? Stella fixed up the spare room the third night."

She filled his coffee cup and set the carafe on the counter. "But you said it was his room like he was living there."

Hooker realized he had let slip something that was going to be a slippery slope toward ruining a great surprise. "Well, he's not dead. He won't be in the hospital much longer. He will need a place to stay where he can be looked after. And he still owes me nine more days of slavery."

She slumped into her right hip. Her eyes wandered all over Hooker's face, looking for even a slight hint of joking. "But why would she do that?"

Hooker couldn't explain these things. The term family was an alien idea for him, as well as to Candy and her brother. A hard life and being taken advantage of had been the norm to Hooker *and* to them. To meet someone like Uncle Willie or Stella and Manny was too far out of the realm of possibility to even relate to, or for Hooker to try to explain.

"You'll have to ask her and make up your own mind about it on Sunday."

She thought quietly and then walked off to pour coffee for the other two people in the restaurant. Hooker went back to reading about how the power range could be increased by polishing the oil channels in a large diesel engine.

"Okay." She stood in front of him.

Hooker leaned back with a thin warm smile. His hazel-green eyes danced. "Good."

"What should I wear?"

He thought of several things at once. The smile probably telegraphed his thoughts. She slumped on to her right hip and closed one eye, giving him a warning look.

"Probably clothes would be a good start." He smiled with a toothy leer. "But a yellow dress would look good. It would look like you were trying to impress them." He smiled and then rolled his eyes. "But if you want to get on Stella's good side, wear some jeans, and be ready to go rooting about in the yard and storage room. She's setting up the outside canning kitchen."

Candy frowned. "I thought people canned in their kitchen in the house."

"Not when you have a dozen people peeling, washing, boiling, cooking, prepping, and bottling a few tons of produce and fruit."

"Tons?"

"They will put up well over five thousand gallons of food between now and October."

"In one kitchen? Five thou... What does that even look like?"

"Well, the storage area at the house is six hundred square feet, and the racks go eight feet with room on top for more boxes. Then there is the barn over at the Pederson place, as well as the basement at the church on third...."

"What is all the food for? An army?"

He reached over and patted her hand. "Stella will fill you in on Sunday. And if she likes you, then she will try to shanghai you into forced labor for the rest of the fall."

She closed her eyes as she raised her eyebrows until they popped her eyes open. "Okay—Sunday." She walked off to make more coffee.

She peeked back around the cabinet. "Five thousand?"

"Gallons." Hooker did the math for her. "Twenty-thousand quart-jars."

The whistle sounded like an incoming bomb. Hooker smiled. His reaction the first year had been much the same. It was a lot of food donated to support any family of a law enforcement worker who was in need. Usually, there was a fireman or two thrown into the mix along the way.

Hooker also knew there would be stacks of pallets of commercially canned goods donated from the farmers and canned gratis by the cannery. Those were held in a commercial warehouse and delivered as needed. Usually, a pallet at a time, or sometimes a truckload spread between the many pantries. It was a lot to grasp the first time around.

He would let Stella describe the non-stop around the clock trucks, and the people and the cooking running from first harvest until almost Halloween. Her telling was a lot more fun. She was a special force of nature, and this was her thing.

Hooker put his finger on the paragraph he was reading. He sensed a body standing in front of him. He looked up and smiled with raised eyebrows.

"I said, I see your uncle loaned you his car. Where are you going tonight... or was it just to come up and see me?" Her voice was playful, but her face showed she really wanted it to be about her.

Hooker leaned back and smiled; the manual forgotten. "All of these months, if I wanted to come up to see you, someone had to schlep me here. Then they would be hanging around."

"And now the cast is off, so you can drive."

"Mae still doesn't have an engine. It's really driving me nuts. Willie has the transfer case torn apart and is seeing if we can't somehow make it all work without the double-clutching." He realized he had just lost her. "It's the way I have to shift with two levers. He wants to make it faster. I keep telling him I don't care, but Willie is Willie, and we're both frustrated we don't have an engine."

"Can't you just go buy one?"

"They stopped making them in the early sixties. So anything we can get will be out of a junkyard somewhere."

"So you came up to see me and study."

"Sort of." He knew eventually, she would know about The Mouse. "I also have to go talk to my sister in a couple of hours."

"You have a sister?" She leaned in. "And I was going to hear about this... when?"

"Now." He shied back, hopefully out of hitting range. Her look was pure hard ice.

"Look, it's complicated." He thought about how to explain his sister. "You know Peter." He jammed his thumb at the door and parking lot.

She nodded slowly.

Hooker pointed toward the booth in the back room. "And you know Jerry."

She nodded.

"Jerry is a peanut butter and jelly sandwich—a little nuts and sweet. The distance from him to Peter is the lunch special with a slice of pie thrown in. To get to my sister, you would have to go to the full sixteen-course Roman orgy, and then some. She is so far out there she scares Peter. Jerry couldn't even start to understand."

"And so I wouldn't have a chance?"

"Candy, of almost everyone I know, you would have the most chance at understanding my sister. Trust me, if there was any way you two *could* meet, you would." He left out where they shared a past of foster homes which should have been havens of safety but were hells of rape and torture. "If I could rescue my sister from her life, and bring her into ours, you two would probably find you have a lot more in common than just me."

She didn't know where to take her mixed feelings. She looked toward the back of the diner at the other damaged goods frequenting the only all-night haven. It came with a waitress who understood the special and delicate needs of the denizens shuffling through the door. And then, there was the one outside, who she gave a package to every morning as she left before the sun rose.

Hooker watched her in her own special purgatory. He returned to his book, and she wandered off to clean something she had cleaned an hour before. It was her shift. Clean the clean, and mother the motherless, tend to her brood, and deal with the few drunks who could make it to Winchester Boulevard.

Hooker looked down the aisle into the back dining-room. She stood talking to Jerry. The man had worked the docks of Alameda Air Station. He had been an up and coming chief petty officer who would have made master chief.

An airplane crash had ended all of it. A small shard of shrapnel the size of a broom handle had rearranged a section of his brain. Jerry had looked up at the sound of the crash. The shard had hit him head-on and passed through the frontal lobe and all the way down one side.

The man now lived with a person he thought was his daughter. His home address and a contact phone number were always pinned to his shirt. He lived by routines you could set your watch by. Every night he would spend four hours and forty-eight minutes at the diner.

He always had coffee and white toast burned more charcoal black than white. He used half a jar of sugar, six little containers of the mixed berry jam, and three napkins. He left two quarters, one dime, three nickels, and a penny. The four-cent tip was something Candy always cherished.

Hooker always wondered what he would do if the prices went up again.

Jerry was Candy's special child. Only he was old enough to be her grandfather. Hooker smiled sadly. Candy, Stella, and Dolly—they all had a lot in common.

The clock ticked over to 1:40 a.m. Hooker looked up. The bars would be closing, and he needed to drive several miles. He started to slip a five under the glass to pay for the dinner and pie but walked toward the back instead. He found Candy sitting in one of the booths, her cheek resting on the heel of her hand.

He sat down next to her. She leaned into him. She sighed. He stroked her hair and kissed it. "I do like your hair the way it is."

They sat there for a few minutes, floating. She turned and looked at him. Her eyes wandered all over his face. She kissed him lightly on the lips. "Go see your sister. I'll be ready at four on Sunday."

He slid out of the booth. It was the best moment life was going to give him today.

The night air washed over Hooker as the glass door sucked open. The late-night summer heat left a charred tang to the more dominant odor of rotting vegetation. Hooker stopped at the car door. He listened with his whole body. It was almost two hours after their regular meeting time, but just maybe. "Peter?"

"Not for another half hour or so."

Hooker turned to see the priest pushing his wheelchair

into the parking lot. It still amazed Hooker the man could maneuver the chair with one hand and a hook.

"Father Damian. It's good to see you again. I thought I had missed you."

The man rolled to a stop. "Normally, you would have. This morning came early with the call of the wild." He rolled his eyes and imitated the bad Irish brogue of his fellow priest Father McBride. "Who would ha' imagined two cats would desecrate the sanctity of it all by screwing noisily under the rectory window?"

Hooker rolled his eyes in mock horror. "Oh, the humanity of such a thing! Shocking. Shocking, I say."

The two men laughed as the priest turned toward the door. "I may have to eat the whole slice of pie I smell."

"Have a great night, Damian."

The man waved the hook over his head as he pulled the door with his hand. Hooker watched the man handle the heavy glass doors with the very fit muscles of the former Special Forces soldier.

The soft breeze rustled through the vegetation at the edge of the lot. But there was no whirlwind of dust and night trash floating across the parking lot.

Hooker opened the car door and sat down. Somehow, it had been just a hollow shell of his usual middle-of-the-night visits to the diner. He laid the book on the floor of the passenger side and turned the key. The big V8 rumbled to life. Hooker nosed the giant of another time out onto the wide boulevard. He gently mashed the pedal, and the growling car surged down the way. The deep bass of the exhaust reverberated off the buildings along the street.

The moon was perhaps a good half hour away from touching the distant tree line. Hooker stood leaning against the front left fender. He knew The Mouse was already here. he could feel it. He made a show of being alone. The driver door was open. His only nod to taking precautions was the sawed-off Remington shotgun cradled in his left arm. The shells were all stacked with thirteen dimes, his variation on the buck-forty dime-load. He had always found the number thirteen to be more lucky than unlucky.

A large shape moved across the night air. The total silence of its flight told Hooker it was a barn owl. He thought about its choice of hunting grounds. He quietly, almost to himself, offered his wishes. "Happy hunting. May your belly be full and your heart strong."

"Nathanial Hawkins never said that in the book, you know."

Hooker didn't flinch. He kept watching where the owl had gone. "I know, but it always sounded so inter-spiritual."

He turned to face his sister as she sat in the driver's seat. Her hands were delicately touching the large Bakelite steering wheel, feeling the smooth coolness. "Hello, Mouse."

She closed her eyes and leaned back into the comfort of the large seat. It almost swallowed her. Hooker thought she had become even smaller and more fragile since he had seen her in the spring. Her skin, always a problem, was now flaking off in thumbprint sized pieces. Her desquamation was getting worse. Even on her face. It looked in the moonlight like she had several eyelids." She was hugging herself to keep from picking at the skin. Her fine hair and the gauze of her clothing leant to the illusion she was all just the layers of skin floating in the air with no substance —more of a spirit than of something corporeal.

The voice was soft as a gentle summer evening. "You were hurt."

"Yes."

"They killed your truck."

He thought and then nodded. "Yes."

"Can you fix her?"

"If we can find a new engine."

"You're not the same without her."

Hooker looked out into the night. He knew she was right. He wondered if he would ever be the same again. Near-death can change a person.

Hooker thought of the Marmon—once, the most powerful truck in the five Bay Area counties, now sitting forlornly in the garage. The proud nose turned on end next to the hollow cavity where the giant engine should be. The dark impotent silence of the once-great truck had also changed its owner. For once, Hooker truly felt his mortality.

"They're not out there."

"Who?"

"My tribe."

"You're alone?"

"I didn't say who."

"The blond one... the one that is always crouched by your leg?"

"Dog." She waved a non-directional hand. "He's out there, somewhere."

"He's not afraid of the mill?"

She chortled. "He's not afraid of the silver in your shotgun either."

"It was a precaution."

"Not from me."

"No... Not from you."

"You obviously got my message."

"Peter gave it to me."

She rolled her head sideways. Her sigh was almost a whisper to herself. "Peter..."

"What about him, Mouse?"

She slowly rolled her head back and looked blankly at her brother. "You hate my name."

"Hate is a strong word. I don't like what it means—a separation between my sister and me. The name is just a name. I just like Clair better... and Sissy even more so."

Her head rolled. She was quiet. "There is a new killer stalking the night."

"You told us what would happen next, and it did. There are questions now."

"Was I part of it?"

"No. We know you weren't. Nor were any of your tribe."

"How would you know that?"

"Because he was a busy boy elsewhere. He has been counting coup on his boots, and he's up to twenty-five now. But we now know he left here and was all over in the Central Valley for the last five or six years."

"He was here before?"

Hooker frowned. "You didn't know that?"

"No."

"Manny, one of the people I live with... would have been his fifth kill, but his partner found him before the killer could carve him up."

She scooted across the seat and leaned up against the passenger door. "Come sit in here. I want to see your face." She waved him in with both of her hands. They glowed in the moonlight. It was from the abnormally high concentration of phosphorous in her skin due to a disease she had had since they were children.

Hooker had a brief memory of being in a chair and blanket fort. A ten-year-old girl who he had started calling sister motioned with both of her hands. *Come in here. I want to watch your face when we talk.* It was the last nice home where they were dumped. He had started calling her Sissy for sister. Clair was the name the adults used.

When the abuse started, the current recipient would become the inside spoon as they comforted each other as they fell asleep, different abuse with different foster homes. But when the talk became serious, they would sit at each end of the inevitable bunk bed so they could see each other's face.

Hooker laid the shotgun on the back seat. He sat down

in the driver's side and closed the door. He turned and leaned against the door and stretched out into the middle of the car.

"Just like in Riverside."

She smiled softly that he also remembered a better time. "Yes."

They sat with their memories. There was no hurry. There was no clock to watch, no radio to answer. The moon started breaking apart as it entered the trees.

"I need your help."

Hooker looked at her and waited.

"I'm dying."

He waited.

"When I become weak, they will kill me."

His heart broke.

"They will kill Dog first. They will make me watch them do it. Afterwards, they will kill me. They will tear me apart, and then eat me for my power. They will crush my bones and suck the warm marrow from inside."

Hooker strained not to flinch or show any sign.

"I will give you the killer."

Hooker waited to hear the conditions. There was always a trade.

"I will give you the killer, but you and the police must kill Dog and me. You must do it in a way there is no doubt. They will be watching."

Hooker couldn't move.

"You must shoot me with your silver bullets. You must use your shotgun. You must stand in the open where everyone can see you kill me. After you have done this, you and the police will get the killer."

Hooker moved his hand to stop her from moving.

She rolled forward in a fluid movement as if she had no bones. The Mouse was more a snake. Her hand was cold on his hot face. She kissed his cheek as lightly as a butterfly landing. "Save me, brother. I love you." She rolled back and was outside the car. "I will come to you here in the dark of the moon. The train moans just past midnight. You have the fortnight."

And she was gone.

CHAPTER EIGHTEEN

The early morning had found Hooker sitting first at Willie's, and then back at Stella and Manny's, explaining what had gone down with his sister. By the time the sun had started its predawn lighting of the sunroom, Hooker was done. Stella had barely stuffed a few bites of leftovers into his mouth before he dragged himself to his room. As he sat on his bed, he remembered making a date for Sunday. With his last energy, he yelled to Stella to remind him about Candy and Sunday later in the day. He had no memory of falling back into the bed.

Hours later, Stella checked in. She gently picked up his legs, removed the last sock, and tucked Hooker into bed. As she softly closed the door, she wondered when he had started sleeping commando.

The evening took on an almost festive flavor, as the brainstorming session turned into an all-hands-on-deck sort of affair. The crime boards had been rolled into the large sunroom and flipped over to make room for the tactical maps. Stella had laid out enough food to feed a small army and was still playing catch-up.

"Manny, I don't think you know John." Willie pointed to the other officer in a white uniform. "John and Alex over there are technically in-ground fire control out at Moffett Airbase, but they both have extensive explosive and bomb-making experience from their days as Seals."

"Glad to have you two aboard."

Manny nodded toward the three men hunkered down with Paul, balancing plates on their knees. "Those three are from the squad that is the fire department interface for the bomb squad. You five probably have a lot in common. All of my expertise was in Nam and Foo Gas."

"Nasty stuff, Foo Gas. The PD lost a couple of officers to it earlier this year." He slowly shook his head.

Manny leaned back just a little more. "My boy and I were the consults on the incident." Manny pointed out Hooker who had awakened and was just coming to the party. His uniform of the day was a crisply ironed white T-shirt, jeans, and bare feet. He was still blinking and trying to get a grasp on who was who.

"Hooker and his Squirt were the ones who finally took down the killer."

The man slapped his forehead. "Romero. Of course! Sorry, I didn't make the connection." He pointed at Hooker and back to Manny. "So the sister is Hooker's, and would make you...?"

"Someone who would like a chance to meet her..." He thought a moment. "It's complicated."

Paul returned to the room. "People, we have a lot to cover and more to figure out. So if you can wind up your sub meetings and clear the decks, we'll get started in about ten minutes. There are bathrooms in any of the bedrooms. Hooker is up and awake, so that makes three heads for use. If any of you know the way to the basement, the plumbers today plumbed out the bathroom in the area across the garage."

"Food?" Stella presented a full plate. Hooker's head swam around and looked at her and then down at the plate. He took the plate and headed back to the dining table.

Stella followed and sat with him. "Do you want some coffee? It'll be ready in a few minutes."

Hooker slowed his shoveling. He chewed and woke up some more. He wiped at his mouth.

"Who are all these people?"

"Your support team, honey." She wiped her hand down along the side of his face. The motherly thumb wiped the bit of burrito his napkin had missed. "Willie and Manny were talking this morning and thought it would be best to make an explosive kill. So they invited people who know how to stop or produce just what we need."

"Which would explain the two Seals out there and Willie?"

She nodded. "Along with a few of the guys from the

bomb squad, a couple of firemen, and someone special Dolly arranged."

Hooker stopped with a fork of food almost in his mouth. He put it down. He looked Stella in the face. Her eyes were dancing between evil and merely mischievous. "Special?" He leaned back and wiped his mouth.

She smiled evilly. "Remember a few years ago, the Shriners were in town, and they couldn't get the Fire Marshal to sign off on the show because the magic act had a lot of flame and explosions?"

Hooker closed his eyes. He was looking for the answer on the inside of his eyelids. His eyes popped open. "The guy got pissed and took it outside to the Spartan arena and blew it up out there."

"No." The quiet voice approached from behind Hooker. "The magician decided to give the show away to anyone who would or could come. It just happened to be over capacity for the stadium. I only blew up the field." The small man walked around in front of Hooker. "But I did make the elephant and brand new Corvette exchange places in their crates." He stuck out his hand. "Thomas Thomason—better known as The Great Boombowski."

Hooker smiled as he remembered the show and the political fallout from it. Three long-time council members never were reelected the next year.

The two men shook. "Very glad to meet you."

"I could have just as easily made them both disappear."

"How did Dolly find you?"

"I think it had something to do with telling the local

Grand Poobah he would never get a parade permit in this town again if he didn't find me. It wasn't hard. His wife and mine are good friends. We live up in Half Moon Bay."

"So you're here to make my sister and her friend both disappear."

"Well, more like a consultant. The heavy pyro-technicians are in there." He nodded at the other room. "I just do smoke and mirrors. They play with the real stuff. And if I understand the circumstance, we're going to have to put on one hell of a show."

Paul called the meeting. Hooker and the magician joined.

"What we know about the group who will be observing is there are somewhere between twenty-five and as many as a hundred of them. They tend to like the near reaches of the salt marshes out near Milpitas and moving west around the end of the bay." He indicated the location on the smaller map.

"Based on that, and looking for a place we could blow up successfully with some kind of impunity..." He placed his hand on the larger map, which looked more like a large blank sheet of paper with a few markings. "As you can see, there isn't much here." He looked up at one of the officers in Navy whites. "John?"

The man stood and stepped to the maps. "Right. What we are looking at was in 1938 an auxiliary air tie-down station for what the Navy believed would be a fleet of about twelve dirigibles. What we got was the Macon, for a short time.

"Originally, there were four of these platforms built out of the slated eight. This is the only one left not plowed over and turned into homes or truck farm. The Navy was still hopeful even after the war and airplanes had proved themselves far more capable than dirigibles. So, for our purposes this month, this is perfect in several ways."

He turned and pointed to the small square drawn in off to one side of the center. "This is the access hatch at what would have been the bottom of the mooring mast where the dirigible would have been tied. The mast is either long gone or never erected, but I checked this afternoon, and the access hatch is still there and functioning."

He reached up and curled a sheet over the top of the board. He brushed it out to hang flat. "This is the blueprint of the access area. The door is here, and as you can see, there are no stairs. It's a ramp. Even a jeep could have been driven down into the warehouse beneath the five-foot thick concrete making up the bomb-proof reinforced pad. The warehouse is about twenty-thousand square feet of space. If the helium tanks had been installed, they were probably removed during the Korean War. We were still using some weather and bombardment spotting balloons back then. So, we have plenty of room to set up a hidden control base and a recovery base where we can spend some time. Any questions?" He pointed to one of the bomb squad.

"What will the Navy let us do out there?"

"The Navy will officially see this as a training mission on an old piece of land and equipment which can be totally destroyed and not impact our mission. In other words, they won't know squat back in DC, and we aren't going to tell them."

One of the firemen raised a finger. "I know the bomb guys are under tight control. What kind of access could we have in the way of material?"

John looked to the other white uniform. "Alex?"

The other officer coughed into his hand in the universal code of every group of men. "C-4."

The group laughed.

"What about large cannon charge, and maybe something that is a lot faster burning like small arms gun powder and even detonation cord?"

Alex frowned with a questioning look. "I'm sorry, you are…?"

Manny interceded. "Gentlemen, I'd like you all to meet The Great Boombowski."

One of the firemen laughed and asked, "Was that a real elephant at the Trojan stadium?"

"Clarabelle? All two and a half tons of her. Would you like to come out to the house and muck out her stall? It will remove any doubt you may harbor about her existence."

They all laughed at the fireman putting up one index finger and crossing it with the other hand.

Alex cleared his throat. "Why cannon charge?"

The small man stepped up to the map. "If I may?"

John stepped back.

Tom circled his hand around the perimeter of the layout map. "Let's assume we have an audience completely surrounding us. There is nothing worse than to plan for your audience to all be out front, and it turns out you have people also behind or to the side of you. So we will look at a theater in the round, as it were."

He took one of the push pins and dropped it into his open hand. Slowly he closed the hand. "Now, our master of the illusion is going to be Hooker." He opened his hand, and there was a small red flower with the pushpin for a center. He took the pin and pushed it into the map. "If I understand things, he will be standing here with a very real shotgun."

He pulled two more pushpins and waved his hand over them, and they became a pink and yellow flower. "His two lovely assistants will start here and run there." He pointed at the access.

"When they are about halfway to the disappear point, he will shoot them. At that moment, it is critical to the show. First, everything must blow up, but in a progression. Let me demonstrate." He shook his body, and in his right hand, a smallish hula-hoop appeared. He shook the hoop, and a small curtain appeared from it.

Stella stepped into the room, carrying a small stand with a top hat sitting upside down on the stand. The magician showed his open palm toward Stella. "Gentlemen, our lovely hostess with the mostess—Stella Romero." They clapped and laughed.

He held up the hat. "Sorry, but there is no rabbit tonight." He placed the hoop over and around the stand and lowered it below the top of the stand. Drawing it straight up with the hoop level, he hid the hat. "If we set everything off all at once, this is what it looks like—very uniform—and very unnatural."

He pointed at Alex. "Admiral."

Alex smiled. "Thanks for the bump in rank, but it's just Captain."

Tom smiled. He knew the rank on the man's shirt. "There are sixteen-inch cannons on the Mighty Mo. How far can they throw a shell?"

"About twenty miles."

"When the trigger man pulls the firing cord, is the bullet landing those twenty miles away?" He redrew the hoop strait up.

"No."

"How long does it take?"

"About forty-five seconds for a class seven gun. Maybe a bit longer out of the Missouri."

Tom now tilted the ring slightly, and as he raised the edge past the rim of the hat, he started making little bombing sounds that grew larger and larger as more was covered. "Boom, boom, boom, boom, boom."

As he finally covered the hat from all watching, there was a flash inside the hat and a billow of white smoke boiled out of the curtain. He let the hoop fall to expose the stand with only a mouse standing on its hind legs and bottom. The hat was gone. He scooped up the mouse, petted it, and threw it in the air. And there was nothing.

"Misdirection, gentlemen." He turned back to the map with the flowers that were now moved. The two had almost made it to the square.

"As you can see, our fugitives from justice are at a critical point." Hooker raises his hand cannon and fires.

He claps his hand together. "In the control center, we set off the charges near him. Now, we don't want to injure our good magician, so we use the slower burning powder used in cannons." He pointed to Alex, who now smiled and nodded. "This looks like the explosion is coming from his magical hand cannon. The smoke and mirrors of these explosions take place each time he pumps a new round into the gun and fires. The explosion must continue around the perimeter of the kill zone—until there is nothing but fire, smoke, and a lot of noise. Inside the hat is a different story. Once the first round of the ring of fire is established, the doors are opened, and the two can run down. But remember, we must convince the audience of what they saw... really happened. So the last round of explosions must end up covering the trap door, thus sealing the illusion."

The man stepped back over to the seat just inside the room and sat down.

The room was silent. Every person was walking through what they knew how to do and how it could fit in. Hooker had never seen so many smart people so struck into silence.

John stepped back up to the center and glanced over at the now deadpan Tom. He looked back at the room, and then a quick glance back at the unmoving Tom. Slowly he looked back around the room. "Umm... uh, any questions? Comments?"

"Question?" The younger of the bomb squad members offered.

John nodded.

The man furrowed his brow. "How did you make the hat disappear?" The room looked at the small man.

He opened his mouth and then closed it. And then he simply stated, "Very well, I thought."

The group laughed at the expense of the young man, but also at the complete showmanship of the magician.

"I think," John started, "in light of the hour, we have a game plan to start with. If you bombers can get together with Alex, we can work out what we have, what we need, and how to rig it. The Seals can work on the final rigging. Meanwhile, the doors right now are mechanical. So I'll work on getting them converted to hydraulic or something that will allow them to open and close in a second or two."

Willie raised his hand. "John, I know where there are about six large rams that would do nicely. They are rated for five-ton so a bank of two on each side should do it. But add a third on each side for safety. This is one act we don't want to go FUBAR."

"Great, Will. I'll have the base maintenance guys drag some power out there. There had to be something at some time, so it can't be hard."

As the group started standing, Stella took control. "Saturday lunch is at thirteen-thirty. Those who are feeling their oats and want to help set up the outside canning kitchen, breakfast will be available, any time after oh-seven-hundred."

She turned on the small magician who still hadn't moved. He was just happy watching all the commotion. "Okay, Tom, where is the mouse?"

He chuckled silently and pointed at her left apron pocket.

Used to men and their games, she stuck her hand in but pulled it right back out. Her face went from shock to scowl. She pushed her hand back in and drew out a small porcelain mouse sitting up on his hind legs and bottom. She smiled and started to return it.

He put his hand up in the sign of stop. "It's for Hooker —to keep his eye on the prize."

CHAPTER NINETEEN

The sunlight streamed through the giant sliding door originally made for observation balloons. The heat of the day pooled on the thick concrete slab, the large one-eared orange tabby sprawled in the center, absorbing the heat. The clanging of metal on metal and the two men talking didn't even cause the ear to twitch.

The two men looked at each other like a couple of goofy kids about to launch their first water balloon in the season's premier catapult. The two were intoxicated from working for thirty-eight hours straight. The glassy eyes and rum-punched grins were infectious.

"Hey!" The sharp voice cut through the open air as only a librarian's voice could.

The two men jerked like small boys caught about to do something they shouldn't. They wavered and turned. The cat's ear then twitched.

The thin woman in a grease-stained undershirt and bib overalls stood in the door to the house. "Not... before breakfast."

The man in the torn jeans and sweaty grease-stained T-shirt swiveled around to look at the man in the pink square-dancing dress and engineer boots. Willie wavered, blinked, and nodded as he shrugged his shoulders. "What the hell. She's probably right." Falling forward to gain momentum, they headed toward the doorway where Maddie had disappeared.

Chet scratched at the scars on his chest where the nerves were still knitting back together. He surged and stumbled after the man in the dress. He didn't have the energy to think of doing anything other than following the leader. Or, in this case, do what the librarian told them to do.

Twenty minutes later, the coffee, scrambled eggs, toast, and bacon had done nothing for their lack of sleep. They sat around the small table, looking at each other through glazed eyes.

Chet finally broke the silence that had been the conversation of the meal. "Dibs on the couch."

Willie and Maddie barely made it to the nearest bedroom. They lay face down where they fell. They would worry about the grease stains on the sheets later.

The phone rang shortly after dusk.

Willie fumbled the phone off the base in the bedroom. "Hunoo?"

"I'm just giving you a heads up if you still need to hide the new engine you kids have been playing with."

Willie was instantly wide awake. "Thanks, Dolly." He hung up the now buzzing phone. He rolled over and sat up. He decided to let Maddie keep sleeping, and then remembered what her front had looked like most of the previous day and through the night. Maddie never had a chance at being a girl. She had three older brothers and a father who knew nothing about rearing anything but grease monkeys and moonshine cooks.

She had never been shy about the oil, grease, and hot fast steel or iron of the family business, but she had the brains. She had turned into the one who called the shots. Two or four wheels, she drove the fastest and had probably accumulated the most speed records as well as the most broken bones.

He prodded her butt. "Hooker is on his way."

He went out to the general living area to find Chet was already sitting up and rubbing the sleep from his eyes. "Come on, Chet. We need to shove Hooker's engine back behind the Speed Wagon."

The two men had just wrangled the half-ton of cast iron and steel to its hiding place and covered it with a dusty old tarp when they heard Hooker pull up in the DeSoto out front. They fell into the grease-stained webbed lounge chairs. As Hooker walked in the giant door, Willie stood and carrying two bright plastic picnic tumblers, headed for the half-open door leading into the house.

"Hey, Hooker," he called out nonchalantly. "Maddie is just whipping up another batch of Hornet Slappers. You care to join us, or are you planning to drive back to Manny's tonight?"

"I'll take a sip of yours, Willie, but basically, I'm off the moonshine for a while."

Hooker saw Chet and veered off to talk to the California Highway Patrol Captain, who was recovering from the same 'dime rash' as his and the Squirt's. All three had looked into the canyon of death, courtesy of the same killer. None of the three had made out any better than the other two, just different wounds.

Hooker shook with his left and stronger hand. "How are the chest wounds?"

"Chest is fine. It's the ringing in the ears and the headaches; they still have me on stand-down. Until I go a month with no headaches, I'm on the shoulder."

"So I see you guys decided to get some time in on the MG."

Willie and Maddie returned with tumblers of mint juleps made with her family's moonshine. Hooker noted she was in clean clothes that looked like they belonged to Willie's boyfriend, Hank. The cuffs were rolled up a good seven inches.

"I'm surprised, Maddie. The boys are out here puking grease and iron, and you stayed clean."

She looked down at her clean clothes. "Oh, I was working at the library. I just stopped by with... um..." She raised a tumbler and smiled. "I just brought some dinner by."

Hooker had laid his hand on the long cold hood of her car, so he knew she had been there for several hours at least. Something was up, and he wasn't going to push it... much.

"So what did you two guys decide on the MG?" He gave Willie a hard look.

The older man in the florid dress and now exposed knobby knees sipped his drink and smiled broadly. "Oh, the Ford piece of shit two-eighty-nine has got to go. We can find a slush box anywhere, and I think it's time to let go of the three-eighteen." Hooker knew Willie was bluffing. He would never let go of any Hemi engine—especially one he had built up as a street racer engine.

Hooker raised his eyebrows and drew down his closed mouth in a wise nod. He bobbed his head and finally landed on Chet again. Chet hid his face in his tumbler.

Bingo. Hooker smiled inside. He had found the weak link, the sellout. "Did you care to raise the stack any higher in this horseshit piling contest, Chet?"

Chet flopped back in the chair. "Aw, damn it all, Hooker. Don't hang me on the meat hook." He quickly looked over at Willie and the large scar on his throat and up the side of his face. Willie's hand was up. No offense was taken.

Willie lowered his tumbler. "Okay, I can see we didn't fool you and you're obviously not going to let it go..." The man nodded at the large heap under a few tarps. "The last run we made down at the drags in Visalia last fall, Maddie blew up the three-forty. She stuck the number five piston straight through the side of the block.

"When the engine seized, it transmitted straight through the power train. I can save the axle, but the pumpkin gears are toast. So, I found a nice little straight-six we can stick in, mount it up to a standard train out of one of the yards, and the old Granny Dart GT will be ready this fall for Candy to go to school."

Maddie finished softly, with conviction. "We wanted it to be a surprise, not only her but for you as well."

Maddie reached over and laid her hand on Hooker's arm. "I'm almost sixty years old. I can give up a nine-second car that is always dreaming of an eight-second car—for a young girl to start her own dream."

Hooker saw more truth in Maddie's face than in his uncle's story. "Are you sure?"

She closed her eyes as she nodded once. She drew her lips in a tight curl against her teeth.

Quietly, Hooker thanked her but turned the all-knowing eye on his uncle. Willie squirmed, but he also knew that what he had just said had to come to pass.

Hooker stood. "I'll let you kids get back to whatever mischief you were up to. I just stopped in on my way up to have dinner with Candy and finish the old shop manual I found on Marmon engines." He turned to leave and got three steps. He turned back, and the three snapped back into their chairs as if they had been reaching for the cookie jar. "Dinner Sunday—sorry, Chet, but you're out. We don't want to overwhelm Candy on her first family date. But Willie, Stella wants you to come early and bring Hank. Maddie, if you would grace us in order to keep Willie in line?"

Maddie smiled evilly. She held the tumbler up. "It would be my pleasure. I look forward to putting a dog collar on William and meeting this young woman." She raised the eyebrow at Willie and then turned back to Hooker. "I think there may also be a few jars available by Sunday."

"Oh, I think there is more than enough moonshine out at the hacienda. Just bring yourself and the boys." He turned as he laughed all the way to the door, more maniacally with each step.

The three didn't move until they heard the DeSoto grow silent down the hill. "You think he suspects?" Chet looked over at Willie.

"Old shop manual for a Marmon, my Aunt Betty's behind!"

Maddie raised her eyebrow as she sipped. "Oh, he has one. If I remember right, it's a 1960 or '61 machining manual. So he's probably looking at the wildcat engine the government built for the Department of Energy transports. They called it the Desert Eagle. If I remember right, it muscled up in the fourteen or sixteen-hundred horse range. If we can figure a smoother through-put on the transmission, it would have more power than you could ever use, and still run some pretty tall gears in the ass-end." She worked some numbers in her head. She had always been good at math, even as a young girl building moon-shine runners and racers with her father and brothers. "I'd say if we can get our hands on one of those new Spicer rigs, and load the back with an over-under, he could end up with a truck capable of hitting at least the better part of a hundred and fifty out on the new flat section of the 101 up near the airbase."

The three laid back in their chairs and thought about the eleven tons of giant yellow and blue tow truck traveling at high speed. Willie rolled his head over, at the same time as Maddie, and looked at the big yellow truck hulking in the gloom. They both smiled slowly, evilly.

"What about the engine we just got?"

Maddie laughed. "That, my dear boy, is exactly the engine they started with. And I have the blueprints to do the rest."

Willie frowned and looked at her. "Where did you get the blueprints for the Desert Eagle?"

"Umm... they floated into my hands a couple of years ago. I was just waiting to see if Hooker was grown up enough to deal with it all responsibly." She harrumphed. "Gosh knows, you aren't."

Willie looked over at the Granny car under the tarp.

Maddie smiled. "The Granny? A straight-six is sitting over at the Contra Costa yard. As far as I've heard, it's clean with low miles on it. Dolly could probably get it released tomorrow. They could probably fill the whole power train, too. And remember, the fan did take out a healthy chunk of the radiator, so we can get one of those sent, as well."

The infection was striking Willie where it always did some good. He began to softly chuckle his evil and sinister laugh. Maddie knew he couldn't control it. It was just something that happened like a cat purring or a dog's hind leg when you scratched its belly. It was just the nature of the beast.

Maddie turned up the evil stove a notch. "We can stick it all on Friday and testbed it by Friday night. It would give us Saturday for a shakedown to Monterey for some seafood."

Willie rolled his eyes, remembering the disaster the last time they had driven home drunk from Monterey in the Granny car. The engine was more than the car or driver could handle, and the black circles on the highway attested to the car spinning three complete circles before it hit the side berm and flipped four times. Both passenger and driver were thrown somewhere about midway through the second flip. Only one deer of the small herd had been hit.

"How about we keep it to lunch and some music at the Boots and Saddle over in La Honda? We can let Hanky do the driving."

The three laughed and drank some more moonshine in the night. A bat flew in the large door, flitted around, and bounced in the air out the back door. A small airplane could have done the same.

The young man out on the freeway had his left elbow on the sill of the old car. Speed was not the intent.

Enjoying the evening air in the convertible was everything, as well as the woman he was heading to meet.

The last of the moon hung low over the south end of the large Bay Area. It had only four more days before it would be dark.

CHAPTER TWENTY

Hooker had never ridden in the back of a truck, much less a military truck. The canvas canopy reeked of wax and old diesel fumes. The truck wove its way sluggishly between piles of mechanical equipment and groups of people. It gently squealed to a halt, more from dust in the large brakes than anything resembling speed or the need for maintenance.

Hooker was dressed in the same work uniform as the Marines with who he had been riding. The two soldiers on the end unlatched and dropped the tailgate. In two files, they all jumped off the end and formed up on the old concrete airstrip. On a single command, they marched off to some undisclosed duty and not of Hooker's concern.

As they moved across the concrete pad, another group moved alongside while Hooker and one of their groups switched places.

Hooker and two others slowed, and the rest of the

group kept marching. The three walked and talked quietly. All around for hundreds of yards, there were companies or groups moving or setting up and tearing down cannons, howitzers, and groups of tents along with radio equipment. The entire old balloon landing site was abuzz with the movement of military practicing being military.

The only strange activity was companies of soldiers marching four and six abreast, carrying large bags of sand or dirt. As they marched along, they were leaking the dirt where they were marching. Over to one side was a group of men filling bags from a couple of dump trucks. Hooker shrugged at the inefficiency of the whole transfer but chalked it up to the military being the military.

Hooker looked around. "Isn't this much activity bound to create a lot of interest?"

John looked around through his eyebrows as his head was down looking at a layout map. "We do something like this—two or three times a year. We could just do all of this on the bases, but this gives us all some needed practice in combined convoys and working the Navy, Marines, and those other guys from down south." The three smiled.

Alex took over. He nodded with his head at the pattern painted on the concrete—the old worn markings Hooker guessed were a carryover from the days of the dirigible. Alex dispelled the theory. They were only painted to look old. "These landing pad markings are important to you. On the night, you must be standing in this circle. Your sister must run over this circle and along this orange arrow. We put some phosphorous in the paint, and at night, it will still be glowing faintly until about one in the morning. After that, the moonlight will confuse the issue enough if the enemy comes snooping around, they won't see anything out of the ordinary."

He nodded at the area where two trucks were practicing getting over two large long humps of dirt. The ridges were about eight feet high. "Those ridges are their set up. If they run between those—they will be lined up on here. In the bay, we have a new buoy with a red over green set of lights. That will be their target. If they get to the break and then run toward the buoy, they will run straight over this arrow. You will chase them and then stop here to shoot. You must stop. This will start the timed process. Once you have stopped, you then cycle your gun. They need to be one hundred feet away from you. We figure they will be running at about four miles an hour, so when you first shoot, they will be about forty feet from the doors."

John took over. "You will know when to shoot by this small red light." He nodded over at a jeep sitting idle with just a driver. As the man pulled an imaginary shotgun up to take aim, a small red light came on. It blinked three times and went dark. "As soon as the light comes on, everything is set to roll with the pull of your trigger."

Alex resumed the explosives run-through. "The charges will ignite from only twenty feet in front of you. Those are all the special charges so they're more flash and smoke than anything else. Those are the magic of Boombowski." They all smiled. "Those lead out both ways and will run as a fan of two arms circling the door zone. As they progress, they will be getting wider and more violent. Once the ignition hits about one hundred feet from you, then the C-4 will start kicking in. This is all being buried by those men marching with the bags of dirt and sand.

"By the time we have wrapped the entire field, the second round will have already started out in front of you again. That is exactly one and a half seconds for you to cycle your gun and fire each time. It will be a fast one-two or cycle-shoot in your mind. You have five shots. The total is seven and a half seconds for everything to happen.

"The doors take one second to open or close. They will start to open one second after you take your first shot. By the second shot, your sister should be at the top of the ramp. We will close the ramp at the fourth shot. With the last shot, we have laid an extra two feet of dirt across the field. We have a field of flat explosives under everything which is timed for the grand finale. When the ring closes for the fifth time, the entire field will end up in the air. We think when it has all landed, there will be at least a foot of dirt cover over the entire door."

"That's a lot of explosives."

"Controlled explosives, but it also means when you shoot the last shot, you need to turn and start running—but you are going to trip. Stay lying down. You will be in the raining earth from heaven zone."

"Why don't I just keep running?"

"Because it's going to feel like you are at ground zero when the San Francisco earthquake hit back in '06. That was about an eight-something on the Richter scale. This might feel more like a nine, and you can't run in it. Just lie down and ride it all out." He looked at Hooker's face and shrugged with a smile. "You can run if you want, but when the field goes off... everyone is going to get knocked on their asses. It's why we'll have mattresses at the bottom of the ramp for your sister and friend."

"So how do we get everyone back out?"

"Did you think we could blow up the world and nobody notices? We will have some police cars here in about fifteen minutes, followed by a couple of fire trucks. That should give the enemy a little time to snoop around, but not long enough to find anything.

"After about twenty minutes, the base will be notified there was an explosion at our old airbase. Only then will we roll a bit of equipment. As the sun comes up, we will build up the number of vehicles standing around, as well as people. There is a manhole over there about a hundred yards. We will extract everyone through it. There will be a bus sitting right over it. It has a hole we cut in the bottom this morning. They are installing sweeper curtains along the underside so nothing will show. It will just look like a shadow.

"We tried to keep you and your sister's parts really simple. We will be watching, and we will control the rest."

Hooker curled his bottom lip into his teeth as he looked around.

John finished it. "It's going to be a show The Great Boomkowski will be proud of but can never talk about. Trust us."

Hooker swung back around. "Oh, I do. I just hope my sister can keep up her end."

Alex nodded in understanding. "It will either be a thing of beauty, or it could all turn FUBAR. Only on the night will we know which way it went."

John thought. "Um, I know this is really out there, but is there any way to bring them over and walk them through it?"

"I don't know." Hooker looked around at the mass of people and equipment in a hyperactive state. "When do you guys finish and clear out?"

"They were done this morning. This was all just camouflage for your being here."

"Okay. I have my meeting with her tomorrow night. I guess I'll see if I can get her over here and run her through the plan. She's not the one I worry about, though. It's her companion. I don't know how he will react or if he can even understand what is happening." He furled his lips. "I guess we'll find out."

A jeep pulled up alongside the three. "This is us. Get in, Hooker. You get to ride like an officer this time."

They wheeled out of the area as Hooker noticed three convoys were forming out of the mass confusion. It gave him hope. Hooker thought about the games his sister used to make up for them to play. The treasure hunt was always a matter of counting. So many steps here, turn, and so many there. She could lead Hooker all over a playground and end up exactly where he needed to be. It was later when he realized that in the early years, her legs and stride would have been much longer than his. By the time you take two or four hundred measured steps, you could be off by as much as a hundred feet, but at her guidance, he always ended up where he was supposed to be.

He remembered standing on a large area laid in cobblestone bricks. To Hooker, they had all looked the same. Then he had counted out the last long set of steps. She had told him to squat, reach down, and pull up the brick. He had expected nothing, but the brick eased out of the hole and exposed a wad of cloth. He removed the cloth and unfolded it. Even today, the battered Tom Mix badge with a broken pin was in his sock drawer at Uncle Willie's house.

He had no doubts about her following directions, none at all.

John leaned forward from the back seat. "We'll let the crew in the bunker know you might be there for a dry run tomorrow night. If you want them to practice the door, then just stomp three times on it or act like you're shooting your shotgun. They will have a heat signature scan done by the Seal team by then and will open if it's all clear. If they don't open, you're being watched."

Hooker nodded.

The ride back from the base had been one of contemplation. Everything was riding on the little things, but Hooker knew if they were going to get this killer off the streets, it all had to go as planned.

Later, as he showered for his first real date, he mapped the layout of the field over and over. Finally, he just sat in the large shower on the small wooden bench and tried to focus on nothing.

Gradually, the field and plans were replaced by a soft smile and a ponytail of mousy blond hair. There was nothing special about the way she looked. Most people would never give her a second glance. She had the hollowed-out face usually associated with people from the Dust Bowl years. However, even when they had met years before, Hooker hadn't noticed her appearance. He had seen how she treated Jerry, an obvious bag of damaged goods. She had stolen Hooker's heart even before he knew her name.

The late afternoon was temperate, still nice enough to leave the top down on the convertible. The DeSoto purred its way up Stupid Hill where greedy contractors had built nothing but stupid houses on streets with even stupider names.

Hooker looked over at Candy. He liked the loose pony-tail she had drawn her hair back into, along with the burnt-yellow cotton blouse—a nice touch of summer, but with deference to the coming fall colors. He smiled—the jeans weren't new.

She smiled over at him. "Approve?"

He laughed. "Tonight, I no longer count. Just remember, you can't sit in Manny's lap on the first date. Stella will love you right out of the box. It's just the way she is. Willie is a mixed bag, and I just hope he behaved himself and didn't wear a dress."

"What kind of dress?" She giggled. Her brother Squirt

had told her about his first meeting with Willie and the really ugly granny dresses he wore when welding.

Hooker groaned. "Awe, beans in sauce. I don't know what to tell you. I've never brought a date home."

She reached out and put her hand on his thigh. "It's all right. I've never been brought home before either."

Hooker realized they were a lot more alike than either had realized.

The large chrome grill of the DeSoto nosed quietly up the street and onto the extra-large parking apron usually reserved for Hooker's eleven-ton girlfriend, Mae West. The large car was dwarfed by the expanse of concrete capable of holding twenty DeSotos.

"Hooker, I don't think you can park here." Her eyes grew wide as she took in the fourteen-foot stucco wall with the protruding black locust logs around the top. The large hand-hewn black walnut gates were standing open to their full nine-foot width. The twin flanking doors stood twelve feet tall. The plaza was lined by votive candles in paper sacks in the Mexican lantern style called luminaires. There was enough afternoon light even though the desired effect was somewhat diminished, it was still romantic.

The fountain glowed. Hooker suspected Stella had scrubbed and polished the tile that morning. It gleamed almost magically in the candle and early evening light. Later, it would be romantic.

"Welcome to Hacienda Romero, the only Jewish Mexican hacienda in Norte Americano."

She looked at him. "You're kidding me, right?"

He raised his eyebrow and nodded toward the equal-sized door on the inside which were the real front doors. The door was opening. There was no turning back.

"You really live here?"

"I think you better ask the lady coming this way."

Horrorstruck, Candy turned to face the smiling and waving woman in bare feet, jeans, and a Mexican peasant blouse. "Oh crap," she squeaked. "She knows you."

Hooker laughed as he got out of the car and came around. Stella stopped at the gate archway. Hooker opened Candy's door.

As they crossed the concrete, Stella solemnly stuck out both her hands toward Candy. "Let me see your hands."

She gently took them and examined them in the light from the hanging bell. The hard calluses and nicks and damage from hard work did not escape her trained eyes. "Hmm, no fork marks." She looked up and smiled. "It looks like his treatment of your brother doesn't run to the whole family." She pulled the young woman in for an official hug. Stella smiled at Hooker.

Stella pulled her arm around Candy's waist. "Come meet the rest of the crazy family."

Stella looked back over her shoulder with an evil smile as she confided, "Dolly is going to hate you for being so skinny, and she won't *even* believe you don't have a fat neck." Stella looked back at Hooker. "What do you even kiss on her? It can't be her neck." She turned back to Candy as they walked into the house, and Hooker groaned seeing Dolly through the window. "Hooker only seems to kiss us women with fat necks... don't you, honey?"

Candy didn't know whether to run screaming into the night or just wet her pants from laughing so hard. The food was amazing, and the non-stop stories, usually at Hooker's expense, were hilarious.

Candy wiped at her mouth and then leaned around Hooker and looked at Stella. "Gosh—I just can't believe we never met each other when we were visiting our boys in the hospital. I guess it was just a matter of I stopped in on my way to work, and you were probably there during the day."

Stella nodded soberly but with a devilish look at the back of Hooker's head. "Wasted time girl—just pure, unadulterated, wasted time—Hooker wouldn't have been such a moving target."

Hooker hung his face into his hands.

Somewhere between courses of the dinner part of the meal, Stella had Hooker come and help her get something in the kitchen. Once he was in the kitchen, she had him fetch something from the pantry. As soon as he started walking toward the pantry, Stella switched Hooker's and her plates and glass and sat down next to Candy. Manny had buried his face in his palm and peeked through his fingers at Willie and Hank sitting on the other end.

Willie watched Manny as he reached out with his right hand and put it on Candy's right hand. Giving Manny a reproving look, he just let a little Nancy slip out as he told Manny, "Now you just shush. We girls might need to talk a smidge." He turned back to Candy. "Now isn't that right, sugar plum?"

Hank closed his eyes and shook his head as he muttered, "Oh boy—here we go."

Hooker returned and sized up the table. He went back to the pantry and returned with two quart-jars with ceramic and wire lids. The contents looked like clear water. Hooker took his new seat next to Maddie. He weighed Candy's seatmates. "You're going to need some of this... and you'll be sleeping in your brother's room tonight." He passed the moonshine down. "Stella can decide which glasses she wants to break you in with."

Willie held up his water glass. Hooker gave him a hard look. "Even with Hank driving, you will behave to some degree tonight."

Maddie gave him an equally hard stare. She understood just how giddy her best friend probably was. He had finally met the nice girl who had seemed to steal his boy's heart. She shared much of the same mix of pride and happiness.

Hank giggled. "Oh, it's okay, Hooker. It makes it easier for me to take advantage of him later."

"Oh, you mean there is a level easier than slut?"

"Hooker!" Stella and Willie both growled a warning at the same time.

Hooker dug into his pants and pulled out a dollar. He handed it to Hank. "For the jar, I'll probably say something else tonight..." Hooker felt Maddie's slender hand patting his thigh in consolation.

Candy hid her mouth behind her napkin and giggled. She leaned over and confided in Stella. "It's too bad Dolly had to go to work."

Stella roared with laughter. "Oh, honey, when my sister and I light into Hooker, it is no laughing matter. I keep him straight, but with Dolly, the only thing he can do wrong is go nuzzle and kiss her and her girls' fat necks." She pushed her hand on the arm of the now laughing Candy. "Where he started that, I'll never know. But lord, do us fat-necked women..." she glanced over at Hooker, "think it's disgusting!" Then she leaned into Candy and murmured. "We love it."

Hank had gotten out his chef's torch and seared the canned peaches on top of the creamy rum vanilla ice cream he and Stella had churned that afternoon. There were just traces of white left in the dishes. The conversations had settled down as the moonshine had mellowed out the carnival of meeting someone new and important in their family.

Stella patted Candy on the arm and spoke quietly. "Bring your glass. I want to show you something even Hooker hasn't seen yet." The men were talking about some logistics of getting something done by the light of the moon. Candy wasn't really following, and so Stella was providing an out.

Stella calmed the look from Hooker with a mention she was just going to show Candy the luminaires and the cactus that was blooming these past three nights. The two women followed quietly by Maddie, walked out the front door. They strolled past and admired the candles and bags, but Stella kept them walking down and around the driveway leading to the large parking area below, as well as the three-car garage.

Two of the garage doors were open, and the light spilled out onto the two pickup trucks parked out in the large parking area next to a couple of very large tents with mosquito netting sides. The trucks were still full of supplies to be off-loaded in the morning.

"We have one more tent to put up. It will be out along there where the crew will prep the food and do any parboiling or blanching. Over the next month, we will generate about three dump-truck loads of peelings and skins. The pits and seeds will all be dried and crushed, but there will only be a few drums of those. All of it will be composted down the hill, and later put into any garden needing or wanting it."

"Hooker told me you did a lot of canning, but I just didn't believe him."

"We are the second-largest canning operation in the city. Metro canning is the biggest, of course, but they do it all year. They also will do about five tons of commercial style canning for us that we can't do." She pointed out toward where the hill came down to the large parking lot. "Later we're going to build a large barn out there. It will house the entire operation, including an outdoor kitchen running the full length of the barn and overlooking the valley."

She took her hand. "Here, come in here. I'll show you

where we store a lot of this food." Maddie smiled warmly. They wound into the garage and around a beige Dodge Dart convertible with red leather interior.

Candy looked at the car. "What a cute car." She looked at Stella. "Is this your car?"

Stella patted the trunk of the yellow Cadillac. "This is my Buttercup. That one is for my daughter."

"Convertibles are nice with this kind of weather. It was nice riding down here in the big car of Willie's. I'd like to have a convertible someday."

Stella smiled back at Maddie and opened one side of the double doors to the storage room. She turned on the light in the almost empty room. Their movements echoed in the large room. "By Halloween, this will be stuffed full all the way to the ceiling with boxes of canned food."

"Wow."

"Yeah, wow. There are five storage areas in San Jose. The wow part is it only lasts about one year. And then we do it all over again."

"And this is all for families of police in need?"

"All of the law enforcement—fire departments, tow-drivers, city and county workers, and the list goes on. We really don't make people in need fit any certain criteria. Goodness knows—people in need are people in need."

Stella looked at the young woman. She walked her into a big hug. "Oh, honey, don't start crying. Not yet, at least."

She turned off the light and pulled Candy back out into the garage. "I want you to see this. I need your choice on something."

As she dragged her around the cars and across the garage, she pointed up the stairs. "We've had the door locked for a week or so, in order to keep Hooker out, but he's been busy lately. The door is a secret door in the pantry. I'll show you how to open it from the other side later."

She opened the door to the apartment and turned on the lights. Maddie let out a little wow.

"Stella, they have been really moving right along on this."

"Well, all the plumbing was in, as was all the wiring. It was just the dividing walls that needed to be put in and wired. But yes, they have really moved it right along. And Hooker never suspected a thing. Poor dear has been exhausted lately."

Candy turned around in the almost finished apartment. "This is going to be where Hooker lives?"

"Not on your life," Stella growled. "He will only be allowed down here if you invite him."

Candy was still looking in the two bedrooms and the large bathroom. She came out of the small hall and looked at where the cabinets were standing to be installed for the small kitchenette. "Do the..."

She turned and frowned. "Why would I invite Hooker down here?"

Maddie quietly smiled, and Stella deadpanned as she faced Candy before stating, "Probably, because it's your new apartment, if you want it while you go to nursing school, that is. As for rent, we can talk after you have a couple of years under your uniform as a nurse."

"But...." She started to tear up.

Stella stood her ground. "Stop. You can't cry yet. Do you want the apartment? Do you want to live here? And, if so, we need to paint—so what color?"

"I like the soft yellow of butter..."

"Then Nebraska home churned butter it is."

Candy nodded numbly as she wiped at her eyes. "Now can I cry?"

Maddie calmly stepped in. Her hands were still clasped together at her legs. "No."

Candy looked with confusion at Maddie who had been very quiet all evening long. Candy knew she was a librarian and a friend of Willie's, but beyond that, she was a mystery.

"If you are going to live here, then you are part of the family." She reached out her hand, dangling a pair of keys. "Here are the keys to your home... and your car."

"But I don't have a car."

"Yes, you do. It's kind of a hand-me-down, but it will always run great. Not as fast as it once was but plenty fast for a student. It's parked right outside in your garage slot. We all call it the Granny car."

The three women came back up through the pantry after they all finished crying. They continued down the 'guest hall' that was Hooker's (and now Squirt's) domain. Maddie broke off and used Hooker's bathroom to wash her face. The other two continued to Squirt's room.

Candy turned around in the room again. "You did all of this for Johnny... for what reason?"

Stella gave her the rolled head stupid zombie act—the inside family joke for all dumb questions. "Like I needed a reason in my own home?" She slurred her answer as she thought a zombie would.

Candy giggled. She hadn't felt this good in a long time. "No, seriously. You didn't even know my brother, and you went out and bought him jeans..." She started opening drawers. "Underwear, socks ... wait... *underwear?* When did he start wearing underwear?" She looked at Stella.

Stella shrugged. "He can go commando for all I care. If he needs a dress, I'll go raid Uncle Willie's closet if it's what the kid wants. I don't care. He's now one of my brood, and I get to do what I want for them." She took hold of Candy's shoulders. "Honey, he saved my Hooker's bacon when it counted most. The kid is a saint." She hugged the girl inside of Candy. "Maybe you don't see it, but the kid is every bit as good as Hooker was at that age. He just needed to have someone tell him that." She pushed back from Candy and looked her in the eyes. "So do you."

Candy fell forward for another hug. "You just have to give us some time to get used to this."

Stella patted her on the back. "You have all the time you need. Just hurry up about it. I'm liking the idea of getting a daughter out of the deal."

They smiled as Candy took one last look around her brother's room, and then turned out the light. "And mum is the word. Hooker has no idea the apartment is almost ready... or about the car."

"I have one question." Candy and Stella stood in the darkened doorway.

"What, honey?"

Candy leaned into her. "How did you know what size jeans he wore?"

Stella let out a roar of a laugh and hung on to Candy. There was so much to teach a daughter.

Hank dragged Willie outdoors when Don and another driver showed up to drop off the new five-ton tow truck for Hooker. He went over the new features on the towing bed, and where everything was. Hooker didn't even think anything was different when Willie and Maddie were chauffeured off by Hank in the DeSoto Hooker had arrived in.

Finally, late—the lights were off. The hacienda settled, and quiet prevailed. Several minutes later, the ghostly figure crept down the short hallway in the moonlight. It slipped into the door, found its bearings, and picked up the edge of the blankets and sheets. The lithe body slid in and found the larger spoon with a small muffled giggle. Anything else in the world could wait.

ooker stood in front of the large truck. It felt strange. Though it was a much larger truck than average, it was also much smaller than the truck he was used to driving. The moon was about a half hour from touching the trees. The hair on the back of his head began to tingle.

Hooker didn't move. "Hello, Mouse."

The voice was at the back of the truck. "It smells brand new, Hooker."

"It is. It's only a loaner until my truck is running again."

She walked around to the front and leaned against the bumper. "I love the moon when it is like this. It is so full of life."

Hooker looked at her. She was tired. It was as if there was no strength left in her. He worried.

She sensed his eyes on her. "Don't worry, Hooker. It will all be over soon."

"We have to go over what is going to happen, but we have to go there. It's at the end of the airbase—the old section."

"They were busy there the last few days. They do these things a couple of times a year. It disturbs the animals."

Hooker wondered if she meant the little fuzzy four-legged ones or the two-legged ones she called her family or tribe. He decided he did not want to know.

"Do you think anyone is watching it?"

She thought. "No." She looked over her shoulder. "It's too bright for most of them... and there would be no food anyway. Not for a few days or so."

"We need to go over there so I can show you what you have to do." He looked past her. "Will Dog be okay riding in the truck?"

She thought a moment and then nodded. "*On* the truck—he'll ride on the back."

Hooker leaned off the bumper and stood. "Well, get him, and we'll go."

She moved around Hooker and headed for the passenger side door. "You're getting slow, brother. He was on the back minutes ago."

Hooker did not even look. Somehow, he knew he wouldn't see the man even if he tried. He opened the door and climbed up into the cab. His sister oozed up into the seat. Hooker still marveled at how she could move as if she didn't have a bone in her body.

He reached for the little silver button on the dashboard out of habit. There was nothing but a new black dashboard. He swore silently and then flicked the key once. The gas engine turned over and rumbled into life. Hooker's right hand wavered in the air where gear shifters should be and then moved his right hand up to the stick on the column. He pulled... Nothing... And then he remembered to step on the brake. He pulled the selector down to drive and eased the truck out of the old parking lot.

The night air was nice as he hung his left arm out the window.

"Do you still eat ice cream with the window down in the winter?"

He smiled. For her, it would be a memory going back to when they were kids. "Sure."

The Mouse laughed. "French vanilla in a sugar cone."

He held up three fingers. "Triple scoop."

The memories with his sister were special. Of all of them, it was ones like this he loved. They were the ones Hooker held on to for dear life.

He looked at her. She was leaning against the glass, looking at the world go by a lot faster than it had been passing for her the last many years. Hooker knew the look —she was hundreds of miles away.

He parked on the old runway. The cracked concrete looked like a filigree of snakes in the dimmed moonlight. The occasional truck on the freeway from a mile away made a sighing sound. The night was alive, and Hooker knew he probably could only grasp a tenth of what his sister was sensing.

Her nose was slightly up. She moved more from the currents of the air than from footsteps. Hooker saw the shadow move low about a hundred feet away.

He spoke to the air quietly. "Dog needs to be close to hear what we have planned."

She turned in the moonlight. Her face glowed from the extra phosphorous in her skin. With enough exposure to light, Hooker knew she would glow in the dark. He also knew the glow was one of the special things about her giving her control over her tribe. They were not sure if she were human or a spirit.

"He can hear your heart beating. You're anxious, and it is very loud and fast."

Hooker knew she was being truthful. He relaxed. "In seven days, we will meet here at midnight. There will be a tugboat standing offshore. He will blow his whistle three times, and then once. That is your signal to be here in ten minutes."

She looked out into the night. Then turned and nodded.

"Dog needs to be very close. We will be meeting out here on the airstrip, and then we will start arguing. When the argument becomes angry, you can start backing up, back up toward those two ridges of dirt. You are going to end up running through the gap. It is very important."

They started walking toward the gap. He pointed

beyond everything and out into the black of the brackish water of the flats. "Do you see the buoy out there? It is the one with a red light over a green light?"

She nodded.

"The buoy is only there for you. You can only see those lights if you are here in this cut between the two ridges. When you run through here, find the buoy, and run toward it. You must always run toward the buoy. It is the only safe place."

He looked at her. It was interesting to watch her. It seemed as though she was ignoring him, but he knew she was paying attention to everything he said and everything around her.

She turned back. "He finds it interesting how the lights hide."

"They are set back into a tube so you have to be looking down the tube to see them."

She nodded with a soft smile. Her little brother was telling her something she had already figured out.

Their life had always been like that. She never told him he was stupid or younger. She just nodded, and he had to accept she already knew what he was telling her, or she was acknowledging the new information. In all of the years, in good homes or ones where names like *idiot* or *stupid* were used interchangeably with your name, she had never shown Hooker anything but mutual respect and love.

He turned and walked through the gap. The dirt had been loosened up from the packing that had gone with the truck training. Hooker could imagine a company of Marines with rakes loosening the dirt, starting on the top and working down. A line of men stretched from one end to the other. He knew this would make it difficult for anyone to sneak over the ridges.

He stopped. Facing the buoy, he looked along the ground. "Can you see the arrow glowing?"

"Dog told me about it ten minutes ago." She looked at Hooker. "Yes, I see it. It is the same as my skin. In an hour, it will fade and no longer be seen."

Hooker took a deep breath and let it out slowly. "When you run this way, you have to be lined up and running on this arrow. I will stop here, at the edge of this circle. You must keep running. When you are about fifty feet away from me, I will cycle the shell into my shotgun. I know you will hear it." He pantomimed the cycling of the pump on the shotgun.

"I will know exactly when to shoot because there will be a small light on the ground facing me. When it turns on, I will shoot. I will shoot every one-and-a-half-seconds. I will have five shells in the shotgun."

A small red light, the size of a dime, came on. The Mouse twitched and whirled on Hooker.

"The light will be my signal. If you see it, it will also be your signal the world is about to end."

He walked her forward, across the lumpy dirt field. They stood looking out toward the bay. Hooker curved his hands and arms in a rising arc.

"All along here are explosives. When they get to about

here, they become very large and violent. They will make an entire ring of fire and explosions seeming to come from my gun. You will, and Dog must be, in the middle to be safe."

They walked forward. "You must keep running. When I shoot the second time..." He raised his arm with the palm up.

The ground swung up, and the twin steel doors silently sprang open.

Hooker pointed. "You are running there. You have three seconds to get there and run down the ramp."

He turned to her. "When I shoot the fifth time, the entire ground will explode. Two feet of dirt will end up covering everything, especially the door."

He pointed down into the ramp where a man was standing in the dim red glow of battle station lights. "There are mattresses at the end of the ramp. Fall and lay on them. The people in the bunker are there to help you. Let them. Please."

He dropped his arm. The doors, large enough to swallow Mae West, followed suit. But for the thin metallic click, it was as if they had never existed.

She stood silent.

He waited.

"We can't do it."

"It's the only way."

"No."

"Why?"

"Because Dog goes berserk with thunder. I can only imagine what will happen when you blow up the world."

Hooker stood looking at her. He had no argument. He had expected her to accept the plan and do it. He had no plan B.

Hooker finally closed his eyes. "Ask him because there is no plan B."

She didn't move. Finally, she nodded. "Yes, it will save us."

An almost naked upright man with a glazing of dirt and sweat and air walked past Hooker. He was nothing more than a slow breeze in the night air. His white blue eyes pierced Hooker's and dredged at the bottom of Hooker's soul. Slowly, he came to a stop behind Hooker's sister. His right hand rested protectively on her shoulder. The man was as if carved of a muddy marble.

Barely perceptible, he nodded.

She looked like she was going to speak, and then didn't. Hooker knew they both knew this was it. This moment would be life or death. If it went as planned, their staged death would be the release from the life they had lived much of their lives. That life would die so they could live. Even though The Mouse said her health would eventually end, she wanted Dog to have a shot at something other than this life in the dirt. Her brother was the key to unlock the door where they now stood.

"Seven days. Midnight. When the boat horn blows three then one." She stepped forward and stood on her tiptoe. Her left hand cradled his cheek as she softly kissed the other. "Be well met, my knight." The night air shimmered, and like Dog, she was gone.

Hooker softly whispered the rejoinder from their childhood. "Or afore the dawn, we lay like scattered wildflowers on the field of battle. Our bones will till the earth, and our blood shall grow the field of honor anew."

CHAPTER TWENTY-TWO

A warm gob of spit splattered on the back of Hooker's neck. The word from his silent mouth was similar, but not the same as spit. He didn't even flinch.

The afternoon had started with strange weather and had just gotten weirder after the sun had gone down. It had not rained all day. It had just thrown the occasional spitball of warm sticky water. Hooker talked nasty at the lug bolt rusted onto the drum of the battered Impala.

Since the early hours, the weather pattern had been reversing the season's 'out to sea' flow of the steamy Sacramento River air. The Central Valley, with its heat and rotting vegetation, created some of the skankiest smelling air. Luckily, the Sierra Nevada Mountains provided a downhill push that would normally drive the fetid air out through the San Francisco Bay and into the Pacific Ocean, where it would mix and push north and back out to the giant air mass of the Gulf of Alaska.

A large storm in the Gulf of Alaska was being pushed down by the dropping jet stream and becoming a driving force of stationary air. A matching or a possibly larger tropical storm coming from the north of Hawaii was being fed by a small tropical front storm pushing up from Mexico. The result was three air masses mixing into the witch's cauldron of the San Francisco Bay. As always, with such a conflict, the riot of air got shoved into the bottom of the bay and over the greater San Jose area and as far north as Moffett Airfield.

On the mountainside of the Coast Range, the highway crossed over to Santa Cruz. The wet air hung there, trapped by the trees.

Hooker heard the gratifying groan of the rusty metal. The lug nut began to turn. The tired old Chevy was once again saved from the junk heap.

High above and almost thirty miles to the north, the Orion P-3 airplane watched the weather, as well as the infrared signatures, gathering at the target site. "Moffett control, this is Watch Eagle."

"Go, Watch Eagle."

"Be advised we have five more bogies entering the field from the southeast."

"Roger, Watch Eagle, five more players from Sierra Echo. Will advise Dugout."

All evening they had been monitoring the movement of warm bodies moving into the area. The count was now close to eighty. Everyone could feel there was another storm brewing. But this one had nothing to do with the weather.

Hooker removed the old tire and mounted the spare. He spun the five nuts on with his fingers and then threw them home by fan spinning the four-way wrench. After ten years of changing hundreds of flat tires, the sequence of one-three-five-two-four was something he did not have to think about, as his hand just automatically set-one skip, set-one skip, set-one skip, until he hit an already tight nut. Then he took one last creak on each nut, all the way around.

He stood and let the jack down. Grabbing the flat, he walked around to the trunk and threw it in. "Get this fixed or replaced in the morning, sir. In fact, we're moving into the rainy season, and these tires won't be safe. You really need five new tires."

Hooker wanted to tell the man it would be almost cheaper to get a new car, but he knew many lived very close to the edge. Although this man might be able to afford the auto club, more than one new or retread at a time might bust his budget.

The woman scowled at the sky that had just spit on her. She hung close to her husband as he handed Hooker his auto club card. "We moved here from Shreveport just to get away from weather like this. Y'all get hurricanes here?" She looked north toward the bay.

Hooker was ever helpful, but he did like to get in a dig occasionally. "No ma'am, no hurricanes. We do get a couple of small tornados out on the flats or at the airports, but no hurricanes. We're pretty uneventful around these parts—just the occasional earthquake now and then." He smiled warmly. "We need them to knock down the old buildings to make room for new freeways."

The old man smiled and tried not to laugh. He turned his head so he could enjoy the joking without being hit by his wife's purse.

Hooker split the signed receipt and handed the man his card and yellow copy. "Y'all have a great night now. Ya hear?"

Hooker smiled as he stowed the floor jack. He over-heard the woman speaking to her husband as he held the door for her. "Such a nice young man, but did you hear what he said about those awful earthquakes? I just don't know about those earthquakes, Arthur."

The man wore a large smile as he came around the back of the Chevy. Hooker, leaning against the side of his truck, returned the smile as the man shot him a two-finger salute. "That will give her something to worry about for the entire winter." They both laughed.

The man opened his door. The woman looked across with a frown. "What were you two laughing about, Arthur?"

"Nothing, Gladys." He closed the door and drove off.

Hooker licked his smile and looked with a jaundiced eye at the black sky. "If this keeps up, in four more nights, the dark of the moon won't matter." He wiped his hands on the red shop rag, threw it back in the side box and closed the door.

As he stood on the running board to get into the cab of the truck, his neck received one more gob of salty gooey spit. He froze and wiped it off. Leaning out, he looked up. "Really?"

High and to the north, a young airman sat at a desk monitoring infrared scanners.

"Moffett control, this is Watch Eagle."

"Go ahead, Watch Eagle."

"We have what appears to be the formation of seventeen approaching from the northwest. I say again, diamond formation inbound from the northwest. They are about half a click out from the playing field and holding."

"Roger, Watch Eagle. Diamond formation of seventeen bogies, inbound, from November Whiskey. Will advise Dugout."

"Also, be advised, we are twenty-eight minutes from bingo."

"Roger, Watch Eagle. Night Hawk Four is on the ramp and will be on station and coordinating with you in under twenty."

The naval petty officer made a log notation and called forward to the pilot. "We will be relieved in about twenty."

"What is the count?"

"It's at ninety-five and growing. It looks like they aren't going to wait until Thursday night. It looks like the war is tonight." He looked at the digital clock above his electronics board. The clock stood at twenty-two-fourteen—still an hour and forty-six minutes until midnight.

Forty miles to the south and five thousand feet lower, the phone rang on the credenza behind Dolly. Her eyes closed, and the muscles around her large heart tightened. Her phone never rang because it was someone nice wishing her a wonderful day.

She swung around and picked it up on the third ring. "Dolly."

"Dolly, it's Danny." He sounded terrified.

"Danny, breathe honey. I'm here."

"Five minutes ago, Sweets was getting ready for work. Suddenly, he is on the floor."

"Ambulance is on the way, honey." She was snapping her fingers at Dina. It sounded more like a gunshot in the dark room.

"I don't need no ambulance. You need to call Hooker. Sweets is running his mouth about Hooker and Armageddon and the world blowing up and dead bodies flying through the air and flames everywhere." He drew in a loud breath. "You need to get ahold of Hooker, and you need to do it now."

"I'm on it, Danny. You take care of Sweets."

She held the phone with her finger on the disconnect button. She let it go and dialed Willie. She let it ring five times and hung up. She grabbed the lollypop microphone off the credenza and checked to make sure she was on the right channel.

"Willie, if you don't pick up right now. I will come pull

your manhood up and out through your throat."

She counted the seconds on her fingers. Her thumb and index finger were out, and the middle was twitching.

"Sounds serious, Dolly." The voice was wrong.

The voice came across on the auto club night radio.

Dolly keyed the mic. "Willie, use the mic hanging behind your head."

The female voice came out of the proper speaker. "Dolly, I tore them all out, and we're rebuilding the cab. What can we do for you?"

"Is she running? And is Betsy loaded and in her holster?"

"We are out testing her now. Stand by one."

"Betsy is ready."

"Hooker is out past The Cats on a flat tire he just finished. The meat sauce is hitting the fan, and he will need Mae. Can she go to war, Maddie?"

Willie came on the radio. "We'll meet him at the diner."

"10-4."

Dolly turned the selector to the shop line in the new truck.

"1-4-1?"

She waited. She knew if he was outside the truck, he would still have the outside speaker on.

Box returned from the office from a visit to his sandbox. He sat looking at his resting place, bouncing around and uncharacteristically moving and working. He grumbled.

Dolly didn't have time for an argument and snapped her finger at the desk. He blinked and silently ascended to the top of the desk, a new place for him. He felt the leather writing pad and then lay down. He would watch the hard work from a comfortable position.

"1-4-1?" She demanded and looked across to Dina.

Dina shrugged. "He cleared the tire ten minutes ago."

"Was he close to Henry's place?"

Dina plugged in a cord. "Teresa, is Hooker there?" She leaned back and nodded. "Yell through the door for him to slap those cheeks and pinch it short because he has a 9-9-9 call." She listened and then pulled the cord.

They waited. Dolly watched the large hand on the big schoolroom clock tick to the seven. One hour and twenty-five minutes until midnight.

"1-4-1." The radio crackled.

Dolly scooped up the lollipop and keyed the mic as she brought it to her. "9-9-9 Hooker. Meet your party at the diner. Be safe, but don't spare the gas. Don has already paid for it."

Dolly could hear the truck starting as Hooker held the mic keyed. "What's going on, Dolly?"

"According to Danny, Sweets is on the floor, foaming at the mouth and Armageddon is arriving four days early."

She could hear the blare of a horn from what was probably a cut off car. "Who am I meeting?"

"All the help I hope you need, honey. You'll know them when you see them."

"10-4. Show me 10-97 in eight minutes."

Dolly raised her eyebrows over her wide eyes as she looked at her girls. "Don must have bought himself one hot engine. Well, it will be broken in by the time he hits Winchester Boulevard."

She snapped her fingers at Karen. "Check the PD roster."

The woman looked up and over as she scanned the roster. Her eyes knew where to look for which officer. "Podel is off tonight." Officer Podel was the least liked officer in the South Bay, and he always seemed to have a hard-on to write Hooker a speeding ticket that would knock him off the street for at least a month.

Dolly smiled. She keyed the lollipop. "Hooker, the poodle is locked in the garage tonight."

She got the 'chink-chink' of a double-tap on the mic key. She could sense that if Hooker had been driving south of the hundred mark on the speedometer, he wouldn't be now. It was now a wait and listen game—her least favorite kind of night.

She leaned back and patted her large chest. Box crossed the gap in one soft jump. The purr-box actuated in mid-flight.

Out on the interstate, eleven tons of giant yellow truck was roaring down the lanes that were clearing ahead of the garish red, yellow, and blue flashing lights. "How about the siren?"

Maddie looked up from the floor where the passenger seat should have been. "We were putting in a siren?"

Willie laughed. He downshifted through the new

splicer transfer gears. They had slid into the lower gear before he realized it. "I guess not on the siren." He rolled the large ivory Bakelite steering wheel as he followed Mae around the cloverleaf. The giant truck cornered like it was a slot car welded to the street. Willie smiled. He knew Hooker would love the new stabilizer bar now keeping the truck flatter in the curves. As he reached the second half of the curve, he rolled in a lot more power. The nose seemed to rise as the automatic exhaust dumps slid back with the higher pressure.

Maddie looked up. "Those work great. I couldn't even hear the PTO run."

"You should feel this new transfer gearbox. What a stroke of genius."

"Why thank you, sir. A girl gets to read a little bit every once in a while." Willie knew tthis was one librarian whose nose was always in a book, especially at home.

"What do you think of the extra horses?"

Willie upshifted and mashed the pedal down. The truck at eighty plus still seemed to lift as the enlarged power slammed into the rear end and was pushed to the asphalt.

The woman squealed with glee and clapped her palms like a little girl. "Oh, yes. Folks, we have a winner!" She didn't have to see outside to know what the sides of the freeway looked like. She had spent too much time north of the hundred mark on motorcycles and cars.

Willie smiled as he backed the truck down to shy of the hundred mark. "If I was a crude man, I would say Mae

West has had a successful nose job. Maddie went back to plugging wires into the new control panel. She stood up and stuck her head out the window and looked down along the undercarriage. She flicked switches. She sat back down and smiled. "Now, if we had music, we would have the fastest calliope in the world."

"How about the floods?"

She flicked a switch and the four large high-intensity lights on top of the cab lit up the freeway wall-to-wall for over a mile. A car a half a mile away swerved and dove for the shoulder.

"How about the back ones?"

They both laughed at the thought of turning them on. Both had a warped sense of humor when it came to auto crashes. Both had their share separately from racing—and then their shared memory of the night they almost totaled the Granny car, as well as themselves, coming home from Monterey drunk, one night...

As they now raced down the freeway in San Jose, the ramp they needed was coming up fast. "Brace yourself." Willie threw on the air brakes, and the world thundered as the air flowed into the diesel engine and provided back-pressure. He romped on the brakes and started jamming down through the gears.

Maddie sat on the floor and watched the shifting and the clutch work. Their week without sleep had paid off. The system was smooth and seamless. She knew Hooker would love the fact they had trimmed the twenty-four original gears down to twenty, but had given him four hundred more horses, and added at least another twenty on the top end. They had also taken out the second gear shifter and replaced the main with what was known as a knuckle buster. All the shifting happened on the one handle.

She saw Willie stomp on the brake, drop four gears, his left foot still floating in the clutch, and she braced for the turn.

Eleven tons of truck with more than half of the weight placed on the rear tires makes a very loud and ugly noise when you do a high-speed drift for a turn. Halfway through the turn, Willie dumped the clutch and mashed the fuel pedal. The driver tires lit up and smoked the asphalt in an effort to gain traction. He feathered the fuel, and all eight slowed down and hooked into the asphalt. For the first time in their lives, the front tires had six inches of air under them for over a second. The touchdown was smooth as the brightly lit, flashing truck roared down the street toward Stevens Creek Boulevard.

Maddie watched Willie's face, and she smiled. She hadn't seen him have so much little boy fun in many years. It did her heart good to see this from her childhood friend.

They swung around onto an empty Stevens Creek and roared down the yellow centerline.

The large clock on the dashboard showed an hour and fifteen minutes until midnight.

They slewed around at the driveway to the diner. The nose of the truck was out in Winchester Boulevard. Willie jammed the shifter into reverse and stomped on the fuel.

Mae's tires burned rubber up into and halfway across the deep parking lot.

Candy's head snapped up at the counter. She watched the familiar giant yellow truck pull backward into the parking lot. She had never been assaulted by all of the flashing and waving lights. The red, blue, and yellow were everywhere. The tires were lit from inside the tire wells, and the colors made it look like the truck was on fire or a mechanical beast from hell.

As the truck rocked to a standstill, a smaller truck crashed up onto the parking lot. It parked at the back next to Mae West. Candy smiled to see Mae still waved from the driver's door on the giant truck.

She started toward the door as she washed her hands in her apron.

Hooker jumped out of the smaller truck and ran toward Mae's driver door as it swung open. He jumped in and closed the door. There was a brief moment, and then the rear tires lit up with smoke as Mae shot out of the parking lot and bounced heavily into the street. More rubber was left as Hooker forced the turn and headed north.

Candy could still hear the tires howling as the giant truck disappeared from her view.

She thought a moment and ran to the phone.

Manny turned down the guitar music they were listening to as Stella answered the phone.

"Hello?'

"Mama, you better call your sister. Hooker just traded

trucks and raced out of here in Mae like the devil was driving."

Stella looked over at Manny. "Thanks, honey. We'll keep you posted." She hung up. She drew her upper lip into a tight roll and bit down. As the lip slowly slid out between her teeth, she looked at Manny. "It's going down."

She leaned against the counter. Her mind was a mass of thoughts. One thought came through clear as Ma Bell could make it. She smiled as she looked over at Manny. *"She called me Mama."*

To the north, the giant yellow truck skidded around the corner and lined up on the freeway entrance. The engine roared, and tires howled as the smoke poured from the wheel wells as if the devil himself were trapped there. The fire and brimstone smelled more like burned rubber as Hooker leapfrogged the gears and exploded onto the freeway.

Willie was teaching from his position in the sleeper part of the cab. "Now when you shift again, you will go back to first as you turn the whole knob right. This puts the splicer into the upper set, and you flick the lever back forward, so you are in the lower side of the upper set. Now you have ten more." Hooker listened to the engine and then made the three-move shift. The gears did not grind, and it all moved smoothly. He mashed the fuel down more and leapfrogged the next shift. As they slowed and made the large cloverleaf from the 280 to the northbound 101, Hooker could see it was all clear.

Mae was only a yellow flash of paint as Maddie had

shut down the lights for now.

Hooker reached for the microphone that should have been behind his head. "Sheets of rain on the street."

Maddie offered the microphone from the dark corner she had been sitting in.

Hooker gave a double take. "Maddie?"

The woman chuckled from the dark floor where the passenger seat was missing. "Just think of me as your flight engineer."

He watched the highway and keyed the mic. "Dolly?"

"Yes, dear."

"Do we have any contact with the base?"

"We're working on it right now, honey. We'll get you patched straight through."

"Thanks, sweetie."

"Just remember, this Wednesday night you're bringing Candy."

Hooker frowned at the jump in topics. Candy was also something not allowed in the dispatch. Dolly's home-cooked food was dangerous enough for the occupational hazard of massive weight gain. "Candy?"

"Cute, scrawny little blonde with no neck but bones?"

"Candy? My Candy?"

"Yes, dear. Your Candy."

Dolly put down the microphone and resumed petting the purring chest warmer. She had a self-satisfied smile on her face. She nuzzled into Box. "Yes, sir, Box. We're going to shake things up a bit... and it's about time."

Karen raised her arm. "Yes, sir, we will be routing you

in a moment. Here is Dolly."

Dolly leaned around, and her fingers danced on the keys of her large phone. She hit the red button and spoke into the air. "This is Dolly. Who am I speaking to please?"

"This is Gunnery Sergeant Cokacheck, ma'am."

Dolly frowned at Karen and Dina. They both shrugged.

"Gunny, did your mother give you a real name?"

The man laughed. "Yes, ma'am. But it's worse than Cokacheck, ma'am. You can call me Gunny or just Dan. It's short for Arachapodanacheck."

"Oh, crap." She looked deadpan with a mix of zombie at the other women.

"Yes, ma'am. That's what my mama always said the nurse said."

Dolly chuckled silently and shook her head.

"Dan, what can you tell me is going on out there? Wait, first... where are you?"

"Ma'am, I am in what we are calling the Dugout. I am the heart and soul of ground zero. We are the control center under the home plate. Everything is now routed through me."

"Are you allowed to fill me in?"

"First, I need to walk you through a series of security questions."

"Go ahead."

"Who was the first black CHP officer in the South Bay?"

"Micha Robinson."

"Is he married?"

"Tall drink of water named Bobby Sue."

"Where is she from?"

"Somewhere around the Okeefenokee Swamp."

"Close. It was the Ochekala. Just for that, you get two more hard ones."

"Where in the heck is the Ochekala Swamp?"

"I ask the questions, ma'am. Next question. Who owns and runs San Jose?"

"I do." Her patience was running thin.

"Where is the only place to be for dinner on a Wednesday night?'

"If I don't have my clearance by now, it's a table you will never sit at."

"Yes, ma'am. You were clear when you got my sister right. My brother-in-law Micha speaks of you like you're a goddess."

Dolly smiled. "Dan, we're tying you in direct to Hooker's private radio. We will back feed you constant to his other radio, so you two can have as close to a full-time conversation. Hooker, are you there?"

"Go, Dolly."

"We're feeding Dan through your sideband but picking you up on the private. You now have Dan constant."

Hooker downshifted for the off-ramp. "Dan, I'm getting off at the lower gate. What's going on?"

"Hooker, we now have over a hundred and eighty bogies showing across the zone. There is a large loose and not so loose cluster out on the end of the old airstrip. We only have minimal eyes on the area, but based on what we see and the disbursement of the infrared signatures, it looks like a confrontation of two factors. This action just started about forty-eight minutes ago. There is no violent movement yet, but the sides are definitely being drawn."

Out on the airstrip, the factions were more heated than those in the Dugout could ever know.

The Mouse stood in the center of a swirling sea of bodies who all knew tonight there would be a massive change in the structure of their lives. She watched the tall man dressed in black. Unlike the other bodies circling in this caldron, he was wearing cowboy boots.

"You dare challenge my authority when you can't even greet the earth with the skin of your feet? What have you done, Raven, joined the Other World? And now you want to bring it here?" She could hear many members of the tribe hiss, breathing with open-mouthed disdain at the mention of the outside world.

Raven preened in his killing clothes. Tonight, his knife would once again taste the blood of a woman. He slowly moved in an arc in front of the glowing Mouse. "You have become weak, Mouse. You have accused me of consorting with the Other World, but it is you who has been doing so."

He called out without turning his head. "Turtle, did you watch her here just a few nights ago with the man who kills with silver?"

The voice oozed from out of the dark. "Yes. They were here, Raven."

"And what did she do, Turtle?"

"She kissed him."

Raven smiled—the smile of a prosecutor during the Inquisition. "She kissed him."

"He is my brother. I can't kiss my own brother?" She turned as she followed the Raven's slow strut. "Who are you to talk about right and wrong? You have been driving a car—a machine."

"Lies!" he hissed. "You tell lies to cover your heresy of consorting with an Other World man with silver in his killing stick."

She seethed. "Swallow. Where are you, Swallow? Tell us about riding in the car with Raven as he went about killing people."

The child walked into the circle of conflict and stood silently. Raven stepped behind her, petted her hair, reached down, and hugged her. "She has nothing to say to you. You are nothing to her. You are like dirt under her feet, and she will drink of your blood and suck the marrow from your bones."

"She won't speak because she is afraid of you. You rule her through fear, not because you care about her."

He continued to pet the child's hair and rub her chest. "I care about my Swallow very much."

"You only care that she will lie in the dirt while you jam your man stick in her ass. That is all you care about."

"At least she is of our tribe."

"Yes, *she* is of our tribe, but you are not. You are an interloper who preys on a child. Everyone else can see it.

You can't even mate with a grown female. She is only now having her first blood. I can smell it on her."

"What does it matter?"

"It matters because she isn't even old enough to realize you're only using her." She looked at Swallow's face. "Tell the tribe what you two have been doing since you came back from the other place. Tell them about riding in the car. Tell them how Raven isn't really one of us but is just a killer looking to fill his own blood lust. Tell us, Swallow... tell us or be banished."

Raven could feel the tightening in the small chest, the stiffening of the spine. He couldn't allow her to speak.

His hands jumped to her head. One swift movement of his hands and her small head snapped almost completely around. The wet snap of her neck carried through the gathered tribe. He released the small body of the child, and it crumpled to the ground like a used rag.

"Where is your evidence now, Mouse?" He laughed. "Go ahead, ask her. You are the all-powerful witch. Make her speak."

The Mouse forced herself not to react to the sudden death. She stood and listened.

If the Tribe was fractured before, it was now splintered. She knew for many, killing was only something one did as a last resort to eat. To others, the body of the tribe was sanctity itself, and killing Swallow was unforgivable. And yet there were those she knew who were ready to follow Raven no matter what.

"You killed Swallow so she couldn't testify as to the

killings. But I already know. You are a wanted man. Not a god, but a man. And you will, by your own actions, bring the Other World down upon us. They will root us out of our holes and hollows. They will take us and force things upon us no Tribe member should suffer."

She pointed her finger like a sword. "You have done this to us. You have killed and done damnable things to the Other World and now here." She spread out her hands at the heap of dirt, skin, and broken bone of what had been the little girl, Swallow.

The Mouse raised her voice as she shouldered the mantle of the high priestess for the Tribe. "We have all stood witness to the evil this man is capable of…" She could feel the Tribe moving in around the center of her and Raven. The storm above only mirrored the storm on the concrete. Her arms slowly rose as she drew in strength.

Her strength was coming, but from a few miles away. The yellow Goliath lumbered around the corner and lined up.

"Ok, I just turned onto the access. I'll be there in under three. Pay attention and be ready for whatever happens." He threw the mic back down toward Maddie.

Hooker swung onto the north end of the old airstrip. He was in sixth gear. He mashed the pedal to the floor, and the front end rose. He leapfrogged the gears up to sixteenth. Eleven tons of steel rolling at one hundred miles an hour is a scary sight in itself. He reached for the dashboard switches. "Crap!" he screamed. "Where are my lights?"

Willie's evil laugh came from the sleeper. "Oh, we have better than the black-out sneak. Maddie, kill it all. Then when I say, I want only the runners." They ran black for a few breaths. Hooker pushed the shifter into eighteenth and mashed the pedal past the hundred and twenty mark. The truck was now chewing up the miles of airstrip like it was about to take off.

Quietly, Willie watched familiar territory fly by. "Okay, give us the red and yellow solids on the undercarriage."

He silently counted to three. "Add in the blues and start the red pulsing in the wheel wells."

Hooker glanced over as he listened to Willie conduct a moving light show from hell. Willie shot him an evil smile. This was his payback for all the wrongs visited on him in his life. There was a lot of payback, and it would be more than just a bitch.

"I want the ring strobes of yellows." The giant tow truck was rapidly closing on the end of the runway, and it was looking like an avenging archangel. "Give me the top strobes and rotators."

Willie counted down, "Three... Two..."

Maddie giggled hysterically.

Willie laughed evilly from the sleeper. "Light us up, Maddie!"

They were a little over a half-mile from the end of the runway and closing fast when the entire truck exploded into a light show. The final touch was when Maddie threw the last set of switches and lit up the runway and everyone on it... all the way to and past the end. A hundred and eighty denizens of the night were full of fight a moment before were now suffering under the hot searing light of a midnight sun.

The charging incarnation was floating on a cloud of light. The thick night air was now dancing with wisps of multi-colored air. The halogen lights turned the phosphorus in The Mouse's skin into a white flame. She stood with raised arms slowly turning toward her strength and salvation, embracing the light. Unlike sunshine, this light did not burn her skin.

The other denizens scattered into the safety of the night.

In the light, Hooker could see a dark figure grabbed her and flung her to the side. The dark figure started to defy the oncoming Goliath from hell but then decided to fight another day. Spinning on his toe, he reached out and grabbed at The Mouse.

She slipped through his hand as another figure raced by and seemed to slash at the taller figure. As the dark figure turned to chase the other man who had just slashed at him, Hooker was close enough to see the cowboy boots.

Hooker timed the end of the line. Stomping hard on the brakes, he whipped the steering wheel hard left, and then back right followed by three pulling turns. His right hand slipped the gears into neutral on its way to slapping the large red button actuating the air brakes all the way around.

The resulting side-slipping truck howled in a deafening anguished scream as all the tires locked in the slide and were forced to the concrete by the weight of all eleven tons of Mae. The sound spurred the runners to run faster than they had ever run before. To compound the crazy, Maddie flicked the one switch she had held in reserve. Gimbaled halogen searchlights randomly swept the area in a crazed pattern.

Hooker's hand reached back along the back of the seat and pulled the short shotgun from its holster. The door swung open with the inertia from the stopping truck. Hooker slid down and away from the rocking truck. In the crazy lights, he saw the cowboy, now pulling The Mouse by the arm.

Hooker gave chase.

The still-healing wounds in his hip and thigh screamed at his attempt to run. He had no choice. Luckily, the tussle between the Cowboy and The Mouse was slowing them down. The two were running and jerking toward the gap. Hooker stayed back just enough to push them, but as close as he would need to be. He knew he didn't dare take a shot. The dimes in his shotgun were entirely unpredictable after the first twenty feet or so.

Hooker could hear his sister screaming something at the Cowboy, and he slapped her across the face.

As she spun from the slap, he turned to face her. Dog raced down from the dirt ridge and reached out and slashed at the Cowboy along the lower back.

Hooker wasn't sure what kind of knife or blade it was, but he saw it sliced open the entire back of the man's shirt, causing the Cowboy to jump forward in pain. He spun, expecting to have to give chase. Hooker saw the empty scabbard on the Cowboy's belt. He guessed Dog had stolen the deadly blade on the first pass.

Dog had slashed and stopped, and the Cowboy turned into the waiting blade. This time Dog sliced across the face. The Cowboy roared and chased after the mostly naked blond man.

The Mouse saw Hooker coming and regained her feet and flew like the wind ahead of him. Hooker gave chase.

As they neared the circle, time and sound collapsed. Hooker saw his sister hesitate. She watched where Dog was running and leading the Cowboy. Her hand reached out hesitantly as if to stop or at least guide Dog back to safety. She looked back at Hooker, pleading.

She knew enough about life and about death. She stepped on the end of the arrow. The red light was over the green light.

She ran.

Hooker stopped. He looked at where she was. He glanced once at where Dog was leading the killer. He jerked the shotgun up and down to cycle the first shell. He aimed at his sister. He then moved the end of the gun higher, and to the right. As the tiny red light came on, he squeezed the trigger.

The world in front of him exploded. He knew as the explosions raced forward Dog had led the Cowboy directly into the line of explosives. Dog had made a choice for himself, his pursuer, and for the life of the woman who was his everything.

As Hooker pumped the next shell into the chamber, he thought he might have heard a scream. He aimed high and toward the left. He pulled the trigger.

He pumped in the next shell and pulled the trigger.

He pumped in the next shell, aimed right again, and pulled the trigger.

He pumped in the last shell. He raised the gun and fired. It no longer mattered. He was spent.

He turned to run. The world turned into white-hot noise. The dark night became the center of the sun.

Something large had pushed him thirty feet before it bounced his body off the concrete. He landed twenty feet farther.

He never heard the sirens. He never saw the cars and fire trucks. He never heard or saw the helicopters. It was Maddie who finally found his body. It just looked like another one of the lumpy mounds of loose dirt.

She sat cross-legged in the dirt, cradling his head in her lap. The man in the bib overalls stood next to them, both holding to their own thoughts.

Willie blinked and looked around in the night. His sight lit on the buoy offshore a hundred yards or so away. He thought it was curious a buoy would have two colors of light on the same side. As he watched, the red light winked out. Only the green remained steady.

CHAPTER TWENTY-THREE

She sat at the head of the table. She wasn't sure why. Some of the ten men were tow truck drivers who had worked with Hooker for years. Ace had taught him how to tow, and Hooker had taught John, the small quiet man, how to tow.

One was a tall young police officer named James Aligo. His pro-football size belied his Filipino heritage. His smile and laughter were infectious more in a steak and eggs sort of way than in a sweets sort of way. His love of life was something you wanted to fill up on—it was good for you.

There were a couple of deputies who had come up through the ranks giving Hooker tows that weren't really his.

Micha was the first black officer for the highway patrol in the Bay Area. The only other woman at the table was his wife. She too had no idea why she was there. Next to her was her brother, a Marine sergeant named Dan. He was as much of a mystery to the rest of the men as were the women at the table. Even Dolly had never sat with them.

The Marine was crystal-clear about why he was there.

Rounding out the table were two shot-up characters. The older, with the white brush cut, was the Captain on the Highway Patrol. He was the man who had hired Micha with never a single regret.

Candy smiled down the table at the other shot-up man. Squirt was out of the hospital on loan. The IV pole still contained several meds, including painkiller. Her brother smiled up the table at her with a wonky expression. She knew if they had had any serious meat, she would have to go down there and cut it for him. She noticed Dolly had cut up his spaghetti as well as the Sicilian sausage from San Jose's oldest deli, Chiaramonte's.

The conversations were subdued. Dolly was her usual self, hovering as her left hand drifted from one shoulder to the next to running her fingers through a head of hair. Her right hand was always full with a pot of coffee. Most of these men would be back at work in a few minutes.

The two hours had flown by.

The end came with Karen calling from the switchboard. "Ace, I'm holding a tow in Willow Glen going to Fremont."

"John, your back up says he is hungry. He just had a tow, and the member sounded young and sweet."

"Chet, you have meds to take before your ten o'clock bedtime."

"James, shots fired at King and Story. Please wear your vest this time."

"Micha, Good Sam called. They want to know where their patent is. Bring him in here for his hug therapy as you leave."

"Candy, it was nice to meet you finally. You're family now, so hugs are mandatory."

"Ace, I'm starting your call in three minutes. Your peanut butt best be in the truck."

Candy put her hands around the purring cat on her lap. "Here, Dolly, let me help clear…"

Everyone stopped what they were doing. Dolly froze at the coffee maker. "Micha? Would you please be so kind as to educate Candy?"

The police officer turned to Candy. He eyed the orange cat and smiled. "The rules are: you never offer to help, you never clear your place, you never get your own coffee, and you sit and act like a guest, or you never come back."

The men, who knew the routine, nodded.

Candy leaned back. "Well, that's just silly. Times are changing, and I want to help."

Dolly turned slowly on her heel. Her suddenly fierce countenance pinned Candy into her seat.

Candy's chin sunk into her chest as she squeaked in a little girl voice, "Or not."

CHAPTER TWENTY-FOUR

The Squirt sat sprawled in the back seat of the patrol car. The IV pole lay precariously over the front seat back, still dangling his bag of medicine. Candy had squeezed in around the pole.

"How are you doing back there, Squirt?"

The young man smiled and rolled his head. "I'm doing fine."

"Bet you are. I bet you are." Bobby Sue had slipped Micha a syringe of morphine and Demerol just in case he was feeling any pain before they got back. Micha just figured why bother with carting the syringe back to the hospital. His wife would just stick it in the Squirt anyway. So he injected the load before they got out the door.

Micha pulled up to the emergency ambulance doors. Two attendants came out. He directed them to take the Squirt back up to room 324.

He parked the cruiser, took off his tie, and opened the

collar on his shirt. He checked the inside pocket of his jacket. He looked at Candy. "You ready?"

"I guess."

They were walking down the hall. The elevators were ahead. "What is it we are really doing?"

The officer bit on his lower lip. He stopped and then took her arm and guided her into the small chapel. The place was as empty as it always was. He sat her down.

"It's hard to explain. Now looking back, it was just the start of another day in what we do. Not that someone dies every day—it's just not uncommon. You never get used to it, but you learn how to take it in stride and move on.

"Back when we were young, and I suspected Hooker was younger than we all thought, there was a really big accident. It was the first rain of the season. It was under the big overpasses going to nowhere, the altars to government waste and stupidity.

"The summer oils and such had built up, and then the little rain had turned it into slippery snot. There was maybe a dozen or so cars. It was a total cluster ..."

Candy nodded and smiled. "Micha, I'm a waitress. I've heard the term clusterfuck before."

If the man could have blushed, he would have. His shoulders relaxed to know he didn't need to dance prissy around things with Hooker's girl.

"Well, it was about an hour clearing things. The rotation had everyone getting a tow but Hooker. Even though he was first to get there, he was screwed by the rotation. But he was Hooker. He just didn't seem to care. He showed up and jerked a few cars around for us, and then broke out his broom. He would sweep until his trashcan was full, and then dump it in one of the other truck's cans. And then back at the cleaning. By the time we were half done, he was soaked. I think he was wearing a jean jacket back then.

"Anyway, we finally got all of the cars towed off. I think Mike told him he was going to dump a bone in one of the parking lots so Hooker could have it."

Micha noticed the frown of confusion on Candy's face. "I'm sorry. So many years, I just think everyone knows the shorthand we all use. A bone is a bonus car. One you got— just because.

"Mike didn't need the tow as much as he knew Hooker could use it. So, he threw him the bone. But as it was, Hooker got two.

"There was a sweet red restored 50's truck parked off on one side. The way it was stopped, you knew it was an accident, but it didn't fit in with the rest of the cars. All the wreck had been in the center dividing dirt. This one was on not only the shoulder, but it looked like the person was trying to drive up the hill to the top of the ramp. It just had a crazy doesn't fit kind of look about it. So after everything had been cleared, Hooker was the last tow truck out there. He waved to me he was going to check it.

"I was right behind him when he got to the door. There was a young blonde girl in the cab. Even in the pouring rain, you could tell at first glance she was a daddy's girl— one of those pretty young blondes who was a cheerleader and the prom queen of her school. Her daddy probably bought her the truck to drive to school in hopes it would scare off most of the riffraff. It was probably the sweetest thing in the school parking lot.

"When Hooker got up to the door, she turned her head and looked at him. I remember him asking her if she was all right. As he opened the door, she just folded out into his arms as she said, *'Don't let me die.'*"

Candy gasped. "She was dead."

The officer tightened his lips and nodded. "We just stood there and cried. There was nothing we could have done. Everything had been internal."

Candy held her hands to her mouth. She had never thought about what kinds of things Hooker had seen in his life and job. He just towed cars. But now she knew.

Micha could see the revelation in her face. "A few months later, I ran into Hooker at the Bold Knight. For some reason, I bought him a drink. I think I even knew he wasn't old enough at the time. It didn't matter. We were sitting there with two shots of whiskey and Hooker asked what we should drink to."

Candy finished the now understood refrain and nodded.

The room was dark, except for the monitor and the nurse's light. The tall nurse turned around at the sound of the door and automatically started her litany. "Visiting hours are over..."

Then she recognized the visitors. "But if I'm bribed

with a kiss from one of California's finest, I might be persuaded to look the other way."

Micha gave her a hug and a kiss. "Candy, this is what my wife looks like at work." They laughed.

"How did you beat us over here?" She looked at Micha.

His wife then asked the obvious. "Let me guess, you gave the drunk the shot, and then tried to get him in the car?" She laughed at the stupid look on her husband's face.

Candy laughed. "It was entertaining."

The tall woman grabbed the ends of her long braids as she laughed. "Oh, I bet it was." She slapped him on the shoulder and muttered, "Dumb ass."

She turned back to her patient. "Let me get the last vitals, and then you can get him drunk." She looked back over her shoulder at her husband and then at Candy.

He nodded. "She knows."

Candy nodded.

"Is he awake?"

The white blob of gauze moved. "I'm awake."

Candy went to the side of the bed. "I'd kiss you, but I don't know where your mouth is."

Another wad of gauze came up and bumped against the lower dark slit.

"Boy, and I thought they wrapped the Squirt up. I don't know if I'm dating the Southside Hooker or the Mummy."

Bobby Sue finished and kissed Micha again. "I'll leave you two. Candy, how about I buy you a cup of coffee?"

Candy thought a moment and then looked at Micha. She knew he would not ask, but he and Hooker needed a personal moment. She turned and took Bobby Sue's arm. "Did I ever tell you how much I love coffee?"

The room was dark, except for the monitor and the nurse's light.

The two men were silent as the one opened the two little bottles. "Here." He held out the bottle where Hooker could feel it was between the two balls of gauze. Micha tapped his bottle against Hooker's.

"Here's to prom queens, may they always be pretty, and daddy's little girl."

CHAPTER TWENTY-FIVE

Fall in the San Francisco Bay Area can be cold, wet, and miserable. Or it can be the most pleasant place on earth.

Hooker dropped off Mae to get her oil checked and to allow Maddie and Willie to put in the new headliner with controls for all the lights and a hidden siren. Candy had dropped off the Granny car for Willie and Maddie to relive a memory by going for fish and chips at the new Monterey Cannery Fish House up on Monterey Highway.

As the sun peeked over the hills and warmed the Bay Area, the old DeSoto cruised at a leisurely fifty, befitting the style and grace of the two tons of classic ride. Hooker's left arm was on the windowsill, as he drove with his two fingers and thumb. His right arm was draped along the back of the bench seat, with his right arm around Candy's shoulder.

Stella had lent her new daughter a silk scarf Manny

had brought back from Japan. The sky blue matched the canopy above and went perfectly with the ponytail. Hooker had even remembered to buy a pair of dark glasses at the Thrifty's while they were getting two triple-scoops of French vanilla in sugar cones.

The cones had almost made it to the city limits.

The new custom leather jacket he had received the previous week fit him perfectly. Danny had a tear in his eye, and Hooker had noticed it. Danny had just told him, "Shut up, fool." Everyone had laughed. But the real surprise had been when Dolly had brought out two other boxes, one for Candy, and one for the Squirt. There were few dry eyes among the eighty close friends on the party deck for Hooker's birthday.

Hooker ran his fingers over Candy's leather jacket. She put her hand up and covered his. She leaned harder into his chest and arm. He could feel her other hand lightly on his jeans. The two smiled in the sun as the deep rumble of the big V8 barely changed pace as it climbed the hill behind Stanford University.

"So, do you like your girl in a leather jacket?"

"I like my girl. It doesn't matter if she is in a leather jacket, waitress uniform, or nurse's scrubs."

She smiled coyly and looked out over the bay as it came into view. "What about in none of those?"

Hooker smiled and couldn't resist baiting the trap and teasing the tiger. "It would depend. What color of underwear?"

Candy chuckled. She had known him long enough to

like his off-kilter sense of humor. She also realized he was comfortable enough in their relationship to approach joking about intimate things, something both of them were still a little gun-shy on.

"Well, I might have to consult with Willie... but I suppose they would have to be color-coordinated."

Hooker hummed and nodded. "Black leather boxers... Are you planning to borrow his...?"

She reached over and found his ticklish spot.

They rode in silence for a few miles, each lost in their own unique thoughts.

Candy shifted and snuggled down deeper into his chest. "You still haven't told me where you are secreting me away to for three days."

He considered. "It wouldn't be much of a secret if I told you when you had only asked for the ninth time, now would it?"

She settled in and feigned pouting. She had never been treated to a real surprise before. She watched the airplane taking off from the San Francisco airport. She thought that one day, they too would fly somewhere. She didn't know where, but it sounded romantic just to fly off somewhere. Maybe somewhere exotic, like Los Angeles or New York.

The city slid by with noise and buildings as they got tall and then not. Candy sat up to watch the park drift by on both sides. The thought of the Golden Gate Park being a long and slender park pierced by major streets still seemed strange to her. She hoped one day she and Hooker could come see the zoo and other things.

She realized that doing things was something neither one of them did—they had always been working.

The Golden Gate Bridge had captured both of their imaginations. Hooker had stopped on the Marin County side, and they walked a way back onto the bridge. Alcatraz Island was a strange mix of serene living space, and a creepy prison.

They stopped in a small town for some lunch and were back on the road. The road was now only two lanes, and Candy fantasized about it being the fifties and the car was new. The large car pushed a lot of air, and they could hear the masses of fallen leaves cheering as they blew through them.

The small sign said simply, The Apple Farm. The large chrome grill slowed and nosed into the narrow driveway. The orchard on the left was large and deep. The trees were almost bare, with only spots of colored leaves hanging tenaciously from the limbs. As they rounded the curve of the driveway, the small hillside on the right gave way to the large expanse of lawn.

The three-story farmhouse rose white on the hillside. The wraparound porch was deep and filled with rockers and gliders, as well as a few tables and chairs. The clapboard siding shone in the late afternoon sun, and the windows were dark with mystery.

As they glided into the parking area next to a couple of other cars, Hooker reached up and waved to the woman hanging sheets on the long clothesline. The woman waved and started toward them. The soft halo of white hair piled high on her head, along with the long dress, gave the impression it was a different time, and the house was new. She turned her head and yelled something toward the large red barn, but they couldn't hear what she said.

"Hooker, so good to see you." The woman fell into his arms. He winced at the hug. She released and stepped back. "This episode or the dimes?"

"The dimes." He turned to open Candy's door only to find her already standing there. He turned as he slid his arm over her shoulder. "Candy, this is Aunt Claire. She is Stella's best friend since..." He frowned, fishing for an answer, "third grade?"

She pushed him aside. "Nice try. We were born in the same room one hour apart." She gently guided Candy away from the leather Lothario. "Stelly and I swore pinkie best friends for life in the nursery." She hugged Candy as she mumbled into her hair, "Welcome to the Apple Farm, Candy. Stella has told me so much of nothing about you. So it must be all true, and you can fill me in on mister silver-in-the-butt here."

She turned back toward the barn. With lungs only rural farm living creates, she called out, "Norman! Bags!" She watched as the man walked out of the gloom of the barn. She turned back to look at Hooker. "He's got himself a new Johnny Popper, and it's giving him the dickens to get running."

Hooker smiled. "I'll look at it while we're here."

As the man walked up, Hooker held out his hand. "Good to see you again, Norm."

"Likewise, Hooker. This is a very pleasant surprise." He walked toward the trunk as the women wandered arm and arm up toward the house. "Let me get those bags for you."

Hooker unlocked the trunk as the man admired the car. "Willie sure does take good care of her."

"Norm, if I didn't know any better, I would think this car was his greatest love. But then, you haven't met his Hank yet. You'll see what I mean at Christmas. You are coming down this year, aren't you?" The man nodded as he reached in for the two small bags.

"Good for him?" The man paused to look for an answer, still the clinical psychiatrist and doctor.

"Very. I don't think I have heard of any night terrors since they became serious."

"Good." He took up the bags again, refusing Hooker's hand. "Love has a curative nature for the disturbed soul."

As they walked, Hooker broke the silence. "How is she?"

The man thought a few strides. "She still has more rough days than good, but I think she also sees the light at the end of the tunnel." He stopped and looked at Hooker, studying his face. "I hope you don't think she will ever be normal—by any stretch of the imagination. The normal girl you remember, just isn't in there."

He turned and looked out toward some trees on the far lawn. "I don't think she will have to be institutionalized, but she will never be a productive member of society." He turned back toward Hooker. "She will always be frail."

"But she isn't dying."

"I can't say. She won't live a long life, but I don't think she is acutely terminal, no."

They stood looking at each other, taking measure. Finally, the older doctor flicked his head back toward the far lawn. "I think you two might want to talk a bit before she meets Candy." He raised the bags. "I've got these. Go see your sister."

Hooker reached out and grasped the man's shoulder in his hand. He bit his lip, thankful for the dark glasses. The man just nodded and turned for the house.

Hooker walked through the grass. His walk was slow and casual.

She wore a powder blue dressing gown. Her head and shoulders were covered by a straw hat with a wide brim. She lounged in the whitewashed Adirondack chair. When Hooker was still thirty feet away, she lay down her book. She looked out across the valley. Her voice was soft as a kitten's breath. "My knight returns well met."

As he came close, she raised her left hand. The white gloves covered to and over her sleeves. He took it and squeezed with the weight of a moth. Hooker bent over and kissed the fingers softly and staying for a few seconds. He could feel her collapse in on herself.

"You were hurt."

"Yes."

"They told me night."

"They shouldn't have."

"I already knew."

Hooker sat on the other chair and leaned back, letting the wood support him. He was so tired. He knew where the conversation would go next.

"Dog took Raven to hell with him."

"That was his name?"

"It was, but he had another name. The name your people are looking for. Try the name Samson Stubbs. I think he had a Bakersfield connection."

"How did you find...?"

She rolled her head and looked at him. Suddenly, her head flopped over, and her tongue lolled out. The image flashed him back to the foster home in Riverside. They had woken up in the middle of the night and turned on the television with the sound almost off. Vincent Price was the last man on earth where everyone had become a zombie.

He chuckled, and then he started laughing. The tension was too much to stop. They were both giggling with bursts of belly laughter as they made faces at each other they hadn't for almost fifteen-years. Hooker laughed, knowing now where the stupid zombie response had started.

As the sun neared the hills, they became quiet. Hooker had moved his chair closer, and they sat holding hands, watching the sun slide beyond the horizon.

"I think he loved me."

Hooker thought about the chiseled marble mud man. "He gave his life for you."

"He saw how to kill evil, and even though he knew it would cost him his life, he still felt it was worth the trade."

"No. He gave you his highest gift—his heart. Taking out the other man, Raven was just what he had to do, but he still gave his life for you."

She looked at her brother. "I can't live with that. I wasn't worth more than him."

"You don't have a choice other than to hold his gift in your heart. The choice was his. All you have to do is accept you're worth his depth of love."

"Would you do it for me? Lay down your life like that?"

Hooker thought.

"Would you do it for Candy?"

Hooker turned and frowned. "You even know her name?" He let his head fall back. "Of course, you know her name. You know Peter."

"Peter and I were... mated... for a while."

"Then...?"

"Peter is a very caring and gentle man. When I became The Mouse, I knew the Tribe would never tolerate such a fragile person. So I had to drive him off."

He listened to his sister's voice. The old connections were there still. "But you still have a fondness for him."

The forward edge of the hat dipped in the gathering dusk.

"You didn't answer me about laying down your life for Candy or me."

He looked at her. "I hope the day never comes where I have to find out. However, I would like to think I am capable of that depth of love."

His sister was quiet. He thought she might have drifted off to sleep.

Dusk was complete, and the dark drifted down on them. Hooker watched. Under the dress, and from beneath the hat, there came a faint glow.

"We should go up. They would be holding dinner for us."

She took his arm as they walked. She rubbed her hand along the leather. She leaned over and put her nose close and breathed deep. The smell of new leather was like no other.

Hooker held the door. As she stepped in the door, she removed her large hat. Her hair was gone. The treatments had started, and she had no hair or even eyebrows.

Candy stood up from the stool and placed her glass of wine on the large island. She walked over with her hands out. Her face was open. Hooker saw it was the same face she always had with Jerry, Father Damian, or even him. It was total acceptance.

He swallowed. "Candy, this is my sister..."

She stepped forward and took Candy's hands. "I've known your name for years. You have looked after so many of my... friends. Please... Call me Sissy."

SNEAK PEEK

A SOUTHSIDE HOOKER NOVEL

UNBIDDEN GARDEN

CHAPTER ONE

T HE DRIVER SWORE in the rain. Everything had gone wrong. The heist, the car, the road, and that didn't include the weather soaking the driver's clothes wet and cold.

The driver tugged on the leg, drawing the body out through the shattered window, and then taking up the second leg like a small burro with a cart. The largest of the bodies, thankfully, was tall but thin. The body bounced and tumbled along the streambed rubble. Only a slight relief came from the swelling of the small December stream. It would become larger with the winter rains. The body floated for a moment and then caught on the rocks of the other side. The driver kept dragging.

The light mist had turned the dirt road to a snotty slide now wept the blood of the driver into larger patches about the clothes the driver wore. The blood from the other man's head curled and danced down the stream, washing away into the late night, screeds of something becoming, and then disappearing.

The driver breathed hard, dragging the body up the small incline to the shallow flood-washed cliff-side cave. Pulling the taller man by the clothes and body parts, the driver fed the warm corpse into the natural tomb. The driver stopped for a moment and looked at the expensive diving watch on the body's wrist.

Quietly, the left hand smoothed over the short hair from the body's forehead. The driver sat thinking of the last few years. Better times.

In the distance, a flash of lightning cracked, and the boom of thunder rolled across the South Bay Area and up into the low coastal mountain range. It wasn't supposed to be like this.

The driver twisted and continued pushing the body into the cramped, shallow cave next to the other smaller body. Finally, the feet were needed to push and roll the larger body up and on top of the smaller to make room for what was still to come. The driver reached in and closed the now opened eye, hand hovering for a moment, and then withdrawing.

Slogging back down the damp incline, the driver once more crossed the small stream, and with dispatch, noted the volume had increased. The hills above would have been getting rain for more hours before. It was now flowing downhill.

The driver kicked at the back door of the car. With a long slender limb, the driver pried the complaining door partially open. Wedging their body into the gap, the driver began to work on widening the access. The screaming of the steel was loud. The driver wasn't worried. The nearest house was probably well over two miles away. And even if it were next door, the sound of the rain and storm would have just made it another noise during a dream in the night.

"Shit."

The last body was pounded into a ball and pummeled down into the leg area between the driver's seat and the back seat. With the car mostly upside down, it was obvious a great force had placed him there. Only the left arm hung free into the space of the car.

After stumbling among the large rocks and flood bed wastage and stubble, the driver clawed around the back of the car, pulling through to the front window. The car had spun-out above, rolled, and then flipped, causing the driver to be ejected on the second roll before the next flip had taken the car over the hundred-foot slope to the stream bed below. The driver marveled at the durability of the car. As 1937 was a great year for Chevrolet, it had also been a terrible year for Chevrolet. The cars were almost indestructible. Now, nearly seventeen years later, they were still running.

The last pitched flip had thrown the car into the ravine eighty feet below and forty feet across the stream bed for one last roll.

The driver stooped and slid upside down through the driver's window. Arching and stretching while feeling for the seat release, it was obvious nothing seemed right upside down. The mutilation on the arm didn't help.

The large black Bakelite knob felt right. The driver tugged without a result. The lever didn't move.

"Shit."

The driver hung from the knob, thinking how the car had rolled over and righted, right hand becoming the left before orientation finally became solid.

The driver's hand jerked, and then jerked harder. The lever moved. A click and the seat jumped forward an inch.

The large body thumped sickly down onto the ceiling.

The driver hung for a moment from the knob. A slight, wan smile crossed the pale, freckled face; the right, lower lip, and the left upper sucked into the teeth at the same time. The driver was still thinking.

Scooting with back down face up, the driver started moving the last body toward the other side. Pushing feet against the window post and moving the body using upper body strength—shoulders, hips, legs, shoulders—each part pushed one at a time.

Exhaustion was taking a toll.

The eyes of the driver flashed open at the sound of a rock as it rolled down the hill and splashed into the deepening water. The cold was setting in, and it hadn't helped drifting off on a nap. The driver wearily eyed the small stream. It was rapidly becoming a much larger stream now moving rapidly.

The driver rolled over, realizing sleep had come with

the driver's head in the face of the last body—the face of the one person who in life had been the most repulsive.

"Shit."

Moving with renewed vigor, the driver pushed the body around until the legs were sticking out of the window. The body was now aligned to cross the now larger body of water. "You better float, you big tub of lard." Thinking, the driver realized the body's coat was insulated and still dry. The driver stripped the body of the warm, dry shirt and jacket.

Crawling out the other window, taking up the two feet, pulling and drawing the body out and onto the water—now waist-deep, the driver was relieved as the body floated.

"Now, if you could just float up the fucking hill, you asshole."

The swearing somehow lent a certain amount of indignant strength. The body fit almost perfectly in the hole, leaving a space for the last objects.

Crawling back into the car, the driver flipped the two custom latches. The back seat swung down, and the four large bags fell from their hiding space. "Shit." The driver, picking up one of the bags and realized it would take three trips. Opening one of the bags, they looked in, and then drawing one of the objects out—the driver whistled low.

As the sun began to glow through the clouds, a lone figure plodded along the road. The driver's fingers were torn up from digging the dirt to fill in the gravesite. This caused the driver to reminisce of times making fun of all the 4-H kids in school and how dirty their hands were—

which was almost as horrid as how bad they always smelled—like wet animals. The farm kids were not much better.

No, sir, the driver had never wanted any part of raising animals or growing things and had damn sure never intended to plant a garden—especially not one as unbidden as the one just planted.

The driver washed off in the now hard-moving cold river. Not even hot water and soap would be able to remove the stain of the night's planting.

The driver turned up the collar of the oversized wool P-coat. It was a very long walk to Salinas down the low coastal mountain range. With any luck, walking the road known as *The Snake* would only take a couple of days.

ALSO BY BAER CHARLTON

<u>Novels</u>

The Very Littlest Dragon: NEW 2019 Editions
(Newly edited editions available: an all-new full-color ebook, a paperback with
coloring pages, and a full-color Collector's Edition hardback)

Stoneheart
(Pulitzer Nominee 2015)

Angel Flights
What About Marsha?
Pirate's Patch
Dry Bridge of Vengeance

—

<u>Southside Hooker Series</u>

Death on a Dime – Book One
Night Vision – Book Two
Unbidden Garden – Book Three
Boomtown – Book Four
One Day Under the Grass – Book Five

Southside Hooker Series: Books 1–5 Box Set
(Collector's Edition hardback & ebook available)

—

<u>Thorny Wallace Series</u>

Death in the Valley – Book One
Light to Light – Book Two

BAER CHARLTON

ABOUT THE AUTHOR

BAER CHARLTON

Baer Charlton graduated from UC Irvine with a degree in Social Anthropology, monkeyed around for a while, and then proceeded onward with a life of global travel, multi-disciplinary adventure, and meeting the memorable array of characters he would come to describe in his writing. He has ridden things with gears, engines, and sails, and made things with wood, leather, and metal. He has been stitched back together more times than the average hockey team; his long-suffering wife and an assortment of cats and dogs have nursed him back to health after each surgery.

Baer knows a lot about many things in this world. History flows through his veins and pours out of him at the slightest provocation. Do not ask him what you may think is a simple question unless you have the time to hear a fascinating story.

You can find more about Baer at his website.
www.baercharlton.com

9 780984 966660